GAME
OVER

Books by Fern Michaels

Return to Sender
Mr. and Miss Anonymous
Up Close and Personal
Fool Me Once
Picture Perfect
About Face
The Future Scrolls
Kentucky Sunrise
Kentucky Heat
Kentucky Rich
Plain Jane
Charming Lily
What You Wish For
The Guest List
Listen to Your Heart
Celebration
Yesterday
Finders Keepers
Annie's Rainbow
Sara's Song
Vegas Sunrise
Vegas Heat
Vegas Rich
Whitefire
Wish List
Dear Emily

The Godmothers Series:

Exclusive
The Scoop

The Sisterhood Novels:

Game Over
Deadly Deals
Vanishing Act
Razor Sharp
Under the Radar
Final Justice
Collateral Damage
Fast Track
Hokus Pokus
Hide and Seek
Free Fall
Lethal Justice
Sweet Revenge
The Jury
Vendetta
Payback
Weekend Warriors

Anthologies:

Snow Angels
Silver Bells
Comfort and Joy
Sugar and Spice
Let It Snow
A Gift of Joy
Five Golden Rings
Deck the Halls
Jingle All the Way

Published by Kensington Publishing Corporation

FERN MICHAELS

GAME OVER

ZEBRA BOOKS
KENSINGTON PUBLISHING CORP.
http://www.kensingtonbooks.com

ZEBRA BOOKS are published by

Kensington Publishing Corp.
119 West 40th Street
New York, NY 10018

All Kensington titles, imprints, and distributed lines are
available at special quantity discounts for bulk purchases
for sales promotion, premiums, fund-raising, educational,
or institutional use.

Special book excerpts or customized printings can also be
created to fit specific needs. For details, write or phone the
office of the Kensington Special Sales Manager: Attn. Special Sales Department. Kensington Publishing Corp., 119 West
40th Street, New York, NY 10018. Phone: 1-800-221-2647.

Zebra and the Z logo Reg. U.S. Pat. & TM Off.

ISBN-13: 978-1-4201-0687-9
ISBN-10: 1-4201-0687-2

First Kensington Books Hardcover Printing: March 2010
First Zebra Books Mass-Market Paperback Printing: July
2010

10 9 8 7 6 5 4 3 2 1

Printed in the United States of America

Chapter 1

The newlyweds looked at each other. Myra was the first to burst out laughing. Charles, looking sheepish, finally grinned and then laughed along with his wife.

"Wearing these silly flowered clothes under all this glorious sunshine, sipping ridiculous drinks with little umbrellas in them, isn't doing it for me, darling," Myra said. There was now a smile on her face, but it didn't reach her eyes.

"We have to suck it up, old girl. This is a ten-day honeymoon, compliments of our chicks, so we cannot return to the mountain until our time here in the Cayman Islands is up. Having said that, what would you like to do when we finish these drinks that are as silly as the clothes we're decked out in?"

Myra adjusted her oversize sunglasses. "We've already walked five miles on the beach. We had our morning swim. We had breakfast and lunch. We gathered shells. Unless you want to build a sand castle, I suggest we meander back to

Mr. Stu Franklin's island paradise, where we can sit on the lanai and sip a scotch and soda. In four hours it will be time for dinner. Oh, goody, I can't wait!"

"Who knew a honeymoon could be so deadly?" Charles smiled.

Myra giggled like a schoolgirl as she linked her arm with Charles's for the trek back through the sand to their honeymoon cottage.

Thirty minutes later Charles made a low, sweeping bow when he said, "Our honeymoon abode awaits us, Mrs. Martin."

Myra tilted her head to the side and looked at the thatched-roof cottage. It was quaint, the thatching covering a red-tiled roof. A Hansel and Gretel island house. It was more than comfortable, with wonderful cross ventilation, billowing curtains, humming ceiling fans, comfortable furniture, and state-of-the-art appliances in the kitchen. The bathroom was a modern wonder, with colored glass, beautiful tile, and a whirlpool tub, along with a double shower with eighteen showerheads. The only downside was there was no television, radio, or telephone.

The lanai was filled with hibiscus and every other colorful island plant. A parrot came by from time to time and chatted them up with his seven-word vocabulary. As Charles had put it, "If we were twenty years old and on our first honeymoon, I'd vote never to leave this place." Myra had seconded his assessment.

"What shall we do now, old girl?" Charles asked his wife as he led her around to the lanai.

He fluffed the cushions on the chaise lounge that was big enough for two people.

A sour expression on her face, Myra said, "What we've been doing every day since we got here, take a nap. I'm napped out, Charles. I want to go home."

"Annie said they were going to turn the cable car off so we can't go back. Dear heart, neither one of us is capable of hiking up that mountain."

"Speak for yourself, Charles. I don't care if it takes me three days to climb to the top. I want to go home."

"Bloody hell, let's pack, and we're out of here. I'll call Snowden to arrange our departure."

Myra was off the chaise and running into the house before Charles could click on his phone. "Thank you, God. Thank you, God," she kept muttering over and over as she threw her suitcase on the bed and, willy-nilly, tossed their clothes in. She rushed to the bathroom and ran her arm across the vanity, and in one fell swoop, the contents went into a small leather satchel.

Done!

"We're good to go, Charles," Myra said breathlessly. "How soon can we leave?"

"Forty minutes!"

"Details, darling, details."

"I just called for a taxi to take us to the airport. We will have private transportation to the mainland, and from there, Annie's Gulfstream will take us home. We will have a two-hour wait once we hit the mainland, but I didn't think you'd care about that any more than I do. Does this work for you, old girl?"

"It does, Charles. It really does. Oh, I feel almost giddy. Dear, you aren't . . . you know . . . disappointed that our honeymoon was so . . . boring, are you?"

"Myra, our honeymoon was deadly boring, but thank you for being so kind. By the way, I'm glad you pushed the envelope. Now, we have to come up with some believable story for our early return. A story the girls will believe."

"They won't believe anything we tell them. You know that. They're going to *know,* Charles. We'll be honeymoon duds!"

Tongue in cheek, Charles said, "And this bothers you, my dear?"

Myra thought about the question. "Annie will be relentless!"

"Well, we're going to have a good many hours to come up with a story that will work for Annie. And the others."

"Can we make it risqué, darling? Annie won't accept anything less."

"I'll put everything I have into it," Charles drawled.

Myra sighed happily. Her world was looking more wonderful by the minute.

Chapter 2

The room looked like an overcrowded gym, with workout clothes, water bottles, and sneakers scattered everywhere, along with sweaty bodies. The only problem was, the occupants in the room were not working out, nor was there any kind of machinery. No treadmills, no Exercycles.

The women were lying in various positions on the floor, glaring and cursing at the evil-looking pole in the middle of the room, the only sign that possibly the pole was the source of exercise. The psychedelic lighting inside the pole added to the snarling that was going on.

Kathryn Lucas rolled over on the floor and groaned aloud. "I am going to take an ax to that damn thing. Then I'm going to kill you, *Mom!*"

Annie eyed the pole, which she and the others had not been able to conquer. "I hate a quitter," she mumbled.

"Quitter! Quitter!" Nikki shrieked. "Is that what you said? Look at us!" she continued to shriek.

"We're black and blue from top to bottom. My butt is so sore, I'm not going to be able to sit down for a month! I am one giant cramp. You better say something, Annie, or I'm going to help Kathryn strangle you."

Annie sniffed. "Obviously, all of you are out of shape. Pole dancing is an art. You need to pay closer attention to the tutorial. I'm way older than any of you, and I've made the most progress. Your performance is pathetic! Now, we're going to get to work and conquer this goddamn pole or die trying. Up and on your feet! I want to see all of you on your feet, and this time turn the music up. We are not, I repeat, we are not going to allow this pole to conquer us. Shame on all of you! We're women. We're supposed to be able to do anything. Wusses!"

"I hate you, Annie," Yoko cried pitifully. "I cannot do it."

"You *will* do it. That's an order!" Annie said as she massaged her thighs, grimacing in pain. "Now, let's see some agility here! You're up, Alexis."

Alexis struggled to her feet, her expression mirroring Kathryn's as she stumbled to the stripper pole. She swiped her hands on her shorts, gritted her teeth, and reached out to the pole. The muscles in her upper arms bulged. The others held their breath as she leaped at the pole and got smacked right in the nose for her effort. She slid to the floor and started to cry. She rolled over to get out of the way as

Isabelle, her face grim, shouted something obscene as she took a run at the pole, grabbed it, and swung around, her long legs wrapping around the pole. The beat of the frenzied music seemed to give her some impetus as she whirled around and around, then fell to the floor in a miserable heap.

"Bravo!" Annie shouted excitedly.

"Screw you, Annie. That's it! Do you hear me? I am never touching this pole again. Ever, ever, ever! If I have to, I'll *chew* it till it falls apart," Isabelle snarled as she, too, rolled out of the way so Nikki could take her turn.

All eyes were on Nikki's grim but determined face. The calves and thighs of her legs burning, she eyed the pole like it was her enemy, which it was at this point in time. She didn't run to it. Instead, she marched up to it, raised her arms, grabbed the pole, her knuckles white. Carefully, she swung her right leg, which was bruised from thigh to ankle, and wrapped it around the pole. Her left leg followed suit. Her jaw tight, her eyes closed, she straightened her back, took a deep breath, and started to rotate her hips to the beat of the music. Somehow or other, she managed to command her body to slither upward, then downward. And then she stunned everyone by doing three full swings around the pole before she allowed herself to slide all the way down in a crumpled heap.

Roars of approval and clapping hands made Nikki burst out laughing. She rolled over and clutched at her ribs. "That's it," she gasped. "I

7

am never, ever going to touch that pole again! You'll have to kill me first."

The others seconded her declaration as they all managed somehow to get to their feet, moaning and groaning at the pain in their abused muscles.

It normally would have taken the Sisters five minutes to slip into their outer gear for the trek across the compound to the main dining room and kitchen, but this time it took almost twenty. They were through the door when Annie's cell phone chirped. She flipped it open and heard a voice command her to send the cable car to the base of the mountain. The Sisters stopped in their tracks when they heard Annie say, "But there's ice on the cable. All right, Charles. I'll do it."

Their pain forgotten for the moment, the Sisters all started talking at once.

"They can't be back already!"

"What kind of honeymoon is over that quick?"

"Maybe something happened!"

"What if the cable car gets stalled?"

"This is not good!"

Kathryn summed it all up by saying, "Now it's Myra's turn on the pole."

Annie was already halfway to the cable car and didn't hear Kathryn's comment.

Annie's hand was on the switch to send the car to the base of the mountain when Nikki reached out. "What if the car gets stuck halfway down?"

"At least it will get stuck going *down,* not coming up. The trip down will melt the ice. Coming up should be a breeze. It was an order from Charles, dear," Annie said, shrugging off Nikki's hand. She pressed the power button, and the hydraulics came to life.

The cable car slid out of its nest and started down the mountain. The women could see shards of ice flying right and left as the car made its slow, steady descent. All eyes were on the control panel, which marked its progress.

Annie's fist shot in the air when the cable car made contact with the hidden platform built into the base of the mountain. The Sisters sucked in their breath as one when the control panel showed the car was on the way up.

"I sure hope that guy Reggie, who Charles had working on the cable car, knew his business," Annie whispered.

"I remember Charles saying he was up on the latest on cable cars and that he worked on them in the Swiss Alps and this sort of thing happens all the time over there," Isabelle whispered in return.

"Why are we whispering?" Alexis whispered.

"Because we're afraid, and talking loud might . . . might . . . Oh, I don't know," Yoko said in a hushed voice.

"Trigger an avalanche of snow?" Nikki said, her voice short of hysterical.

"Anything is possible. However, I think unlikely," Annie snapped in a normal tone of voice.

And then the cable car slid into its nest, and everyone heaved a huge sigh of relief.

The Sisters rushed to embrace the newlyweds and chastise them at the same time for their early return. Everyone started talking at once as the girls struggled to carry Myra's and Charles's luggage back to the main building through the snow.

Inside, the babble continued as Annie made her way to the kitchen to remove two long trays of brownies she'd set the timer to bake while she and the others worked the pole. She turned on the burner on the stove to heat the hot chocolate she'd prepared ahead of time.

The Sisters did their best to ignore their aches and pains, their bruises and abrasions, by bombarding the newlyweds with questions about their honeymoon.

"It was pleasant," Charles said.

"No, it wasn't. It was boring," Myra said.

"We ate a lot and walked on the beach," Charles said.

"Charles ate a lot, whereas I ate healthfully and sparingly, and we *trudged* on the beach," Myra said, correcting her new husband.

"We read a lot," Charles said.

"That's not quite true, dear. I read a lot. Somehow Charles found someone who allowed him to use his fax machine, and he read reports that came in to him at the speed of light."

"You look tired, Charles," Annie said pointedly.

Charles looked around. Well, he didn't just fall off the watermelon truck. He knew when he wasn't wanted. He pretended to huff and puff as he pulled on his jacket and made his way to the door. He was halfway there when he turned and came back. He kissed his wife soundly on the cheek and said, "Now, don't be giving away what we really did on our honeymoon. Some things should remain sacred, old girl."

Myra blushed a rosy hue as she waved her husband toward the door. The minute the door closed, she said, "It was a *water bed!* Do you believe that? We couldn't . . . what I mean is . . . We got *seasick.* We slept on the floor after . . . well, after we found out it was a water bed. Charles was so . . . *inept.*"

Annie poured the hot chocolate. She sniffed. "That's probably more than we really need to know, dear."

"Hogwash. That's all you really wanted to know, *dear,* and you know it," Myra retorted. "Let me sum it up for you, Annie. The sex end of the honeymoon was a disaster. Charles has a bad back. He had most of the blankets and covers. One night I slept on the beach, because the sand was soft. But, I got sand in every orifice of my body, and I will never do that again."

"My-raaa!" Annie screeched.

"Oh, hush, Annie. You are reveling in the details of my honeymoon. But I am now willing to make a wager with you. I will wager my pearls against your pearls that I can master that . . .

11

that stripper pole with all the lights in it. I'm ready and willing to take on all comers. Do we have a date for the recital yet?"

The Sisters' eyes popped, their jaws dropped, and Annie sat down with a thump and immediately regretted it.

"Your . . . heirloom pearls! Your one-of-a-kind, priceless pearls? The pearls you feel naked without? Those pearls?" Annie managed to gasp.

"Yes, Countess de Silva, *those pearls,*" said Myra.

"Are you telling us you . . . you practiced on a stripper pole while you were on your honeymoon?" Nikki managed to squeak out as she recalled her own dismal performance and the aches and pains that had followed her efforts.

"I am saying no such thing. Charles was glued to me the entire time, except for the night I slept on the beach. I wouldn't have even known where to look to find a pole to . . . practice on."

"Then how . . . ?" Yoko managed to weigh in.

"Just you never mind, honey. So are you going to take my bet or not, Annie?"

Annie eyed her old friend warily. She tried to read something in Myra's expression but saw nothing to ease her fear that Myra had some kind of secret power that would make fools out of all of them. She had no choice but to take her old friend up on the wager. She tried to work some excitement and jubilation into her voice when she said, "You're on, Myra!"

Myra laughed, to Annie's discomfort. "Maybe

we'll be able to take our show on the road. After the recital, of course."

"Drink your hot chocolate and shut up, Myra, while I try to figure out if you are snookering me somehow to get my great-grandmother's pearls, which are just as lovely as yours. You just want a matched set," Annie sniped.

Myra smiled.

The Sisters shivered.

"Let's talk about something else, ladies," Nikki, ever the diplomat, said. "Has anyone heard from Lizzie? I wonder how her first four days at the White House are going. We should have heard something by now."

The others said they hadn't heard a word from the Silver Fox.

"Maybe Lizzie can't make personal calls from the White House, or maybe she's afraid the walls have ears," Yoko said.

"She's nine to five. Her nights are her own. She could have called us last night or the night before. But there is Cosmo, so maybe she wants her free time to be with him. The last time I spoke to her, she said he would be here for a week, while, as he put it, she got her feet wet at Sixteen Hundred Pennsylvania Avenue," Alexis said.

"The New Year started off with a bang in D.C. There is all kinds of stuff going on that the president has to deal with. I guess that means Lizzie has to deal with it, too. Like, for instance, yesterday I saw in the paper online that one of the

Supreme Court justices is going to retire when the court goes into recess. Then today the paper said that rumor was false. That's a whole big megillah for the president. I hope they pick another woman this time if it turns out to be true in the end," Isabelle said.

"Yesterday I read that President Connor is cleaning house. She's giving staffers a chance to resign and waiting to see how that offer flies. Wonder what that's all about," Nikki said.

"Maggie said when President Connor took office, she listened to the wrong people, and staffers and positions were hired under pressure. She's going to correct that situation, and Maggie thinks Connor waited until Lizzie was installed as chief White House counsel to do anything. Makes sense to me," Annie said.

"Well, I'm off to the hot tub," Nikki said as she got painfully to her feet.

The others quickly rose and, at the last minute, looked at Annie and asked whose turn it was to clean up.

"Myra and I will do it," said Annie. "Run along, girls, so I can pick Myra's brain about that wonderful honeymoon she just returned from five days early."

Myra watched as the Sisters stumbled their way to the door. "What's wrong with them, Annie?"

Annie sighed. "I might as well tell you, Myra, so you can laugh your head off. We have all been practicing on that . . . on that damn pole, and none of us have actually mastered it, so you are probably going to win my great-grandmother's pearls. All of us, me included, are black and blue, and muscles we didn't even know we had are protesting. That pole seemed like such a wonderful, fun thing. It looked so easy. Trust me when I tell you it was not easy. I have no idea how the women in those clubs do it hour after hour. I'm not kidding you when I tell you it's killing us. I was wrong, Myra."

"Then why didn't you tell the girls you were wrong? Have Charles call . . . what's his name . . . oh, yes, Reggie, to take it out and toss it over the mountain."

"And admit I was wrong! Is that what you're saying?"

"Well, yes, Annie, that's what I'm saying."

"I was never a quitter," Annie sniffed. "I'll do the recital on my own, with or without an audience. If I embarrass myself, it will teach me a lesson when I get another harebrained idea. Can you really work the pole, Myra?"

"I think so. I took that tutorial you gave me and put it inside a book I was reading. Charles didn't have a clue what I was reading. I memorized it, and every chance I got, I tried it on a tree in the backyard of that house we were staying in. I realize a tree is different from a stripper pole, but I have the . . . moves down pretty pat. I might be making a fool of myself, too, but you did say we should cut loose and try all these new things. You better not be telling me you were wrong, Annie."

"You want another brownie, Myra?" Annie

said as she shoved a whole square into her own mouth.

"Why not?" Myra said as she reached for the sugary treat. When she finished the brownie, she looked up at Annie and asked, "You want to try the pole this evening or wait for tomorrow?"

"Oh, God, Myra, I don't have it in me to go at it tonight. Tomorrow will work just fine. Don't you want to join your new husband?"

"Why? He's sound asleep in a real bed. Did I ever tell you he sleeps sideways? He does. I have to go to bed first in order to claim my space. I'm probably going to sleep on the couch."

"No, you never told me that, and again, what's with all this sharing you're doing all of a sudden?" Annie grumbled. "I don't have anything to share, if that's what you're hoping."

"Oh, go to bed, Annie. I'll finish cleaning up. I want to sit here and think a bit. Something is niggling at me, and I want to try and figure out what it is. It's good to be home, my friend."

"Glad to have you back, Myra. Good night. Give Barbara my regards."

Myra smiled.

Chapter 3

It was twenty minutes past the lunch hour when the bailiff informed Assistant District Attorney Jack Emery that the presiding judge was canceling the afternoon court session. Jack waited a full minute to see if a reason would be given for the cancellation, but none was forthcoming. "What about court tomorrow?" he asked.

"Your office will be notified first thing in the morning."

Jack shrugged and started to pack up his briefcase, just as the defense attorney from the Prizzi law firm was doing.

"I heard at lunch that the judge's denture broke, and he hightailed it to the dentist. Don't count on tomorrow, either," the other attorney said gleefully.

Jack shrugged again, and since the courtroom was now empty except for him and opposing counsel, Jack turned his cell phone on. It rang almost immediately. He listened to Harry Wong's excited voice. "You making this up,

Harry?" He held the phone away from his ear and said, "Okay, I'm on the way. What? How hard is it snowing? Oh. How many times do I have to tell you there are no windows in the courtrooms here in the courthouse? I'll pick you up in twenty minutes."

Outside, it was snowing lightly, the wind gusty as it blew Jack along to the courthouse parking lot, where he spent ten minutes clearing off his windshield and back window. He'd be glad when spring rolled around. He hated cold and snow with a deep passion. Inside the car, with the heater working at peak capacity, he reached over to the backseat for his duffel bag. He yanked at the bag and pulled out his battered sneakers. He tossed his Brooks Brothers loafers onto the backseat, slipped his feet into his Nikes, put the car in gear, and peeled out to the road. Forty minutes later Jack carefully maneuvered his car into the narrow driveway in back of Harry's dojo.

"Don't you ever get anything right, Jack? You said twenty minutes. It's been forty minutes. My ass is frozen. And . . . I suspect Cosmo Cricket is not the kind of man one keeps waiting. This is your fault."

Jack snorted. "Who told you to stand outside? Certainly not me. If your ass is frozen, the blame is all yours. One can sit on a pointy stick and twirl when one issues mandates. The weather is not cooperating, and what the hell does he want to see all of us for, anyway? Just get in the damn car, Harry."

"It was an invitation, Jack, not a mandate. He didn't elaborate. Just said it was important."

"How do you know Cricket invited Ted, Espinosa, and Bert?"

"You are stupid, you know that, Jack? They all called me because your phone was off since you were in court. You remind me on a daily basis that you don't answer when you are in court. So they called me to get in touch with you. I hate talking to you when you go all snarly on me. So, just shut up and drive. Wake me when we get to Old Town."

"Damn it, Harry, don't you dare go to sleep on me now," Jack said as he carefully inched over to the right lane to avoid getting stuck behind a sanitation truck. "What did the guys say about the invitation?"

"Nothing. Cricket didn't tell them anything more than he told me. Just that he would appreciate it if we'd meet with him. Oh, yeah, he said not to mention the meeting to Lizzie, but he called her Elizabeth. I said okay. I wasn't comfortable with saying okay, but I did it because he caught me off guard. The others said the same thing. Now I feel disloyal to Lizzie."

Jack didn't like Harry's fretful tone. When Harry was fretful, things happened, things that he invariably got caught up in. "Cricket is Lizzie's husband, Harry. Maybe he's planning some kind of surprise for her. As guys, we have to stick together. Just look at you, Harry. Where would you be if I didn't step in to help with your decorating?"

"Eat shit, Jack."

"Stop being so damn testy, Harry. It's not becoming to a man of your dubious status and physical capabilities. Pay attention to the GPS so I know where the hell I'm going. Did Cricket indicate what our destination is to be?"

"No. Just the address, and it's about two miles down the road. You're making good time, considering the weather." Just then his cell rang. Harry mouthed the word "Ted" and listened. He grunted something and hung up. "Ted said Cricket made him promise not to tell Maggie about this little outing. He's worried about making that promise."

"What the hell is going on, Harry? We only met that guy . . . what . . . three times, and suddenly he's enlisting our aid for something that concerns his wife. I'm just not getting it."

"That's because you're stupid, Jack. Men call other men when there is a crisis in their relationship. Even I know that. Either Cricket wants us to be part of something he's planning or he wants our advice, which I doubt. I feel duty bound to tell you I am going to tell him not to pay any attention to any advice you might offer."

Jack ignored Harry, as he usually did. "I bet it has something to do with Lizzie's new position at the White House. I wonder how he *really* likes that. You know, is he jealous? Are people calling him for favors? That kind of thing. You know what, Harry? Suddenly I am not feeling good about this meeting."

"Yeah, me, too. Okay, hang a right at the next

corner, go all the way to the end of the street, and make a left, then another left, and that should put us on Morning Glory Lane. The number on the building—maybe it's a house— is seven-one-one. Talk about your old lucky gambling numbers," Harry said.

"This looks like a pretty high-end neighbor-hood," Jack said as he let his gaze go to the houses on large lots, separated from one an-other by spacious lawns. "What, two acres each? No immediate neighbors to gossip with over the fence. I wager these babies go for four or five million. I bet Ted will know."

"That's it!" Harry said, pointing to a string of cars parked in an immense driveway. "Guess we're the last to get here. This is your fault, you schmuck. I hate being last. All the good stuff happens when you're first. When you're last, no one wants to rehash everything that went down in your absence."

"Will you just shut the hell up, Harry? I hate it when you go off on a tangent. So what if we're last? I'd rather get where I'm going safe and sound than be dead on arrival."

Jack got out of the car and made his way up the long driveway. He looked to his left and saw that Cosmo Cricket was standing in the open doorway, waiting for them. Cosmo shouted against the wind, "Thanks for coming out in this weather, gentlemen."

Jack knew Harry was muttering something obscene, even though he couldn't hear it. Harry's lips were moving, which was never a good thing. Actually, it was pretty much of a bad thing.

Hands were shaken; then they were inside a monstrous empty house that seemed to Jack like a gigantic cave. It was warm, which was, he supposed, a good thing. He eyed Cosmo Cricket as Lizzie's husband lumbered his way to the back of the house. "A moving stairway would be nice," Jack muttered as Cosmo's massive body preceded him and Harry. Jack later swore that the house trembled.

Again, hands were extended as all the men shook, their expressions curious at this particular summons.

"How big is this house?" Espinosa asked.

"Sixty-five hundred square feet. I bought it back in September of last year and had it gutted. Elizabeth doesn't know I bought it. It's supposed to be a surprise," said Cosmo.

Harry stiffened. "Women do not like this kind of surprise. Just ask old Jack here."

"I've heard that. That's why I asked all of you to come here. You've all been to Elizabeth's house. I can barely move around in there. I thought . . . So, are you saying I shouldn't have done this?"

Cosmo looked so worried that Bert took pity on him. He started to talk, and the others weighed in, offering advice.

"It's a stunning house, and I think Lizzie is going to love it. But leave the decorating up to her," Bert said.

"She might not like driving this far, and I

can't see Lizzie taking the Metro. That might be a problem. Of course, you could get her a chauffeur," Espinosa said. "You know, as part of the surprise."

Cosmo was looking more worried by the moment.

"There are surprises, and then there are *surprises*. Maggie likes to be part of all decision making. I don't know, Cricket. This might be a hornet's nest," Ted said.

When Cosmo looked at him, Jack decided to take the high road. "Knowing Lizzie the way I do, I think she's going to love this house. The fact that you bought it for her with the best intentions will go a long way. Lizzie is the kindest person in this whole wide world." He waved his arm about. "We can attest to that. So, if for some reason she doesn't like it, you sell it. It's that simple. But I wouldn't tell her to sell her little house. She loves that place, too. She makes us dinner, and we eat in the kitchen. Lizzie likes cozy and intimate." Jack realized he was babbling and held back whatever he was going to say next.

Cosmo sat down on the window seat in the breakfast nook, a look of pure panic on his face.

"Don't listen to Jack. He has no decorating experience at all. Were you going to call in a professional decorator?" Harry asked.

"I didn't get that far in my thinking, Harry. I got the certificate of occupancy yesterday. As you can see, the house is ready to be moved into. The minute I had that paper in my hand, I real-

23

ized that maybe I had overstepped my bounds a bit." Cosmo looked around the kitchen and muttered, "This is not cozy and intimate."

"But it could be," Ted said. "Maggie says a kitchen should reflect the owner. She likes green plants, lots and lots of green plants. Bright colors, the right furniture, and copper pots are where it's at. Lizzie has a good decorating eye. I like her little house and have always felt comfortable when I'm there. You know, you can take your shoes off and feel at home. Then again, maybe it's Lizzie herself who makes you feel at home. Shit, I don't know," he finished lamely.

The others pondered this startling bit of information and nodded sagely.

"Yeah, well, that isn't all you need. You need coordinated place mats and napkins, and the candles have to match. Then when they get stubby looking, you have to replace them. It's all about scent and ambience." Suddenly Jack saw something in Cosmo Cricket's expression that he couldn't define. "This isn't about the house at all, is it, Cricket?"

Cosmo lumbered to his feet. He turned around to look out the bay window at the falling snow. "You're pretty astute, Emery. You're right. It isn't about the house. Well, it is, but it isn't. You know what I mean."

Suddenly he had everyone's attention, their antennas fully extended. They waited for the Vegas attorney to enlighten them.

Cosmo cleared his throat. "No one knows

what I'm about to tell you yet. It won't make the news till tomorrow, maybe the day after. Then again, they might hold back on it until later. People sometimes have a tendency to boast that they have friends in high places, and for the most part, it's probably true. I have a few myself, as I'm sure you all do, too. This one friend . . . is very high in the pecking order. She called me late last night and shared what she knew with me."

"How high is high?" Ted asked, the reporter in him on high alert.

"The top. There's no place else to go from that particular slot," said Cosmo.

This is like pulling teeth, Jack thought. A chill ran down his spine. "And does Lizzie know about that call?"

"No, Jack, she doesn't. She was sound asleep when the call came in. I was scheduled to go back to Vegas today but changed my plans. Elizabeth thinks I'm on my way back. I didn't exactly lie to her. I am leaving, weather permitting, this evening."

Bert's eyes narrowed. "Are you telling us someone so high up on the totem pole called you, I'm assuming in the middle of the night, and the FBI doesn't know about it? Who is that person?"

Cosmo held up hands that were as big as catchers' mitts and shook his head. "Actually, Bert, there were two calls last night. I guess I should have said that in the beginning. The first call involves the person and a personal decision he decided to make. He wanted me to know before anyone else."

"And . . . ?" Jack said, prodding.

Cosmo took a deep breath. To the others, it seemed like all the oxygen in the room was suddenly sucked out. "Justice Douglas Leonard called and said he's resigning in June, when the Supreme Court session ends. His wife, Florence, has a terminal illness, and he wants to spend his time with her. But the more I think about that call, the more I think . . . it just didn't ring true somehow. He said he was going to call President Connor at five o'clock this morning to tell her. President Connor called me at five thirty and told me she already had a short list ready should a vacancy crop up. Elizabeth is at the top of the short list. Elizabeth knows nothing about this. The president called to give me a heads-up, and I guess to see if I would give her any opposition, which I didn't, because I was in a state of shock."

Cosmo sat back down, his shoulders quaking.

"Holy shit!" was all Jack could think of to say.

"Lizzie Fox Cricket a Supreme Court justice! Man, it doesn't get any better than that!" Ted said.

"Do you think Lizzie will want the position?" Jack asked carefully as he watched for Cosmo's reaction.

"I don't know. I know I'd certainly give it some serious thought if I were under consideration. I'm afraid for Elizabeth. My position in the gambling mecca of Las Vegas may not help her.

She would make a top-notch justice. There was something about that call, though, that is bothering me. Maybe I'm too jaded, but the thought that maybe it was a setup of some kind did cross my mind."

"Jesus, I can see the headlines now," Bert said.

Ted whirled around, a snarl in his voice. "I hope you aren't referring to the *Post*, Bert. Maggie will be front and center, and you have to admit, she has a way with words. The *Post* will be on Lizzie's side, and woe to those who oppose her."

They all started to talk at once as they extolled Lizzie's virtues and how criminal they all thought the vetting process was. The final summary was that Elizabeth Fox Cricket was a legend in her own time, and only a bunch of fools would even consider rejecting her nomination. Cosmo sighed as he heaved himself to his feet.

"So, what's the game plan, Cosmo? What do you want us to do? That's why you called us all here, right? Do you want the *Post* to get on it? Are we supposed to keep quiet? Do you want us to call the mountain? We need a plan here, big guy!" Jack said.

Cosmo threw his hands in the air. "I don't know. That's why I came to you five. I thought you might have some advice."

Ted Robinson stood tall, squared his shoulders. "The best advice I can give you is to let Maggie and the vigilantes handle this. We can stand in the wings, but this is right up their alley.

If you want it to happen for Lizzie, turn it over to them. That's a big if."

The others murmured among themselves and ended up agreeing with Ted.

"I think the big question is, do you want this for Lizzie? You personally?" Jack asked.

"It's going to change our lives if it happens," Cosmo replied. "I will support Elizabeth one hundred percent if it's what she wants. Listen, thanks for taking time out of your day to come out here and talk to me. I'll let you know if I hear anything, and I'd appreciate it if you'd all do the same."

The guys agreed as they trooped to the door. It was still snowing lightly.

Bert turned around as Cosmo locked the front door. "I think this magnificent house is befitting a justice of the Supreme Court." He clapped Cosmo on the back and said, "Fly safe."

The others made their way to their respective cars.

"That was a mindblower, wasn't it, Harry?" Jack said as soon as they were settled and back on the road.

"If it happens, I don't think Lizzie will take it, Jack."

"Don't be so sure, Harry. It's what every lawyer aspires to, the highest position of its kind. A job for the rest of your life. You get to make law. I know Lizzie is outside the box, over the top of the box, and way out there, but she's going to think long and hard about it. If the job were offered to Nikki, I would be jealous as hell but happy as hell for her. Cosmo's right, though. Their lives will change. I'm glad I'm not him. He's just plain miserable right now. Just out of curiosity, Harry, what would you do if it were Yoko?"

"Run for the hills. I'm a simple guy, Jack. I think I would always feel I didn't measure up to all those legal brains that would be part of her life. And it would be a separate part of her life, one I couldn't share. I wouldn't like that at all. It's just my personal opinion, but I think Lizzie will turn it down if it's offered to her. On the outside she's all glitz and glamour, and I would never underestimate her legal expertise, but inside, Lizzie is home and hearth and simple, like me. If you laugh at me, Jack, I will kill you on the spot."

Jack let his mind go back to that long-ago night when he found Lizzie at the cemetery with a bunch of frozen violets in her hand. She would have frozen to death if he hadn't picked her up and taken her home. "I think you're right, Harry."

Chapter 4

Maggie Spritzer looked around the empty newsroom. Then she looked at the bank of wall clocks that gave the time all over the world. To verify the time, she looked down at her Cinderella watch, a funky gift from Ted eons ago. Ted was late. She walked over to one of the newsroom windows and looked out at the falling snow. *Enough with this winter weather already,* she thought.

Maggie whirled around when she suddenly realized she wasn't hungry. She felt a wave of panic at this strange phenomenon. She tried to remember the last time she wasn't hungry but couldn't come up with a time or a place. Where was Ted? More to the point, why hadn't he called in all afternoon? She hated it when the Hardy Boys, as she secretly thought of Ted and Espinosa, didn't check in. Therefore, something was up somewhere.

It was totally dark outside. She stared at her reflection in the darkened glass. Down below and across town, she could see a mass of twinkling lights. She knew the roads and sidewalks would be a mass of wet slush.

Maggie looked at the bank of clocks again. Either dinner with Ted was going to be canceled or he was running late, which wasn't like him at all. Normally, Ted was pretty good about following her rules. She'd give him another ten minutes, and then she was outta there.

Ten minutes later Maggie was pulling on her red ladybug rubber boots, another funky gift from Ted, and getting ready to leave the office. She looked up and said, "If you ever turn your cell phone off again for five hours, you'll be in the unemployment line. Are we clear on that?"

Ted shuffled his feet and looked properly chastised. Espinosa, who was standing next to him, backed up a few steps to get out of the line of fire. He knew that a verbal barrage was going to be engulfing Ted shortly. Maggie stood up, her red boots the only splash of color in the room.

"The weather isn't all that good, Maggie. I don't think we have to worry about our dinner reservation. I'm sorry, okay?"

"Cancel the dinner reservation. I'm not hungry. I haven't heard an explanation, *Teddy*."

"What do you mean, you're not hungry? Are you sick?" Ted asked, hoping to divert Maggie, which he knew would not happen.

"No, I'm not sick, and I am as mystified as you are about why I'm not hungry. You look guilty. I'm going to count to three, and I want to know what you're keeping from me. Freeze, Espinosa," Maggie barked when she saw her star photographer trying to inch his way backward into the newsroom.

"It's personal, Maggie. I'm sorry I turned off my cell, but nothing happened, and the world didn't come to an end."

"Don't try feeding me that line of crap. You do not have anything personal going on in your life, and we both know it. Tell me now or regret it."

There was such menace on Maggie's face, Ted turned white. "Jesus, Maggie, will you please cut me some slack here? This is a guy thing, okay?"

"So, who cares? I'm a girl. Last chance."

"Oh, shit! Listen, if I tell you, will you keep it a secret?"

"No!"

Ted's shoulders slumped.

Espinosa leaned against the wall. "You're weak, Ted," he said through clenched teeth.

Ted inched himself into Maggie's office and sat down. "My life is on the line here. If those guys find out I blabbed to you, I'm toast."

"You're ashes if you don't tell me right now."

"Okay, okay! Don't go getting your panties in a knot. Espinosa, Jack, Harry, Bert, and I got a call from Cosmo Cricket. He wanted us to meet him at a location in Old Town in Alexandria. Cricket bought this big old fancy, high-end house for Lizzie back in the fall, had it gutted, and it's now ready to move into. He wanted our opinion. We gave it to him. We told him whatever he did, not to decorate it, because that's the woman's job. Cricket was real nervous. Now he wishes he had told Lizzie or not even bothered to buy the damn house. He's on his way back to Vegas, if his plane left on time. We promised not to tell Lizzie or anyone. Anyone means you, too."

Maggie stared up at her best reporter, her best friend, her lover, and said, "Do you think I just fell off the turnip truck? Now, give me the rest, the real reason he asked you all to go out there."

Ted squirmed in his chair. He gave it one more shot. "Maggie, that's it. Call Cricket yourself or the others. They'll tell you just what I told you."

"I'm not sleeping with them, and I won't be sleeping with you, either, you schmuck. Now, tell me straight up."

Ted took a deep breath. "Lizzie Fox Cricket is on Martine Connor's short list to be nominated for the Supreme Court. One of the justices, Justice Douglas Leonard, who is a very close friend of Cricket's from way back, is going to retire when the court term ends in June. Well, it's not definite. Things keep switching up, so maybe yes, and maybe no. If it's yes, Lizzie gets nominated. That's why you have to keep it quiet, in case it turns out to be a bad rumor."

"And you didn't call me on this?" Angry sparks flew from Maggie's eyes. "What is the first rule of a good reporter, *Mister* Robinson?"

"Tell your boss the news so they . . . *she* can decide if she wants to go to the mat with it and get out a special edition. Reporters don't take sides. They just gather the news, and you print it. Jesus, Maggie, I gave my word."

"You had no right to give your word. The only right you have is not to reveal your source. That I respect. But you gave me your source at the outset, so that cancels that right." Maggie kicked off one of her ladybug boots.

"What? You can't run with this, Maggie!"

The other boot hit the floor. "One reason, just one, why I can't go with this. It's not too late. I can get something out if I hustle."

Ted stood up, a defiant look on his face, his shoulders squared, as though he were ready to go to battle. "Lizzie doesn't know, Maggie." It was all said so quietly, Maggie had to strain to hear the words.

Maggie stared at Ted as she tried to figure out if he was lying to her or not. "How could she not know? She's been working at the frigging White House for four days now. She's Martine Connor's best friend! There are no secrets in the White House. Or in this damn town, that's for sure. How could she not know, Ted?"

"I can only tell you what Cricket told us. She doesn't know, Maggie."

"I have to call the mountain. I'll do whatever Annie says since she owns this damn paper."

Espinosa decided he needed to weigh in. "Don't do it, Maggie. Please. This is Lizzie we're talking about. Don't screw it up for her. Sometimes headlines aren't where it's at. People count. You know that. Like I said, this is Lizzie's life you're diddling with."

Maggie sat down and pulled on her boots again. Ted and Espinosa were right, and she knew it. She would have thought it through and . . . She was *almost* sure she wouldn't have run with the news. She shivered. She'd been a hair away from maybe doing something disastrous. Damn, maybe something was wrong. Something was happening to her. She still wasn't hungry, and she had almost made a serious mistake. Something hot burned behind her eyes.

"Let's go get something to eat," Ted said, hoping to drive the awful look from Maggie's face.

"No, you guys go. I couldn't eat anything if I tried. I'm going to stay here for a while. I need to think."

"Then why did you put your boots on?" Ted asked.

"Because my feet are cold, not that it's any of your business," Maggie said. "Be sure to stop for some cat food. If you recall, you asked me to remind you this morning you were all out. Look, I'm sorry for jumping all over you two. I'm not liking this at all, but I do understand, and to show there are no hard feelings, go out to dinner, use your expense account, and eat till you're stuffed."

"Are you sure, Maggie?" Ted asked.

"Yes, I'm sure. Go on before I change my mind."

Maggie could see the elevator from the newsroom windows. She waited till she saw the doors close and the numbers light up overhead before she picked up her phone and hit the speed dial.

"Abner, sweetie, I need some help here. I need us to keep an open line, and I want the information as you get it. By early morning if possible. Let's not go to the wall on this. This is one of those name your price and it's yours. Of course, if you try to screw me, I'll have to kill you, but not before I splash your face all over the front page of the *Post*. This is top secret, classified, need to know, the whole ball of wax. You following me here, Abby?"

Abner Tookus, Maggie's supreme hacker bar none and one of her best friends in the whole world, simply said, "I had a new DVD I was going to watch tonight."

"Boo-hoo. Listen up."

Abner Tookus listened. And then he whistled. "A month in Hawaii. I loved that last trip you gave me. Black American Express card to use while I'm there. First-class tickets for two, five-star accommodations. And a new Porsche when I get back. Silver, black interior."

"Done," Maggie said.

"Why am I thinking you're getting me cheap?"

" 'Cause you're stupid. A deal's a deal."

"Maggie . . ."

"I have your back, Abby. At any point if you feel . . . you know, uneasy, shut down, cover your tracks, and our deal is still a deal."

"That will never happen, Maggie. I'm too good. That's not what I was going to say or ask. I was thinking maybe instead of the Porsche, a check for a down payment on some beachfront property in Hawaii."

Maggie hung up, but not before she said, "Remember, an open line on that other cell you have. I'm leaving here now, so just keep talking even if you don't hear me."

Twenty minutes later Maggie exited the *Post* building and walked straight to her transportation, a Town Car with a driver, the most beloved perk of her being the EIC of the *Post*. If she had looked behind her and to her right, she would have seen Ted and Espinosa huddled in the side doorway of the *Post* building.

"Goddamn it, I knew she was going to do this!" Ted hissed.

"I might be stupid on my stupid days, but how did you know she was going to come out and get in the Town Car? She does that every day. She's probably going home," Espinosa said.

"I know because I would be doing the same thing she's doing. I'm a reporter, or did you forget that? Maggie at heart is still a reporter, and she is *not* going home. Five will get you ten she's going to Lizzie's house. Well, do you want the bet or not?" Ted hissed again.

"Nah, that's a sucker's bet. So, does that mean we're going to follow her? And, why should we if you're so sure that's where she's going? It's cold out here, and I'm freezing. We'll have to pay a taxi some big bucks, that's providing we can even flag one down. I'm all for a three-inch-thick steak, some nice greasy fries, and French onion soup. C'mon, Ted, Maggie isn't going to blow it."

"Yeah, Joe, she is, but not in the way you think." Ted called Espinosa by his given name only when he was really and truly worried about something.

"Do you mind spelling that out for me, Ted? How can she blow it but not blow it?"

"She's going to tell Lizzie she's on the short list. They're females, Joe. Females stick together, no matter what. They'll screw us over in a heartbeat, and you damn well know it. The one thing Maggie won't do is tell Lizzie the information came from Cosmo Cricket. I'd stake my life on that. The screwy thing is I can't really get mad, because if a secret involved you, Jack, Harry, or Bert, I'd be doing the guy thing, too."

"So does that mean we're going to go get that steak?"

"Yeah, that's what it means. And before you can ask, no, Maggie won't call the mountain. She knows she stepped over the line with me."

"You are so weak when it comes to Maggie," Espinosa sniffed. "I hope I never turn out like you."

"You should be so lucky. Right now you should be worshipping the ground I walk on."

Espinosa gave his buddy a hard shove, which pushed him into a snowbank under a lamppost.

* * *

Lizzie Fox looked down at her watch when she heard her front doorbell chime. Then she looked at the dinner she had just served up. She shrugged as she made her way to the door, where she looked through the small cut-glass triangle that passed for a peephole. Maggie! She mentally calculated the amount of the surefire, quick stew recipe that was in the warming pot. Certainly there was enough for Maggie. She flung open the door, looked at the falling snow, and said, "You're just in time for dinner. Homemade stew, warm rolls, soft butter, crisp salad, and sorbet for dessert."

"I'm not hungry, Lizzie."

"Are you sick? What's wrong? What are you doing here, anyway, at this time of night? My, God, did something happen on the mountain? Is Ted okay? Talk to me, Maggie."

Maggie kicked off her boots and shed her down jacket. She trailed behind Lizzie to the kitchen. She eyed Lizzie's bowl of food but didn't bat an eye. Instead, she opened the refrigerator and picked up a bottle of water. "Go ahead and eat. We'll talk when you're finished. Everything is fine. Nothing is an emergency."

Lizzie started to eat but realized she'd suddenly lost her appetite. She stirred the food around and watched Maggie out of the corner of her eye.

"So how do you like working at the most famous address in the world?" Maggie asked.

"It's a job, Maggie. New people came on board when I did, so in a sense we're all getting to know each other. Tobias Daniels is a great guy, and he's going to be a superb chief of staff. We've known each other for years. He genuinely likes the president, so that's a definite plus. Lowra Dilic was a great pick for press secretary. I've known Lowra for a long time, and she's a great team player. I'm just glad Marti took my advice. I heard through the grapevine, that's the White House gossip chain, that the old chief of staff is going to be indicted along with Baron Bell. I didn't hear any other details, but Marti got rid of him just in time."

"Have you met anyone important?"

"Nope. The prime minister of Israel was there today. So was some Muslim leader. I see Marti's schedule every morning, and she doesn't have a spare moment. I have no idea when she gets a bathroom-and-lipstick break. It's a killer schedule. This is absolutely not for publication, Maggie, but something has Marti's knickers in a twist. She came into my office, admired my window view, said hello, then just stared at me for five whole minutes. After that display of something or other, she kind of nodded to herself and told me not to work too hard and that she was glad I liked my office. Oh, she brought me a poinsettia plant for my desk. I thought that was a little weird, but I can't shake the feeling that something is going on. I asked Toby, and he said he didn't have a clue. I think he would have told me if he did."

"So, you like it there, huh?"

"Actually, Maggie, I don't like it there. I only took the job to make sure POTUS keeps her promise to the vigilantes. I gave her six months. She knows what she has to do."

"What if she hasn't kept her promise at the end of the six months?" Maggie asked.

"Then the girls can go at it, and I'll help in any way I can. Just like you will. Do you want to tell me why you're here so I can quit messing with this food I'm not going to eat?"

Maggie made a production of going through her bag, looking for money. She finally ended up with eighty-seven cents. She laid the coins out on the table. "I'm hiring you, and this is my retainer. Unless you take credit cards."

Lizzie bolted upright. "Are you in some kind of trouble, Maggie? Did something happen at the paper? It's not Ted, is it?"

"None of the above, Lizzie. I'm not sure if I should be here, but we all belong to the same . . . club, so to speak. Plus . . . women have to stick together, don't you agree? By the way, no one knows I'm here, and I'd like to keep it that way. Also, I probably should have called the mountain, but I didn't."

"I absolutely do agree that we should all stick together. Why don't you just tell me what brought you out here on this miserable night so we can go at it and make it right?"

Maggie started to shred one of the paper napkins on the table. "We're good on the eighty-seven-cent retainer?"

"We're good on the retainer, Maggie."

Maggie sucked in air and let it out with a loud *swoosh*. "Okay, here goes. Buckle up and listen carefully."

Chapter 5

Ted Robinson walked to the curb and whistled shrilly. Luckily, a cab pulled up almost immediately. Both he and Espinosa climbed in. Ted leaned over the seat to speak to the driver. "We want to go to Georgetown, but with a stop at Andolino's on the way."

Ted leaned back and buckled up. "Espinosa, call Andolino's and order takeout for five. Spaghetti, meatballs, and sausage, with three orders of garlic bread, salads all around, and two six-packs. I'll call Bert, Jack, and Harry."

Harry was the only one of the three who kicked up a fuss, which prompted Ted to say, "Listen, you ninja terrorist, I don't have time for this bullshit. Just be at Jack's when we get there. Espinosa and I are bringing dinner, and, no, if you want that tofu shit, bring your own, we're eating Eye-tal-yun. That is so rude, Harry, and God or Buddha is going to punish you for talking to me like that. Bye."

"He's going to kill you, Ted. You know that, right?"

"Jack will shoot him. I'm not worried."

Espinosa laughed so hard he choked, and Ted had to pound him on the back.

When Espinosa finally got his breath back, he asked, "Do you want to be fried or planted?" Then he went off into another choking fit of laughter.

Ted stared out at the falling snow and thought it was tapering off. His thoughts turned to Maggie. He wished he wasn't so gutless. He turned to Espinosa, who was staring out his own window. "Straight up, Joe, would you have caved in to Maggie the way I did?"

"Yeah. Maggie has the full electric charge. The best we can hope for is a sputtering spark, which doesn't say a whole hell of a lot for us."

Ted almost strangled himself when he squirmed and wiggled to face Espinosa. "What's your best guess? Did those guys call the mountain? Did they spill their guts? I need to know your thoughts so we don't go confessing to something they did, too. You getting my drift here?"

"I am. The short and long answer is *yes*. I'm also thinking my ass is going to go in a sling when Alexis finds out she's the only one who didn't get a call. Do you think I should call her, Ted?"

"Hell, yes. Talk sweet. Tell her you were in a dead zone, and the phone keeps dropping calls. We're here. Anything else you want besides what you ordered?"

"Yeah, two bags or boxes of cannoli. Make sure they have chocolate on the top."

The cabdriver slid to the curb, and Ted hopped out. He was back ten minutes later, his hands gripping two very fragrant shopping bags full of food. Two six-packs were tucked under his arms. The cab was moving before he could buckle up.

"What'd she say?"

"Nothing. The call went to voice mail. I told her to call me and said it was very important, crucial actually, along with critical, and to get back to me as quick as she could."

"Okay, your ass is covered. Do you really think the others blabbed?"

"Absolutely they blabbed. You can take it to the bank." Espinosa wondered if what he was saying was true. "Look, you're good at bluffing and lying when you have to. You're a reporter, for God's sake. Just act like you know they did it and go on from there. Harry is not going to kill you. He might hurt you a little, but he doesn't want to go to jail. Relax."

"We need a new circle of friends, Joe. Haven't you noticed how stressed we are of late?"

"I thought you'd never mention it," Espinosa grumbled. "By chance, do you mean someone like Charlie Farrell and his gardening wife, or do you mean Matt Oliver and his social-climbing spouse?"

"Jesus, we'd die of boredom and be drinking sherry out of little glasses at four in the afternoon. Forget I mentioned it. We should think about maybe taking Xanax or something. Nah, with our luck we'd get addicted. Harry isn't *that* violent."

"Yes, he is."

"Shut up, Espinosa. We have only a block to go, and we'll be at Jack's house."

"Just out of curiosity, Ted, have you given any thought to Maggie finding out we're going to Jack's house? She's going to come home sooner or later, and she lives just two doors away. Plus, she's going to see the bill for the credit card you charged all that food on. Dinner was just for the two of us, not for five, and Andolino's is expensive. She's going to figure it out."

"You had to say that, didn't you? Don't I have enough on my mind without worrying about my expense account? We're here. You take the beer, and I'll carry the food." Ted inched himself out of the cab and handed the fare to the driver, along with a generous tip, compliments of the *Post*.

"It looks like it stopped snowing," Espinosa said. His jittery-sounding voice did not go unnoticed by Ted.

Espinosa jiggled the two six-packs of beer as he rang the doorbell with his elbow. When the door opened almost immediately, he stumbled through the open doorway. Jack stepped aside.

"It quit snowing," Espinosa said.

"That's nice to know. I was going to turn in early tonight. What the hell is it with you two? Can't you get enough of me during the day? Whatever this is all about, it better be good."

"Yeah, right. Like you think I'd spring for dinner for five people at Andolino's if it wasn't important? Plus the taxi fare and tip. Is everyone here?" Ted asked.

"All present and accounted for," said Jack. "Harry is in his killer mode, and he also brought weeds and tofu and that shitty green tea. Guess we can save his share for Maggie."

Ted snorted. "Believe it or not, Maggie has lost her appetite. I'm worried about her."

"And well you should be. We'll save it, anyway," Jack said, leading the parade to the kitchen, where Bert and Harry were waiting expectantly.

Bert sniffed appreciatively. Harry nibbled on his weeds. Ted refused to make eye contact with Harry as he started to take the boxes out of the bags.

"We don't even need dishes or silverware. Everything is included. No fuss, no mess," Espinosa said, taking his place at the kitchen table.

"We can talk after we eat. The food is still hot, so let's enjoy it," Ted said.

The guys fell to with gusto. Thirty minutes later the kitchen table was clean, and the fifth meal was in the refrigerator. Harry packed up his weeds in a little plastic bag and stuffed it into a pocket of his baggy pants. All eyes turned to Ted.

Ted squared his shoulders and worked up a case of ripe indignation. "You guys just couldn't wait, could you? You promised Cricket not to blab, and what do you do? You damn well blab! Don't deny it! So much for guy power! No wonder women don't trust us. Well, say something. I'm embarrassed to be sitting here with you. You can't be trusted."

"Now hold on here, Ted," Jack blustered. "You better be careful when you bandy accusations about. Where do you get off saying something like that?"

He looks guilty. They all look guilty. Ted felt so giddy, he thought he was going to black out. He risked a glance at Espinosa, who looked like he was going to fall off his chair in relief.

"Maggie." Ted leaned back on his chair and crossed his arms over his chest. "You gonna lie to my face or man up?"

"Okay, okay. I'm the head of the goddamn FBI. I had no right to make a promise like that. How'd that look if it got out?" Bert said lamely.

"We're part of a team here. I had to tell Nikki," Jack said. "You think I want those girls coming down on me, and that's exactly what would happen if they found out after the fact."

"So what are you going to do about it?" Harry asked quietly.

"Not a damn thing," Ted said cheerfully. "It's what Maggie is doing as we sit here talking. She's on her way to Lizzie's house. She was leaving when Espinosa and I left the paper. We both heard her give Lizzie's address to her driver. Hell, she's been there now for about an hour. Now, gentlemen, being as smart and astute as you are, why do you think Maggie went to Lizzie's house in this weather at this hour of the night, and more to the point, why isn't Maggie hungry? Well, say something."

"The woman hasn't been born that you can trust," Jack said virtuously. "Women stick together like glue, and they *can* keep a secret."

"That's what women say about us," Bert said, pity ringing in his voice. "Except for the part about us keeping a secret. Obviously, we failed the test."

"I did not divulge any secrets, nor did I call Yoko," Harry said.

All eyes turned to Harry in disbelief, but no one said a word.

"What? What? A man is measured by how he keeps his word. I gave mine to Cosmo Cricket. I take something like that very seriously. Why are you looking at me like that?"

"Well, Harry, what do you think Yoko is going to say? How is she going to feel when she finds out you didn't think enough of her to alert her to what's going on? What about all that crap you guys are always spouting about losing face?" Jack said. "Man, I would not want to be in your shoes right now."

"Up yours, Jack. Yoko feels the same way I do about honor and lying and giving one's word," Harry retorted.

"That was back in the Dark Ages, buddy. She's a member of the vigilantes these days, or did you forget that? She's damn well going to wipe up the floor with you. Ah, you aren't looking worried, Harry. Big mistake." Jack cackled.

The others looked at Harry with pity.

Harry squirmed in his chair. "You guys are bullshitting me, right?"

"Nope," the foursome said in unison.

Ted got up, picked up his backpack, and started for the door. "My work here is done. I enjoyed your titillating company and dinner, even if I paid for it. Have a nice evening, boys. Uh-oh, it's snowing again," he said to no one in particular. "Espinosa, call us some wheels."

"Never mind calling for a taxi. I can drop you off," Bert said, coming up behind them. "I got a parking space two cars up."

"We accept," Ted said magnanimously. "I have to stop at the convenience store near the apartment for some cat food. I can make my way on foot after that. You want to stay over, Espinosa?"

"Yeah, I think I will," Espinosa replied.

Inside the car, Ted finally got the courage to ask, "How's Harry? Is he staying the night at Jack's?"

"Looked to me like he was crying when I left. He was begging Jack to help him out, and Jack was extorting all sorts of promises out of him. That's all I know, boys. Hey, do you think spring will ever get here?" Bert asked.

"Someone should remember to call Jack in the morning to see if he's still alive," Espinosa said. "I can't believe you guys squealed."

"Well, you did, didn't you?" said Bert. "Isn't this the kettle calling the pot black, or whatever the hell that saying is?"

"Actually, Bert, we didn't squeal," Ted lied and was glad it was dark inside the car, so Bert couldn't see the lie in his eyes. "Maggie did to us what we did to you. She wormed it out of us, but I think she already knew. They're women, for God's sake, and you can't trust them."

"So, what does this whole sorry episode mean to us guys? To Lizzie? To the girls?" Bert asked.

"Damned if I know," Ted said.

"Not a clue," Espinosa said.

Chapter 6

The Sisters were gathered in the conference room as they waited for Charles to join them. They were talking among themselves in hushed whispers.

Annie was listening intently to the conversation around her, one eye on the door so she could alert the others when Charles was about to appear.

"I'm not sure what we're supposed to be feeling here," Kathryn said. "Should we be happy for Lizzie, or is this something that's going to work against us and her? Especially her."

Nikki, the only lawyer in the group, sat up straight. Her voice was tight with emotion. "It's every lawyer's dream to be nominated to the Supreme Court. We all live and breathe for that to happen. But having said that, Lizzie isn't *every lawyer*. Plus, she just got married. She'd be on one coast, and Cosmo would be back in Nevada."

"Well, he did buy that big new house for

Lizzie, so that has to mean he's contemplating living here," Alexis said.

"They'll crucify Lizzie in the vetting process. I can see it now. She represented the vigilantes. She married Nevada's most famous lawyer, who just happens to represent the gambling industry. It will be a three-ring circus," Isabelle said.

"The big question is, will Lizzie even want to go to the Supreme Court?" Yoko asked as she chewed on her thumbnail. "We all know she turned down a federal judgeship, saying she preferred to work in the trenches, so to speak. I don't want to see those people chew her up."

"None of us want to see that happen," Myra said.

"Then we need to prevent it, don't we?" Annie said grimly. "But first we need to find out Lizzie's reaction to this news."

"I can tell you exactly how Lizzie is going to play it," Nikki said. "First, she's going to be stunned speechless. Then, at warp speed, she's going to see everything that could and will go wrong. Her first worry will be us, then Cosmo. Then she'll make that little snorting noise she makes sometimes and say, 'No big deal.' But it is a big deal. It will all seem like a dream for about ten minutes. Then she's going to get angry. With us and with Cosmo, because we found out before she did, and Cosmo acted like the man he is and didn't go to her right away."

The Sisters looked at Nikki in awe.

Annie cleared her throat just as Charles appeared in the doorway. They all looked at the heavy load of files and folders he was carrying. He offered up a greeting and went straight to the bank of computers lining the far wall.

"Enough already, Charles. It's late. We're all tired. Please, join us and tell us what is going on," Myra called over her shoulder.

And then the Sisters all started to babble at once.

Charles clapped his hands over his ears, a signal for quiet. "I understand your concern, your worry. Now, let's sit down and try to come to some sort of resolution where Lizzie is concerned. To begin with, I want to tell you I have a seed of an idea, but it will require my leaving the mountain for a day or so. Now, one at a time, tell me your thoughts and your concerns and where and how you think this is going to play out."

"That's an absolute no-brainer, Charles. First and foremost, we don't want to see anything happen to Lizzie. We don't want her splashed nine ways to Sunday, and we don't want to be the ones responsible for her not being confirmed," Annie snapped.

"With all your resources, surely you can find a way to do *something*, dear," Myra said.

"I suppose in the back of all our minds, we're wondering how this will affect the pardon Martine Connor promised. We all know the only reason Lizzie took on the job of chief White House counsel was because of us. Pro bono, no less," Kathryn said. *"For us,"* she added emphatically.

Myra leaned forward. "I would like us all to take a vote right now. As of this moment, our pardon, which is really iffy to begin with, goes on the back burner, never to be brought up again until we have Lizzie on whatever road she wants to walk down. I want to see a show of hands." Myra smiled when she saw eight hands shoot upward, Charles's included. "Then it's settled. Lizzie is our priority. The moment we find out which way she wants to go on this . . . honor . . . we go to work."

"It's one o'clock in the morning, girls. I say we hit the sheets and convene first thing in the morning," Nikki said.

"Then I'll say good night and good-bye," Charles said as he gathered up what looked like a fifty-pound briefcase. "I will call every few hours. Call me if you make any carved-in-stone decisions. And, no, I am not telling any of you where I'm going, not even you, Myra." He kissed his wife and blew kisses to the others as he marched across the room and out the door.

"Charles, it's one o'clock in the morning!" Myra said weakly.

"Best time to travel, old girl," Charles called.

The Sisters grumbled among themselves as they gathered up their jackets and boots for the trek across the compound to their living quarters. Some of the comments were: "Charles *never* leaves the mountain, like in *never.*" "It has to have something to do with Lizzie. He'll turn himself inside out for her." "He never moved from the computer all day. It was like he knew

58

what was going to go down before it did, and he was preparing for this."

And then came the big question posed by Annie. "How long before the secret gets out and Lizzie's name is worldwide?" When there was no response, Annie huffed and puffed her way across the compound, Murphy nipping at the tops of her boots.

Inside their quarters, Kathryn ripped at her outer clothes, tossing them in a pile by the front door. Murphy immediately claimed her down jacket as his bed for the night. "Who was the fool who said we should get some sleep? With all this going on, I'll probably never sleep again. Well?"

"I think it was me," Myra said.

"No, it was me," Nikki said. "Look, we don't *have* to go to sleep. It was just a suggestion. We can sit here all night and hash it out to death, but we don't have enough information to do that. Until we hear from Lizzie herself or Maggie, there's nothing we can do. We don't have information, we don't have a plan, and Charles is obviously up to something he thinks will help, so we can't undermine whatever that may be. Ergo, the best thing to do is try to go to sleep."

"Why don't we try calling Maggie?" Isabelle asked.

"That's not a good move," Alexis said. "She might still be at Lizzie's house or maybe even staying the night. Girl talk of the most serious kind. We can't rock that boat right now. That's my opinion."

"Maggie will call when she has something to report," Yoko said. "I don't know if I should be happy or sad for Lizzie. She just got married, and she's so happy. Now her world is going to turn upside down."

"Lizzie can handle anything," Isabelle said.

"No, Isabelle, Lizzie can't handle everything. Did you forget that time Jack brought her to the mountain from the cemetery? She'd given up. The press is going to go back to the day she was born. They'll bring in that whole Mafia thing," Nikki said.

"But . . ."

"Nikki's right," Annie said. "This is just a wild guess on my part, but wherever Charles is going, I think it has something to do with Lizzie's background. I want all of you to think about something. Then we're going to bed, whether we like it or not. Right now, at this moment in time, we ourselves are outrageously famous. We can spread the word that we want Lizzie nominated. If we're to believe our own press, politicians shudder and run for cover when our names are mentioned. Just the fact that we're *on it*, so to speak, will speak volumes, and don't forget Maggie and the *Post*. Now, if Lizzie decides to pass on the nomination, and the press and the Washington insiders go after her, we go after them. *One at a time.*"

Myra got up and started to wring her hands. "Annie, dear, when we broke into Baron Bell's offices, what was the name of that senator you said had a thick file in that old safe?"

Annie's eyes sparked. "Ah yes, Senator Lantzy. He sits on every committee and is quite powerful. He has a voice in the Senate, and his colleagues listen to him. And we have the file on him that Baron Bell made sure never saw the light of day! Ooooh, I'm starting to get excited, girls."

"Ah, I'm suddenly seeing some light and perhaps the beginning of a plan," Nikki said. She yawned elaborately. "I think I might be able to sleep now."

The yawn was contagious as the others followed Nikki out of the room. Only Myra and Annie remained.

Annie reached down into the bowl of candy and popped a handful of M&M's into her mouth. When she finished chewing, she said, "Cough it up, Myra. Where did Charles go? And don't even think about telling me you don't know, because if you say that, I am going to snatch those pearls right off you and drape them around Murphy's neck. He will eat them, and there go your beloved pearls."

"I think, and I say I think, he went to see Hank Jellicoe."

"I need more than that, or those pearls belong to Murphy," Annie snapped.

"Henry Jellicoe of Global Securities, also known as Hank to his friends. When Hank was known as HJ Securities and just starting out, he did the security for my candy company. When Charles came to the States, he took over, and Hank moved on to become Jellicoe Securities.

Over the years he built the company, until today it's known as Global Securities. He's got offices all over the world. His yearly revenue, Charles told me last year, was in the billions. You want security, you go to Hank Jellicoe. He hires only the best of the best. Ex-FBI, ex-CIA, ex–Secret Service. Then he debriefs them and retrains them at some secret location. He pays his people astronomical sums of money, and there's a waiting list to get hired. Anyway, he and Charles are great friends. Oh, did I mention his people also do, or at least they used to do, security for the White House when big doings are going on? Impeccable reputation. Oh, one other thing. He keeps files on everyone. You think J. Edgar had files. Ha! According to Charles, what J. Edgar had was kindergarten stuff compared to Jellicoe. You happy now, Annie?"

Annie nodded sagely. "Okay, you get to keep the pearls. By the way, Myra, I have yet to see you on the pole."

"This might be a very good time for us to retire for the evening, Annie dear," Myra said as she headed to the door to go back to the main building, which she shared with Charles.

"Why don't you stay here this evening? There's an extra bed in my room. You don't want to be alone, do you?"

"Oh, Annie, I thought you'd never ask. You're right. I hate being alone." Myra hugged her old friend, and together they walked down the hall to Annie's room. "About that pole . . ."

* * *

Three hundred miles away as the crow flies, Maggie Spritzer stared at Lizzie Fox. People, she thought, really did go into trances. Who knew?

"Lizzie, you need to say something. I don't even care if you tell me you hate me for coming here and telling you all this. Just say something, okay?" Maggie watched, fascinated at the way Lizzie's throat muscles worked and the way she tried to lick at her dry lips.

"I don't know what to say. The whole thing is . . . bizarre. Why me? It must be some kind of trap. It has to have something to do with the vigilantes. They'll hash that over forever. Then they'll start digging into my background and run with my husband's family. You know how that went down. Doesn't matter if we were innocent bystanders or not. Cosmo. I don't understand why . . . Oh, poor Cosmo, he must be in such turmoil. They'll go on the attack and chew him up."

Maggie laughed. "No, they won't. You have the most powerful weapons there are on your side. You have the *Post*. You have the vigilantes. You have all of Vegas and all those important people Cosmo knows. I'm thinking they're going to be treating you with kid gloves."

Maggie leaned across the table and took Lizzie's cold hands in her own. "The big question, Lizzie, is, do you want to be an associate justice of the Supreme Court? You know as well as I do, it's not what you know. It's who you know. The best thing you could have done was take on the job of chief White House counsel pro bono. Cosmo bought you that big, wonderful new house, so that's out of the way. You two can commute just the way you're doing now, if it's what you want."

"Oh, Maggie, if it was only that easy. I made a promise to the girls to get their pardon. I won't be able to work behind the scenes to make that happen. I will be under such scrutiny. I do not like people watching me. Unless I want them to watch me. But to answer your question, I've always had this picture in my mind of myself in my black robe, sitting with the other eight justices. I was always sitting in the middle. I think every lawyer ever born sees himself sitting on the highest court in the land. Yes, yes, a thousand times yes, I want that. But not at the girls' or Cosmo's expense. How long do you think I have before the word gets out?"

"I think you have plenty of breathing room, Lizzie. No one knows about Justice Leonard's decision but Cosmo and the president, and, of course, the girls. The president is going to sit on it for a little while. Don't forget, this is all new to her, too. Remember now, you can't let on you know. That means you cannot call up Cosmo and talk it to death. At least not yet. The other thing is, do not get angry that Cosmo held out on you. I want your promise on that."

Lizzie nodded.

"You know what? I think I'm hungry. No, I'm ravenous. What do you have to eat?"

Lizzie laughed. "My larder is full. Did you forget

Cosmo was here? I have some of everything," she said, jumping off her chair and running to the refrigerator. "I have ham, roast chicken, a potato-cheesy-onion casserole that Cosmo loves and made himself. All kinds of vegetables and fruit. Beer, wine, soft drinks, or coffee."

"A little bit of everything. I'll make the coffee. Are you going to join me?"

"Damn straight. We need to celebrate. Oh, Maggie, do you think it's even remotely possible that one day soon I will be sitting on the Supreme Court, just the way Sandra Day O'Connor did? She was my idol, you know. Still is."

Maggie turned away from the sink, where she was measuring coffee into the pot. She set it down and placed her hands on Lizzie's shoulders. She looked deep into her friend's eyes and saw only honesty, integrity, and hope. "Honey, us *women* are going to put you there if that's what you want. As Annie would say, you can take that to the bank. You know the bank I'm talking about, the one that is owned by a woman in the District."

Lizzie burst out laughing and almost dropped the ham she was holding.

The two women high-fived one another before Lizzie started to slice the ham.

One impossible dream coming up, Maggie thought happily.

Chapter 7

Even in the dark, with all the snow and the ground and tree lighting, Charles Martin thought it was the most beautiful spot in the entire world. He remembered thinking the same thing some thirty-odd years ago, when he'd been brought here as a guest of the owner.

Back then he'd been told this place was called Lord's Valley by the owner. These days it was called Jellicoe Valley. There was even a quaint sign five miles back, right underneath the road marker, that said so. This time he was coming as an uninvited guest.

Charles sucked in his breath, knowing that all manner of eyes, human and electronic, were on him, even though the night was pitch-black. He wondered just for a moment if he should get out of his Hummer and wave a white flag, but he didn't have a white flag to wave. He supposed a handkerchief would do it. On second thought, the wisest thing to do was probably just to sit there and wait for someone to come and get him.

The thought no sooner passed through his mind when he heard a light tap on the window. He pressed the power button and said, "You're good."

The man ignored the compliment. "Welcome to Jellicoe Valley, Mr. Martin. Mr. Jellicoe said to ask you what took you so long."

Charles chuckled. "A little of this, a little of that. Thirty years isn't all that long."

There was no return chuckle. "Follow me, sir. Be sure to stay on my tracks. We don't want any unnecessary explosions. Mr. Jellicoe is partial to quiet, especially at this time of night."

Claymore mines. Unlike Fish's spread in the Nevada desert and his pretend mines, Charles knew there were indeed mines surrounding Hank Jellicoe's hundred-acre spread here at the foot of the Allegheny Mountains.

When he'd been here a lifetime ago, it was just wild brush, scraggly trees, and a rustic three-room cabin. As he bounced along behind his escort, Charles tried to remember exactly when he'd seen an architectural rendering of Jellicoe's spread, as he liked to call it. Someone brave enough at the time had taken some aerial shots of the man's property, then had the audacity to publish his drawings in *Architectural Digest*. Why he'd never submitted the actual photos he'd taken was something that was never explained. Nor was the man's disappearance ever explained to anyone's satisfaction. He had heard, but was never sure if it was the truth or not, that *AD* had paid through the nose for invading Hank Jellicoe's privacy. Along with sending a note of sincere apology.

It was a wise man, or, in some cases, a wise woman, who learned that you did not bring down the wrath of one Hank Jellicoe, aka Jellicoe Securities, aka Global Securities. At least if you valued your life.

There were more lights now. To Charles's keen eye, it looked like a winter wonderland with all the lighting, the shimmering snow, and the fragrant pine trees. Christmas-card perfect. The cabin was still there, nestled among a copse of pine trees. He turned to the right and saw *the house*. Gabled and turreted, it spread out for what, Charles thought, could be several city blocks. The house was lit up from top to bottom. And there was a light on on the front porch. And it was a porch, one that wrapped around the entire house, from what he could see. Just like Motel 6, Hank had the light on for him. Good old Hank.

Charles strained to see beyond the house and thought he saw a row of garages, a stable, which made sense because Hank loved to ride early in the morning. Hank also liked to swim, so he knew somewhere there was a heated indoor pool and probably one outside, too. A tennis court was somewhere. He was sure of it. Just the way he was sure there was an airplane hangar and a helicopter pad, and if there was any deep water around, a yacht would be moored somewhere. Hank Jellicoe had it all going for him.

The four-wheel drive in front of him came to a stop. The man climbed out, his AK-47 slung over his shoulder. Charles knew the drill. He remained in the Hummer until the man approached his vehicle.

"You can get out now, Mr. Martin. Mr. Jellicoe is waiting for you. He held dinner for your arrival."

"Very sporting of him," Charles said. He reached behind him for his bag, but quicker than lightning, his escort had his arm in a vise.

"No need to carry your bag, Mr. Martin. I'll bring it up."

As soon as you go through it, you mean. Charles slid out of the Hummer and made his way up the steps to the old-fashioned front porch.

The monster cathedral-style door opened, and there stood his host. "What the hell took you so long, Charlie? Thirty years is a long time."

Charles winced at being called Charlie. If anyone else but Hank Jellicoe had called him Charlie, he would have decked him on the spot. The men shook hands the way men do, then pounded each other on the back the way men do, before Jellicoe led Charles into the main part of the house.

It was a man's house, all leather and wood and polished wood floors. It smelled like a man's house, too. The scent of burning wood, pipe and cigar smoke hung in the air, but it was not unpleasant.

"Come along before dinner is ruined. We've been keeping it warm until you got here. We have all night to palaver. Venison is on the menu. I remembered how you like venison. A bunch of other stuff, too. And I made the pie myself, Charlie. It's every bit as good as yours. Wait till you taste it. Used the apples from the root cellar, so it's as fresh as can be. Got a secret ingredient in there, which you are never going to figure out," Hank Jellicoe said by way of greeting.

Charles looked at his host and grinned. "We'll see."

Henry, Hank to those near and dear to him, Jellicoe was a tall man, six-four or so, with snow-white hair, weathered skin bronzed by the sun, wrinkles that were more like trenches, and the sharpest blue eyes ever to grace a man. His teeth, whiter than snow in his dark face, could light up the night. He boasted that his weight, 180 pounds, was the same as it was the day he turned eighteen. He was lean and rangy, sinewy from his neck to his toes. Dressed in his favorite garb of worn, tattered, and battered jeans and a plaid flannel shirt, with boots he had specially made for his size-sixteen feet. Charles knew for a fact he had the strength of an ox. But what Charles respected most about Hank Jellicoe was that he was an honest, fair, and generous man.

The three traits Charles most admired in a man. Or woman.

Jellicoe escorted Charles to a long table set for two. "First things first, Charlie. I want to get it out of the way. Tough break about your son. I did what I could. I want you to know that."

"I know you did, Hank. I tried to get word to you."

"I got the word."

And that was the end of that conversation.

Charles sat down and opened his napkin. "Has there been any . . ."

"Don't go there, Charlie. *That* topic is not up for discussion."

Charles looked into the sharp blue eyes and gave a nod.

Jellicoe shook out his own napkin and leaned back when his server placed a huge platter of food in front of him. "So you finally tied the knot. I have a wedding present in the hall closet. I hope Myra likes it. Heard you didn't much care for that water bed in the Caymans."

Charles burst out laughing. "Is there anything you *don't* know?"

Jellicoe grinned. "Nope. Does Myra know you're here?"

Charles stopped chewing on the delectable venison and said, "I thought you just said you know everything. Myra is fine. No, she doesn't know where I am, but by now I'm thinking she's probably figured it out. There's a special place in her heart for you, you know that, right?"

"I do. I would move heaven and earth for that lady. In part, she's responsible for who and what I am today. I don't forget things like that. And the . . . girls?"

"For someone who knows everything, there seems to be a few gaps in your intel, Hank. The girls are fine, but we find ourselves in a bit of a quandary at the moment."

Jellicoe nodded.

"So, are you on a hiatus, vacation, what?" Charles asked. "I remembered you always liked to be home for Christmas and took a wild chance I'd actually find you in residence. What do you call this place these days?"

Jellicoe laughed. "I call it my house. One of my operatives said it reminds him of a mall. I like space, Charlie. Lots and lots of space. Don't know why that is. It just is. I do love Christmas. I had a big tree with colored lights. Did the whole drill, wreath on the front door, candles in the windows. Presents under the tree for the help. It was depressing as hell. How's things on the mountain?"

"It gets confining at times, but we've adjusted. Every so often we develop a raging case of cabin fever. What's the word on Pappy?"

"Contented on that mountaintop in Spain you swapped out. I've been trying to entice him back into the fold, but so far I'm not having any luck. You want to do an intervention?"

"No. He has three youngsters these days. Kids need to know their father and see him every day. You and I both know that. Leave him alone, Hank. How long are you going to be here before you trot off somewhere?"

"Well, the plan was for me to leave here at the end of the week, but when I found out you were on the way and the why of it all, I put those plans on hold. We'll get to that later. You ready for my pie now?"

"I feel like I should loosen my belt, but, yes, I'm game. You still think I won't be able to figure out your secret ingredient?"

"Ha! I would have made a hell of a pastry chef, but this crazy-ass sweet tooth would do me in. I try to limit my sugar. We aren't getting any younger, you know. Now you have to watch your triglycerides, your good and bad cholesterol, all that crap. Just so you know, mine are all within normal boundaries. How are yours?"

"Perfect."

"My ass they're perfect. Look at the weight you put on, Charlie. All you do is sit behind a computer."

"When I get back to the mountain, I'll fax you my medical report. Like I said, they're perfect, which leads me to believe yours are not."

Jellicoe flinched. "You always were a show-off, Charlie. Well, here's our pie. It's my turn to show off. Eat hearty, my friend."

Charles did eat hearty and savored every bite of the delectable flaky pastry. "Almost as good as mine, Hank."

Jellicoe threw his head back and laughed. "I guess we could have a bake off if you hang around here long enough. So, what's the secret ingredient?"

Charles snorted. "Pomegranate. Did you really think I couldn't taste it? Maybe, I'm thinking, a quarter cup of the pulp."

"Son of a bitch! How did you figure it out?"

"I tasted it, you son of a bitch!"

Jellicoe was still pretending to be outraged when he said, "Coffee and brandy in my study and a really good Cuban cigar."

"I'm your man," Charles said, pushing back his chair.

Settled in front of the fireplace, which rose all the way to the ceiling and held half an oak tree, which sent sparks shooting up the chimney, Hank Jellicoe poured hundred-year-old brandy into a snifter and handed it to Charles. "To the best of the best," Jellicoe said, clinking his glass against Charles's snifter.

In spite of himself, Charles was flattered. "At pie baking," he quipped.

Jellicoe roared with laughter. "That, too! So, talk to me, Charlie."

"It's about Lizzie Fox. Lizzie Fox Cricket these days."

Jellicoe roared again with laughter. "Now, who in the world would ever think old Kick could get himself a filly like Miz Lizzie? Sure as hell not me. I have to tell you, I was dumbfounded. I sent a smashing present to the newlyweds. Got a sweet handwritten note from the new Mrs. Cricket. I love that little lady like she was my own daughter. You know that, Charlie, and I think of Kick as a son. But then you know that, too. Articulate and fill in all the little ifs, ands, and buts. I'll take it from there."

Charles talked. For an hour. With no interruptions. The 140-proof, hundred-year-old brandy bottle was down to the quarter mark. The oak log was still burning as brightly as both men's eyes.

Jellicoe reached for a second cigar, clipped the end, and handed it to Charles. He did the same for his own. Both men puffed contentedly. "The big question, Charlie, is this. Does Lizzie want to go to the Supreme Court? If she does, we have the power to put her there. If she doesn't, this is all moot."

"Lizzie never puts herself first. She's worried about the vigilantes. She's worried about Cricket. There's the commute from Vegas to here. She might want it so bad she can taste it, but she won't lift a finger to help herself if she thinks it will cause one iota of trouble for the vigilantes or her new husband. That's why Lizzie is Lizzie. Ten years ago, when you needed her, she pulled it together for you and didn't take a fee. At least that's the story I heard at the time. She said—correct me if I'm wrong—'I might need a favor someday, and I expect you to come through for me.' We both know she'd never ask, so it's up to you to honor that favor, don't you think?"

"You son of a bitch! Where do you get off telling me I would even think about not honoring the favor, and I know she'd never ask? Do you hear me? I know that, Charlie."

"No need to get your knickers in a twist, Hank. I'm just saying. Do you still walk in and out of the White House like it's your summer home?"

"Well, yeah, when I'm in town," Jellicoe drawled. "I like the new president. We get along just fine. She told me to call her Marti. I'm Henry to her. She likes biblical names for some reason. But she did say Hank suits me. Yep, we get along just fine."

"Now why doesn't that surprise me, you old reprobate?"

Jellicoe grinned from ear to ear. "Back to business. But first off, did you ever sleep in the Lincoln Bedroom? I did, and it sucked. But the company more than made up for it."

"That's more than I needed to know, Hank."

"No. You needed to know that." Jellicoe was all business now. "Game over, Charlie. You want Lizzie on the Supreme Court, she's there. Anything else?"

"Well, I think I might want to know what the fallout is going to be."

Jellicoe pretended horror at the statement. "And what makes you think there will be fallout? Have you ever heard of *any* fallout from anything I've ever done over the years?" Not bothering to wait for a reply, Jellicoe said, "No, you have not, and there will be none this time, either."

It was a guarantee, pure and simple. Charles accepted it.

"No sense in letting this fine brandy sit in the

bottle. We might as well finish it and head for bed. Tomorrow is another day. Actually," Jellicoe said so quietly, Charles had to strain to hear the words, "there is one other thing, Charlie. I personally saw the pardons on the president's desk. I just wanted you to know that. Now, when and how she's going to handle it, I don't know. Let me clarify that. At this precise moment I do not know how she's going to handle it. Tomorrow or the day after might be a different story."

Charles nodded and got up. He tossed his cigar into the fireplace. "Cosmo will come out of this intact?"

"Better than ever. He'll be a household name. What? You doubt me, Sir Malcolm?"

"Not for a minute."

Both men slapped each other on the back as they made their way out to the hall, where there was a moving sidewalk that would take them to the west wing, which housed the bedrooms.

"Were you drunk when you designed this house, Hank?"

"In a manner of speaking. I was thinking more of my declining years and bad knees and the like. Got four elevators, three moving sidewalks. Works for me."

Two moving sidewalks and one elevator ride later, Jellicoe opened the door to a massive suite of rooms. "When I had this room designed, I had Myra in mind. I always hoped she would come to visit someday."

"All you have to do is invite her, Hank, and

she'll find a way to make the trip. This is just a wild guess on my part, Hank, but Myra is the one you should talk to about—"

"Good night, Charlie."

"Good night, Hank."

Chapter 8

Stuffed to the gills, Maggie tossed and turned in Lizzie's guest room, the cell phone that was live—with Abner Tookus on the other end—clutched in her hand. "You there, sweet cheeks?"

Maggie strained to hear a mumbled response. "Where do you think I'd be at this hour of the night? Why aren't you sleeping, anyway?"

"Because I don't want to miss anything. Do you have anything?"

"Of course I have something. I do not run a Mickey Mouse operation. You know that. I hope you didn't call me just to chitchat."

"Well, what do you have?"

"Stuff. I have stuff. I am not giving it to you in dribs and drabs, because it won't make sense, and that's not how I work. You know that, Maggie."

"That Porsche is starting to look like a Kia, Mr. Tookus."

"You win some. You lose some. Go to sleep."

"I can't sleep. That's why I'm calling you. This is important, Abby, and I'm only as good as my sources, who, I might add, rob me blind." When there was no response, she said, "Okay, okay, I'm going to sleep, but if you get anything, shout. I'm a light sleeper, and I'll hear you."

Maggie reached up and turned off the light. Then she turned it back on. She pulled out her other phone from under the pillow and called Ted. When she heard his groggy voice, she said, "Did you remember to get the cat food?" She thought she heard Ted mumble something; then she heard him snoring. She looked over at the little digital clock on the nightstand—3:20. She realized she was hungry. She didn't think Lizzie would mind if she went down to the kitchen to raid the refrigerator. If she spent thirty minutes eating, another twenty taking a shower, she could call her driver and be at the paper before it got light out. She shook her head as she pulled on her clothes. She'd never been able to sleep in a strange bed, no matter how comfortable it was.

She crept quietly down the stairs and headed for Lizzie's cozy kitchen. She blinked when she saw Lizzie sitting at the table, coffee cup in front of her. Maggie backed up and was about to leave to go upstairs so as not to invade Lizzie's private time when Lizzie motioned for her to sit down.

"I couldn't sleep," Maggie said. "Guess you couldn't either, huh?"

"I doubt I'll ever be able to sleep again,

Maggie. I have never in my life been in such a turmoil."

"Do you want to talk about it?" Maggie asked as she poured the last of the coffee into a cup.

"No offense, but no. I was just sitting here thinking about how Cosmo and I made a promise not to keep secrets from one another. Now he has one, and so do I. I don't know how it's going to be once I show up at the White House. The game plan has now changed, with what you told me. Even though no one is supposed to know, I'm not sure I believe that. You and I both know there are no secrets in this town. The White House leaks like a sieve. I'm still getting my feet wet at Sixteen Hundred Pennsylvania Avenue."

"Lizzie, you took three cases all the way to the Supreme Court, argued them, and won all three. That tells me you can handle this. Is there something in particular worrying you?" Maggie asked as she sipped at the coffee in her cup.

"No, Maggie. It's just such a shock. I need time to . . . to, you know, think about it, let it sink in. I'll be fine. Like I said, once I get on with my day and the shock wears off, I'll come down to earth."

Maggie smiled. "Why would you want to come down to earth? You should be soaring with the eagles and enjoying every second of it. This is like winning one of those big lotteries where the odds are a *kazillion* to one. Lizzie, look at me. Stop worrying about everyone else, and enjoy this moment in your life. Don't blow it. Don't take the edge off it, either. Enjoy every single nanosecond of it. Promise me."

Lizzie sat bolt upright in her chair. She laughed then, the tinkling, melodious sound she was known for, as both her clenched fists shot upward. "You're absolutely right, Maggie. Thanks for bringing me up short. I promise. I think I'm going to wear yellow today. You know, spring, sunshiny, flowers blooming, that kind of thing."

Maggie grinned. "I looked out the window before I came downstairs. I saw snow flurries under the streetlight. There's a flower shop on Independence Avenue that opens at seven o'clock. Stop and buy some tulips for your desk."

"Well, aren't you Miss Sunshine herself this morning! I'll do it. I love tulips, especially at this time of year."

"Well, now that we have the immediate problems of the world solved, I think I'm going to head home, since I'm already dressed. I might try for some springy attire myself. Thanks for the hospitality, Lizzie."

The two women hugged one another before Lizzie headed up the steps to the second floor while Maggie called her driver to pick her up.

Twenty minutes later Maggie was settled in the back of the luxurious Town Car and headed to her house in Georgetown. She spent the entire ride home wondering what surprises the new day would bring.

* * *

Lizzie Fox drummed her fingers on her desk, her gaze on the window and the lightly falling snow. She tore her eyes away from the wintry scene to look at the spring tulips sitting on her desk, her thoughts a million miles away. She'd bought several bunches of the colorful blooms, one for the president, one for Jackie Hollis, the president's private secretary, and the last for Tobias Daniels, the president's chief of staff. She'd been rewarded with smiles and effusive thanks. But that moment was gone, and she had a full day's worth of work piled on her desk.

Lizzie removed her jacket to reveal a bright summer yellow silk shirt. It was a yellow day, no doubt about it. As long as you didn't look outside.

It was midmorning when Lizzie looked up to see Jackie Hollis standing in the doorway. Lizzie scribbled a few more notes but motioned for the elderly woman to come in.

Jackie Hollis was the mother of six and a grandmother of eight. Her office was decorated with pictures of her brood in every possible setting. She had unruly gray hair, cut very short, twinkling eyes, and a firm jaw. She wasn't exactly a dragon guarding the portals of Martine Connor's domain, but she came close. She played no favorites and donated to homeless shelters all the goodies people heaped on her in hopes of a tad of favoritism. She dressed conservatively, in suits of beige and gray, with colorful blouses. Lizzie suspected she had dozens of suits, in different styles, but she never ventured outside of the gray and beige color range. If she had a fault, it was that she smoked and was known to sneak outside with the help of the Secret Service agents, who, as she put it, covered her butt, with no pun intended. On more than one occasion the president and her closest ally scurried off to some unseen location to take a few quick puffs, with no one the wiser.

"I thought you might like some coffee, Lizzie," Jackie said, holding out a cup with the presidential seal emblazoned on the side. "I just made it."

Lizzie smiled. "I never turn down a cup of coffee. If you have time, sit down, and we can chat. I'm overdue for a break."

"I do have about ten minutes," the older woman said as she settled herself in Lizzie's one comfortable chair. "Do you think it will ever stop snowing?"

Lizzie laughed as she tried to figure out if Jackie Hollis was privy to the president's secret, her secret now. If she was, she was wearing one of the best poker faces she'd ever seen. "The weatherman said it's snowed every day since Christmas." Was it her imagination, or did Jackie look uncomfortable?

Never a paranoid person, Lizzie realized she had become one. Secrets could be a terrible thing. Then again, there were secrets, and there were *secrets*. She crossed her ankles under the desk and hoped she wasn't giving off any kind of bad vibes or signals to the woman sitting across from her.

The two chatted a few more moments about Jackie's Christmas with her grandchildren and how they'd frolicked in Rock Creek Park with their new sleds and sled boards.

"Lord love a duck, I almost forgot why I came down here, Lizzie."

In a pig's eye you forgot, Lizzie thought. She smiled.

"The president asked me to have you pull the contracts for Global Securities and bring them up to me. She said there's no big rush, but I sensed there is a rush, so when you have time, get them to me. It won't be a problem, will it, Lizzie?"

Lizzie almost fell off her chair at the mention of Global Securities. She knew Hank Jellicoe. Back in the day, she'd handled his legal work. When he went global, it had become a 24-7 job and had left no room for other clients. She'd worked for months, parceling out work to attorneys she trusted to give Hank the service he demanded and needed. To this day, she still handled some of his more private matters.

"Not at all." It would be a problem, though, because she had no clue where outside private contracts were kept. She knew without anyone having to tell her that Global Securities' contracts were private and best kept that way, private. She knew they would be somewhere under lock and key, that was for sure.

The fussy little lady paused in the doorway, turned, and said, "Thanks again for the lovely tulips, Lizzie. You really brightened my day today. And before I forget, you look like a splash of summertime sun. I love color. As famous and wonderful as this house is, it's a dark place. I hope I didn't take up too much of your time this morning."

"Not at all, Jackie. I welcome a break from time to time."

Now, what was that all about? Ah, yes, contracts. Ever mindful of the unseen eyes and ears that surrounded her, Lizzie went back to what she was doing, but her mind was not on the job at hand. Clearly, she was going to go out to lunch today, snow or no snow. She needed to call her husband to talk about Global Securities and one Hank Jellicoe, one of Cosmo's oldest and dearest friends, and she didn't want to do it from the White House. Cosmo might be able to give her some feedback because, while she had a professional relationship with Hank Jellicoe, Cosmo had a personal relationship with the head of Global Securities. Global oversaw all of Vegas's internal security, even though most people thought it was casino security. Interestingly, when the vigilantes cleaned up the situation at Babylon, during which time Lizzie met and fell head over heels in love with her wonderful husband, Global was preparing a sting of its own to root out the corrupt security operation in that casino. When you talked billions of dollars a day, you called Global Securities to protect those billions.

It was 12:45 when Lizzie parked her car at her favorite dry cleaners. She reached behind her for her cleaning bag and walked into the shop, knowing full well someone was watching her. She'd been bringing her clothes to Tillie and Leroy Chen since the day she'd settled in Washington. Over the years, she'd handled their legal work, bringing elderly family members to America. There was nothing Tillie and Leroy wouldn't do for Lizzie. She knew the couple would let her into the small back room that was used as a mini office so she could call Cosmo without anyone listening to her conversation. They'd even bring her tea and rice cakes before they closed the door for her privacy. Tillie and Leroy Chen were what Lizzie called good, honest people.

Lizzie was greeted warmly and immediately ushered into the small back office. Rice cakes, tea, and a cell phone appeared as if by magic; then the door was closed quietly. Lizzie sighed, thankful that Tillie had immediately picked up on her need for some privacy.

"Hi, Cricket," Lizzie said by way of greeting. "Just dropped off my cleaning, and I'm having tea with the Chens. It's snowing out again. What's the weather like in Vegas? Cold is good." She laughed, the tinkling sound Cosmo Cricket so loved. "Aside from just wanting to hear your voice, I want to give you a heads-up. The president has asked me to pull all of Global Securities' contracts and hand them over to her private secretary, which I will do when I get back to the office. You might want to alert Hank. This is as much as I can tell you. Once I touch those files, I cannot and will not be able to talk about them. It's that old devil attorney-client privilege. Now, tell me how much you miss me and how you love me more than I love you so we can argue." Lizzie listened to the voice on the other end of the phone, and her world turned right side up. She smiled, she laughed, she grinned, and then she blew kisses into the phone before she broke the connection.

Lizzie wished Maggie was with her so she could eat the rice cakes and drink the tea, but since she wasn't, she scarfed them down, not wanting to hurt the Chens' feelings. She slipped a hundred-dollar bill under her teacup because the Chens would never accept payment for cleaning her clothing. She closed the door quietly behind her to find Tillie Chen waiting for her, with her cleaning hung neatly in plastic bags. They bowed to one another without a word spoken.

Thirty-five minutes later Lizzie was back in the White House, with a little sack of honeyed rice cakes, which she turned over to Tobias Daniels, who thanked her profusely for the snack. She knew without a doubt that someone would check the dry-cleaning bags, but there would be no sign her car had been invaded when she climbed in for her return home at five o'clock.

Now, how best to find those pesky Global Securities files?

Chapter 9

"We look like a bunch of bedraggled cats caught in a rainstorm," Annie said sourly as she poured from the third pot of coffee. "Charles has been gone for three days, and we haven't heard a thing. It's the weekend, the sun is shining, and the snow is melting. I think we all need to put on our happy faces and *do something*. If none of you can come up with something constructive, then we need to adjourn to *the pole*."

That statement grabbed everyone's attention. The Sisters all started jabbering at once.

"Just because we've heard nothing of importance doesn't mean we can't make plans. We're coming up to the second week in January, and Lizzie has been on the job as chief White House counsel for a whole week now. But we all know her thoughts are elsewhere at the moment, which means we need to work on our own strategy as far as our pardons are concerned," Myra said briskly. "Let's bundle up and go over to the command center and see what we can come up with."

Jackets and boots on, the Sisters were at the door when they heard the sound of the cable car sliding into its nest. The dogs in the lead, they all ran outside to greet Charles.

"I'm hungry," Charles said by way of greeting as he hugged his wife.

They all trooped back to the dining hall, where Annie set out fruit, muffins, and sausages and made fresh coffee. The rule was, they never talked business until a meal was finished. With one meaningful look from Myra, Charles wolfed down his food in record time.

"Where did you go, and what if anything did you accomplish?" Nikki asked.

"I went to Pennsylvania, ladies. To a little-known place that was once known as Lord's Valley but is currently called Jellicoe Valley. The man who resides there is named Henry Jellicoe, Hank to his friends. Hank used to handle the security for Myra's candy company, until I took over. It was all a long time ago, but Hank and I remained friends. Hank is now Global Securities. What that means is, he provides top-notch security for American-based companies all over the world. He represents a few foreign enterprises also. He has a five-star reputation.

"I went to see him because of Lizzie, to see what could be done to guarantee her seat on the Supreme Court if she's nominated. If Lizzie wants the position, I think I can almost, and I say almost, guarantee the appointment is hers. But bear in mind there are no guarantees in this life that she will be voted in. What we have going in our favor is that word has not yet leaked out, so that gives Hank and us, and by us, I mean you ladies and Maggie, along with the *Post*, time to help things along when needed.

"I was at the foot of the mountain when I got a call from Hank. It seems he has a source in the White House, an aide to the president, who passed along something none of us want to hear. It seems the president has been working on your pardons, and the files have been on her desk in the Oval Office for some time. The source says he checks them from time to time. Yesterday afternoon the president had a meeting with her top advisors, and it did not go well as far as the pardons are concerned. Every single advisor in the room, as well as the national security advisor, voted no. The files are no longer on the president's desk but are now in a drawer." Charles winced at the collective intake of breath around the table. He waited to see if there would be a verbal outburst, but there was none forthcoming.

He went on. "It is Hank's and my opinion that the president was doing her best where the pardons are concerned. Now, however, we surmise that she thinks that the Lizzie appointment will appease all of you, and you won't do anything to ruin it. It's like putting the egg before the chicken, because had the president not

Fern Michaels

heard from Justice Leonard first, what would she have done about the pardons? She could, of course, stomp her foot on everyone's neck and just issue them and take the blowback. Or she's going to listen to all those advisors and let you all hang out to dry, thinking Lizzie is more important. A stall for time is how Hank and I are looking at it at this moment in time."

Annie stood up, her expression fierce. "Charles, that scenario simply does not work for me. I have plans for my life, and that includes the pardon President Connor promised, and I have no intention of having those plans thwarted. Are we clear on the matter?" Ice dripped from her words.

Charles allowed a small smile to tug at the corners of his mouth. "I'm very clear on the matter, Annie. It's the president who isn't on our wavelength."

"Then I suggest we do something about it," Myra snapped. "And the sooner the better."

"Hear! Hear!" the Sisters shouted in unison.

"Before you arrived, Charles, we were on our way to the command center to work out a plan to do just that," Annie said. "We are more than willing to work Lizzie into our plan so that whatever we come up with works for her as well as for us." She walked over to the door and pulled on her boots and her down jacket. "Time is money, girls!"

The Sisters hustled, Charles bringing up the rear.

96

Ten minutes later the Sisters were settled but grumbling, Kathryn's voice the loudest. "I feel like chewing nails and spitting rust. The president damn well promised us a pardon. She's reneging and allowing her advisors to call the shots when she has all the power. If we were a priority, our pardons wouldn't be sitting in her desk drawer, now would they?" Kathryn took a deep breath and rushed on. "Next week the pardons will be moved out of the desk drawer to a file cabinet, and the week after that, the file cabinet will be moved to the basement, never to see the light of day again. This is *unacceptable!*"

Murphy and Grady growled at the same time, their hackles rising at the fury in Kathryn's voice. Kathryn reached down to stroke the big shepherd's head. He calmed almost immediately.

Grady sidled over to Alexis, who said, "Kathryn is right. It is unacceptable, and it sucks. If there is one thing I hate, it's a liar. The president lied to us. After all we did for her. I, for one, appreciate what she's trying to do for Lizzie, but that does not let her off the hook with the pardons. It's apples and oranges."

"So then, what we're saying here is, we want to take on the White House and the president as well, is that it?" Nikki asked. She sounded calm, as though she were discussing plans for an afternoon stroll in the park.

"Then I suggest we sit down and set up a working plan, with the full knowledge that if things don't pan out, we'll be spending the rest of our lives in a federal prison," Isabelle said. Her tone and voice sounded like she was following through on Nikki's plans for that afternoon stroll.

Yoko was more succinct. "Then let's do it!"

Charles swiped his hand across his stubbly chin. He should have shaved, he thought, but everyone was so anxious to get down to business, he didn't have the heart to delay his explanations. "Let me make sure I understand what all of you are thinking. You plan to invade the White House and what? Just walk out with your pardons? Is that what you're saying?"

"That's exactly what we're saying. If we write it down on paper, will reading it in black and white make a difference to you?" Annie demanded.

Charles smiled, recognizing the challenge Annie had just presented. "Then I say we sit down and get to work. But first, a favor, if you don't mind. I'd like to take a shower and shave first. I will need thirty minutes. When I return, I will have coffee for all of us. In the meantime, feel free to, uh . . . bat some ideas around until I get back."

The room was totally silent until Murphy and Grady barked, the signal that Charles was out of the building.

"Are we out of our minds?" Myra asked.

"Even if we are, who will notice?" Annie said. "Why are you all looking at me like that? You think we can't invade the White House and walk out with our new lives? I am suddenly embarrassed to admit I know all of you."

"Annie, waltzing into the White House is not like tripping into Wal-Mart," Alexis squeaked. "I'm all for it if we can come up with a foolproof plan for our getaway."

"Darling girl, we won't need a getaway if we have the pardons in hand," Myra said sweetly.

The others stared at their fearless leader, their eyes wide, their jaws slack and agape.

"What about Lizzie?" Nikki asked.

"I think Lizzie's future is in good hands, and I really don't see what we could do to help her, anyway. Considering our current situation, that is. In the end, trying to help her might do her more harm than good if it ever comes out that we were involved," Kathryn said.

"By the same token, we cannot do anything that will interfere with the process to confirm Lizzie once it goes public," Yoko said. "We agreed that Lizzie comes first."

"Yes, dear, we did agree to that, and there is no reason why we can't multitask, is there? I'm sure we're more than capable of creating diversions if need be. We're women. Remember that," Myra said.

"All we need is that foolproof plan," Annie said.

"That's not as easy as it sounds, dear," Myra observed.

"This is what we have going for us at the moment. Us, now, not Lizzie. We have Maggie and the *Post*. In itself, the *Post* is a very powerful weapon. We have Jack, Harry, Bert, Ted, and Espinosa. We also have a few others that we've more or less deputized. Nellie, Elias, Pearl, Rena Gold, and Paula Woodley, Cosmo possibly, and Fish. I don't know how any of them can be incorporated into whatever plans we come up with, but there you have it. And ourselves and Charles, of course," Nikki said. Nikki stood back to view all she had written on the huge chalkboard.

"Diversions, dear," Myra said.

"Secret Service," Yoko said. "It should be noted that Harry has contacts all over the world who are as versed in martial arts as he is. I am speaking only of the top tier. They would love nothing more than for Harry to request their help. The Secret Service is no match for Harry and his colleagues." She smiled.

"How sure are you on that?" Kathryn asked skeptically.

"I am one hundred percent certain that Harry and his colleagues can render the agents helpless at the White House. All of them. What I cannot guarantee is how they can get inside. That's our job. If we can get them in, then it's all over." Yoko smiled again.

Kathryn thought it an evil smile. Then she laughed. "That's good enough for me. We'll need time to get Harry's people here."

"All it takes is one phone call or one e-mail. Harry's friends will be on the first available flight," Yoko said.

Nikki added Yoko's information to the list just as Charles entered the room and took his place behind the bank of computers. He looked over at the chalkboard, processed what was written. He nodded. "You forgot Avery Snowden and our people. And don't forget Maggie's computer guru."

Nikki scribbled furiously. "Anyone else we can count on?" When there was no comment, she dusted the chalk from her hands and took her seat.

Charles walked over to the chalkboard and said, "This is what we have to work with. At the moment. Hank Jellicoe has promised us help if we need it." He wrote the name Hank at the bottom of Nikki's list. "Hank can give us the agents' positions, the shift changes, the command center, how to dismantle it, or at the very least render it inoperable, in whatever time is allowed. He and his people excel at high-tech malfunctions. He is also a familiar face at the White House and has served three presidents, including Martine. He will not arouse any suspicion with his frequent trips in and out of the White House."

"Now all we need is a legitimate reason to appear at the White House. Is there such a thing as a public schedule?" Annie asked. "Festivities? Movie stars appear from time to time and require security. Baseball figures. Connor is a Pittsburgh Pirates fan. Maybe something along the lines of an invitation before the season starts."

"Maybe Lizzie can put a bee in Connor's bonnet if she can make it sound like good PR. But I'm thinking anything she comes up with will be suspect now since the pardons are in the desk drawer rather than on the desk. I know Lizzie and the president are friends, but when it comes to survival, in this case, the administration's, you look out for number one. I don't trust her. The president, not Lizzie. Lizzie I would trust with my life," Kathryn said.

"What goes on in the spring at the White House? We should start there," Alexis said.

"Cherry Blossom Festival. Several Japanese contingents arrive annually, since the Japanese are the ones who donated the trees along the Tidal Basin," Myra said.

"Valentine's Day."

"Saint Patrick's Day."

"April fifteenth, tax day."

"May first, or May Day, with a maypole. Memorial Day."

"That's too long to wait and plan for. We want this over and done with as soon as possible. The big question is, do we move before or after they announce Lizzie's nomination?" Annie queried.

A ripe discussion followed, but no concrete decision was forthcoming.

"Let's just get our ducks all in a row, decide what we want to happen at the White House, then make it happen. With the *Post* in our corner, Maggie has the power to put pressure on the White House to create an event," Myra said.

"I have an idea. Let's call all our people and host a get-together for next weekend. We can't assume everyone will be on board. We need to confirm it all," Kathryn said.

The Sisters gave a rousing cheer of approval of Kathryn's suggestion.

"Take care of it, ladies," Charles said.

Chapter 10

The streets of Georgetown were dimly lit from the sodium-vapor lampposts. No one was walking a dog; no lone pedestrians were meandering about. There were no cars to speak of on the roads. Nothing unusual, since it was 3:10 in the morning.

Harry Wong was wide awake in the backseat of the taxi that was taking him to Jack Emery's house in Georgetown. As he stared out the window, he did see dim yellow lights shining indoors at some of the houses. There were many porch lights, probably on timers, that winked and went totally dark at some preset hour. Jack's house was one of those. As the taxi pulled to the curb, Jack's front light flickered and went out. Harry leaned forward, paid the driver, and got out of the taxi. He leaped over a pile of snow on the curb and landed on the sidewalk, which was free of snow.

Always alert, even in the wee hours of the morning, Harry looked around to see if he could pick up on some infinitesimal sound. The night was quiet. Even the sound of the taxi's engine had faded as the driver turned the corner, his red taillights glowing in the dark night. Satisfied that nothing, not even a stray dog or cat, was going to interfere with his late-night visit, Harry made his way up the front steps and rang the doorbell. He waited, knowing that Jack was a sound sleeper. He rang it a second time, waited a few seconds, then lifted his foot and kicked in the door. He shrugged when a high-pitched shriek of sound permeated the air. He could see Jack outlined in the dim foyer light, his hair on end, gun in hand.

"Move and you're dead!" Jack shouted, loud enough to wake the dead.

"Stop being so damn dramatic and turn that stupid alarm off. The neighbors are all awake now. If the cops show up here, you're the one who is dead," Harry shouted, to be heard over the screeching alarm.

"What the hell! You kicked my door in! Do you know what time it is, Harry?"

"Of course I know what time it is! If you had answered your door, I wouldn't have had to kick it in."

When Jack made no move to turn off the alarm, Harry walked over to it, clenched his fist, and smashed the security panel. The sudden silence was deafening.

"Did someone die? What? You better start talking, you son of a bitch, or I really am going to shoot you. Don't go thinking you can catch the bullet in midair, either."

"You want to bring it to a test? Ha! I didn't think so. Get dressed. We're going over to Maggie's house."

Jack still looked dazed as he ran his hand through his spiked-up hair. "I can't go anywhere until the alarm company calls. Otherwise, they send the cops to investigate. I could have you locked up for what you did, you . . . you ninja terrorist!"

The phone rang.

Harry listened as Jack said, "No, I set it off. I got in late and forgot I had the alarm on. Yes, of course. My mother's maiden name was Terrance. Thank you. Yes, I will be more careful in the future. Thank you again."

"Your pajamas have yellow ducks on them," Harry said, guffawing.

"You have a problem with yellow ducks, Harry? My aunt gave me these pajamas. They're high-grade flannel and very comfortable, not to mention warm. What kind of nephew would I be if I didn't wear them? What the hell are you doing here, Harry?"

"Put your jacket and boots on. We're going to Maggie's house. I figured it all out. I'm not going through this twice, so get a move on."

"You want me to go to Maggie's dressed like this?"

"I hope you don't expect me to carry you. Move it, Jack!"

Jack picked up the cushion on the sofa and wedged his gun down into the back. He yanked at his ski jacket, hanging on the clothes tree by the front door, as he slid his bare feet into a pair of rubber boots sitting in the boot tray. "This damn well better be good, Harry. I'm holding you responsible if anyone breaks into my house while we're at Maggie's."

"Don't you *ever* shut up?" Harry grumbled as he stomped his way from the house.

"Look! You woke up the whole damn neighborhood," Jack said as he waved his arms wildly about. "These good people are all worried about a home invasion, and it's all your fault. Even Maggie has lights on."

The front door opened before either Jack or Harry could ring the doorbell. "You kick in my door, and your ass is grass, gentlemen," Maggie remarked.

Stunned, Harry looked at the fiery little redhead, who was glaring at him. "How'd you know I kicked in Jack's door?"

"I'm a reporter, that's how. I had woken up to go to the bathroom, and I always look out the window when I'm peeing. Tough if that's more than you need to know. I was going to call the police, until I recognized you. What are you doing here? Did someone die? Oh, I like your jammies, Jack."

"A gift from my aunt. That's what I asked, and he didn't answer me," Jack said smugly. "He said he wasn't going to repeat his story twice. Are you making breakfast?"

"Why didn't you just kill him?" Maggie said to Jack as she shuffled to the kitchen. "You want breakfast, go to Denny's. Coffee is all I'm offering. If whatever you came here for isn't good, I'm going to plaster your faces all over the front pages of the *Post* and label you both terrorists. So, talk. I can listen while I'm making coffee."

Harry Wong was a stubborn man. He sat down and waited until Maggie settled herself next to Jack.

"Yoko called me a little while ago. I was meditating. What that means to you both is I was on a higher plane and receptive to all manner of universal messages, aside from what Yoko was calling me about. She told me about Charles's visit to one Henry, also known as Hank, Jellicoe, who lives at the foot of the Allegheny Mountains in Pennsylvania. He owns and heads up Global Securities. The man has had the ear of several presidents, including the current one. It appears he has the run of the White House, and he confirmed to Charles that he and the president have a *thing* going on. Meaning an *intimate thing*."

"You woke me up and kicked in my door to tell me *that*?" Jack snarled.

Maggie looked appalled. "You should have killed him. That front page is almost a definite now, Harry."

Harry leaned back in his chair and glared at his two friends. "Am I the only one with a brain here? Why aren't you getting it?"

"Getting what?" Jack bellowed.

"It's all a game! There is no Supreme Court appointment in the offing! It's all a setup!"

Maggie and Jack could only stare at Harry. Maggie found her tongue first. "And you're basing this on the fact that Charles went to see the head of Global Securities and he's maybe, sort of, kind of, sleeping with the president. Is that what you're saying?" A vision of the booty she'd promised Abner Tookus danced behind her eyelids.

Harry shook his head. "No. It was what happened when Charles returned to the mountain. Actually, Yoko said he was at the base of the mountain when he got a call from Jellicoe, who has a source, a stool pigeon if you will, inside the White House. The source is an aide to the president. The source said that since Christmas the presidential pardons for the girls have been on the president's desk. As of yesterday, they've been relegated to a desk drawer. That's one step away from being put into a file cabinet, which will then be moved to the bowels of the White House, never to see the light of day again. In other words, the president is reneging on her promise to grant the pardons.

"It seems on January second, the president had a meeting with her closest advisors, and it got extremely heated, with threatened resignations if she went through with the pardons. The advisors called granting the pardons political suicide. Did I mention that the pardons are signed? They are. Desperate to cover up, the president came up with the Supreme Court bit to tide her over until she can find a way out of her own mess. There is no appointment, Jack! Do you hear me, Maggie? It's all a setup!"

"My God! You not only said whole sentences, but you said paragraphs...you...you silver-tongued orator, you!" Jack quipped.

Maggie looked like she was in a daze as she poured coffee, got cream out of the refrigerator, and fumbled around in the cabinet for the sugar bowl. "It makes sense if you stop to think about it. But, how cruel to do that to Lizzie. They're supposed to be friends. We damn well put her in the White House. This is definitely pissing me off, guys."

"See, you still aren't getting it," said Harry. "Lizzie is not supposed to know anything about this. At least for the moment. At the appropriate time it will be leaked. The president has to appease Lizzie because she knows Lizzie is tied to the vigilantes. Connor either doesn't understand or refuses to understand Lizzie's loyalties to the girls."

"So what do we do now?" Jack asked as he gulped at his coffee.

"How the hell am I supposed to know, Jack? I just delivered the news. You're the one who always comes up with ideas and plans that don't work," Harry said as he, too, sipped at the strong coffee. He was going to ask for tea, but one look at Maggie's face had told him not to bother.

"Who's going to tell Lizzie it was all a . . . a game?" Maggie asked.

"Don't look at me," Harry said.

"Don't look at me, either. You're the one who couldn't wait to run to her house to tell her in the first place. Guess you're it, Maggie," Jack said.

"I'm not telling Lizzie anything. At least not right now. First, I'm going to have Ted and Espinosa do a little fishing. Does either of you happen to know where Justice Leonard hangs his hat when he isn't in Washington? And we're going to want to know about his wife Florence's medical condition. Once we have that information, we can go after him to find out what he was promised to take part in this little charade."

"Harry, did you tell Yoko you . . . uh . . . figured it out? Maggie, I have no clue about Justice Leonard. He could live in a tent, for all I know," Jack said.

"No. Because I didn't figure it out until after we hung up, and I was back to meditating," Harry replied.

"Damn good thing," said Jack. "What that means is you can stay in the boys' club. Shit! Do we call Cosmo or just hug this stuff to our breasts? What are we supposed to do with this information?"

The trio looked at one another, their faces glum.

Finally, Maggie said, "I don't know."

Harry shrugged.

"Harry, your best guess here. How long before Yoko puts it together and tells the girls?"

Harry shrugged again.

"The girls are not going to like this one little bit. Whose side is Jellicoe on. Do we know?"

"Yoko said Lizzie's side, which means our side. But he was conned, too, is what I'm thinking," Harry said. "We have to keep Cosmo Cricket in the loop. I think Maggie should be the one to call him. Makes it more professional."

"You dumb shit! Maggie is not supposed to know, just the way Lizzie is not supposed to know. Cosmo doesn't know we all ratted him out. Maybe we could sic Ted and Espinosa on him," Jack said.

"Hold on here! I'm not calling Cosmo Cricket, and I have plans for Ted and Espinosa as soon as it gets light out," Maggie said.

"Where does that leave us, then?" Jack growled.

"Sitting in Maggie's kitchen, sucking our thumbs, that's where," Harry said. "This is not good, Jack."

"No, Harry, it definitely is not good. The girls are going to go nuclear when they put it together. I just don't know if they'll be more pissed that Lizzie isn't going to the Supreme Court or that they aren't getting their pardons."

"Both," Maggie snarled. She wanted to cry when she thought about Abner Tookus and all she'd had him do. Now she was going to have to

113

explain the large expenditure to Annie. Her insides jumping all over the place, she reached behind her for her cell phone, which was charging. She punched in Abner's number and waited.

"I want a freebie, and I want it right now," she demanded. "If you don't give it to me, I have this guy sitting here in my kitchen who will kick your ass all the way to the moon, and he won't be there to catch you when you land. Do not say one word. Just listen and get back to me in thirty minutes. Yes, I said thirty minutes. I want to know where Supreme Court Justice Leonard lives when he is not in Washington. I want his and his wife's medical records, and I also want their financial statements, plus their address here in Washington, or wherever they live during the nine months of the Supreme Court term. Thirty minutes, or you're on the way to the moon.

"Gentlemen, I am hungry. In fact, I am starving. And since there is no way I am going out to breakfast, I am going to cook. How do eggs, bacon, and pancakes sound? I'll even brew you a pot of tea, Harry. Jack, you make another pot of coffee and nuke the bacon. Make the whole pound. Harry, you're in charge of the toast, and, yes, I like toast even when I have pancakes. I also have a melon in the fridge, which you can cut up."

"Go for it!" Jack said happily. "That person you just called, he can get all that in thirty minutes?" His voice was so skeptical, Maggie actually laughed when she really felt like crying.

"He probably already has it and will wait a full twenty-nine minutes before he calls, but, yeah, he's that good. His fees are astronomical, but he always comes through. Plus, he is in love with me but won't admit it."

Neither Jack nor Harry knew what to say about that, so they just looked at each other and rolled their eyes.

"What? You don't believe me? You don't think anyone but Ted Robinson could love me? Well, he does. Love me, I mean." And then she burst into tears.

Jack and Harry started to twitch, unsure what their next move should be. Maggie solved the problem by swatting each of them with a spatula.

Things settled down in the kitchen as the trio worked together to put breakfast on the table. The conversation mainly concerned Lizzie and how disappointed she was going to be that her possible appointment to the United States Supreme Court was all a hoax.

"I bet if we tried, we could get Justice Leonard to resign and make it happen for Lizzie," Harry said thoughtfully as he snatched a piece of bacon to nibble on.

Jack stopped what he was doing; so did Maggie. It was Jack, though, who gave voice to the question. "What do you have in mind, Harry?"

"Well . . ."

Chapter 11

Yoko stared at the cell phone in her hand for long minutes before she slipped it into the pocket of her robe. She'd been wide awake all night, long after the others were sound asleep. That was why she had called Harry. He'd answered on the first ring, even though it was three o'clock in the morning. At the time she had smiled, knowing they were on the same plane, and he knew that she would be calling, just the way she knew he was waiting to hear her voice. She and Harry were soul mates, destined to find each other and to love one another into eternity. There was no doubt in her mind that it was all true, and she knew there was no doubt in Harry's mind, either.

She stared into the dancing flames as her being literally transported itself to somewhere else that she couldn't identify. She sat down in front of the fire, relaxed, and assumed the lotus position. She didn't have to be told that Harry, who was three hundred miles away, was doing the same thing. No, he was moving. He was going somewhere.

Something was wrong. Something she had missed when she spoke to Harry a short while ago. Jack's house. Harry kicking in the door. She smiled. What was it she had missed? She leaned forward and saw images in the flames, images that she didn't recognize but that were somehow vaguely familiar. Maggie's house now. Jack in his pajamas with little yellow ducks on them. She smiled again. The flames flared, then died down.

Yoko blinked, then blinked again. In one graceful movement, she was on her feet and headed to her bedroom, where she dressed quietly and let herself out of the building. She crossed the compound to the dining hall. The first thing she did was build up the fire, even though it didn't seem as cold as it had been when they all retired for the evening.

In the kitchen she made a pot of tea and waited for it to brew. She reviewed the events of the evening, her call to Harry, the urgency of that call. She pulled out the cell phone she'd transferred to her jacket, the same cell she'd used earlier to call Harry, and stared at it thoughtfully. Should she call him and . . . say what? Ask him what it was she'd said to him that warranted a trip to Jack's and Maggie's houses in the middle of the night?

Her tiny fingers drummed on the kitchen counter, tiny fingers that could kill, maim, or incapacitate. Something was wrong. That much she knew. But what? Her thoughts were lightning fast as she blinked and did everything in her power to bring whatever it was to the forefront of her mind.

It was all wrong. They had too much information. "They" meaning Charles, the Sisters, Maggie, and the boys, as she called them. Way too much information. There were too many people involved in something that was supposed to be a secret. *All wrong. All wrong. All wrong.* It was . . . almost like there was a puppeteer in the wings, tugging and twisting everyone's strings. A master puppeteer? If so, not only was it all wrong, but it was also a game. Games had winners and losers.

Yoko stopped drumming her fingers on the countertop. She stared into the dining room from the huge cut-out kitchen window. Winners and losers. The winners were obviously . . . who? The president of the United States and Justice Douglas Leonard? The losers . . . who? Well, one didn't need to be a rocket scientist to figure that one out. The answer was so obvious, Yoko wanted to scream. The losers were Lizzie and the vigilantes and anyone involved with either the vigilantes or Lizzie herself.

Yoko's mind was feverish now as she shifted and collated what she knew. How devilishly clever of the president. The Sisters were not going to like this news, not even one little bit. Annie would go nuclear. Kathryn would go ballistic, and the others would bite down and figure a way to close in for the kill. As would she.

The clock overhead read 5:50. Charles would

be arriving soon to prepare breakfast. Maybe she could help out while her thoughts whirled and swirled. She'd always been good at multitasking. Today, even at this hour, should make no difference. But first, she was going to call Harry.

Harry's usual greeting of "What can I do for you, my little cherry blossom?" did not make her smile and hunger to be in his arms. "Harry, listen to me. It's all wrong. It's a game. They're trying to ruin Lizzie and get rid of the vigilantes at the same time."

"I know. I knew you'd figure it out. Maggie is going to give me a lift back into town. We're almost certain we'll all be coming to the mountain either later tonight or tomorrow. Everyone has to clear their schedules. The best part is, *they* don't know we're onto them. Did you tell Charles or the girls yet?"

"I was going to do it after breakfast. I'm in the kitchen now. Charles should be arriving any minute now. The girls are *not* going to like this. I think we should agree not to say anything to Lizzie, at least not yet."

"I'll tell the others. Maggie's ready. I'll see you soon."

Yoko set the phone on the counter and started to squeeze oranges. When the crystal pitcher was almost full, she added crushed ice and set the juice in the refrigerator. She was mixing the dough for sticky buns, Charles's favorite, when he walked into the room.

"What did I do to deserve this?" he asked, smiling.

"I couldn't sleep. Listen, Charles, it's all wrong. I spoke to Harry, and he and the others agree. But it was Harry who figured it out. I was a little slower."

"I know, dear. I couldn't sleep, either, so I've been over at the command center, working on things. I figured after breakfast was time enough to alert the girls. By the time they get here, they might have all figured it out themselves."

"I don't think we should tell Lizzie, at least not yet. But we need to vote on that, and it is just my opinion. Harry said they were all going to try to come to the mountain tonight or tomorrow." Yoko's expression was bland as she watched Charles mix pancake batter. "We should have figured it out right away," she grumbled.

"How so?"

"Harry figured it out. It felt wrong from the beginning. I'm the first to admit I know very little about politics, but if it was so, what would Kathryn have said? Out of the box, and yet none of us picked up on it. We all just ran with it."

"It's only a matter of hours, dear. We know *now,* and that's all that matters. Always remember one thing. Everything happens for a reason. I hear the girls. Remember, we do not discuss business until breakfast is over."

Yoko laughed as she slid the tray of sticky buns into the oven. "I'll set the table now."

*   *   *

Maggie stared at her star reporter and star photographer. While they were neat and clean, their hair slicked back, it was obvious they hadn't gotten enough sleep. Not that she cared. "I have a rather *cushy* job for you two." If she was hoping for delighted smiles and a gung ho attitude, she didn't get either.

"You have that look, Maggie," Ted said. "Who do we have to kill? I hope to hell you aren't planning on sending us to Iraq or some such place."

"Nothing that exciting, boys. I have here," Maggie announced, waving a thick stack of papers in the air, "all you will need to make my day a happy one."

"Highlights please," Ted said. "Do we have time for breakfast?"

"You do have time for breakfast, and pay for it yourself today. These," she said, waving the papers in the air, "contain the current address of Justice Douglas Leonard and his wife, Florence. As you can see, they reside on Connecticut Avenue when court is in session, although Mrs. Leonard goes back and forth to Vermont quite often. She stays a week or ten days at a time. They were both in Vermont during the holidays. The Leonards' financial records are all here. At one time they had a robust brokerage account, but it is very *anemic* right now. Another twelve months, and that account will be nothing more than a memory. And it has nothing to do with the economy. Justice Leonard was diversified, and the account held steady until two years ago. In the last two years, there have been many, many things sold and converted to cash. This is just a wild guess on my part, and I am no accountant, but from what I'm seeing here, the Leonards are living paycheck to paycheck at the moment. Mrs. Leonard does not work.

"We were told—oops, you boys were told—by Cosmo Cricket that Mrs. Leonard had health issues and that's why Justice Leonard was going to retire. Not true, according to these medical records. Florence Leonard is healthy as a horse. Ditto for Justice Leonard. The kiddies, of whom there are four, are all grown and have thriving careers. The family meets over the holidays, and the rest of the year, they all go their separate ways. Neither Justice Leonard nor his wife appears to be a doting parent or grandparent.

"Where did all that money in the brokerage account go? I'm thinking, and again, this is a guess on my part. Mrs. Leonard has a gambling problem. She can do it right from her own home. Or else the justice himself is into some heavy-duty porn on the Internet, or they could both be secret gamblers. The third choice is that someone is blackmailing them, but I'm not buying into that. That's it, boys. Come up with some cover story and run with it. Do not, I repeat, do not, come back empty-handed."

Ted reached for the papers in Maggie's hand and shoved them into his backpack. An idea was already forming deep inside his head as he and Espinosa made their way to the elevator.

Over a huge breakfast, the kind Maggie had

cooked for Harry and Jack, Ted ran his idea past Espinosa. "We just march up to the door, hold out our IDs, and say we're doing a feature article on the justices' wives to run in the Sunday edition. We lead her to believe she's the most important wife, and if she's as vain as most women are, she'll jump at the chance to be featured first. What do you think, Joe?"

"It's not very original or even clever, Ted. What if she has to check with her husband or some crap like that? Women have to get their hair done, pick out new dresses, that kind of thing."

"It's that old early bird who gets the worm. If she goes that route, we tell her we can't get back to her till the end of the week, because we have appointments with the other wives and the two husbands whose wives are justices. Or, better yet, we can say we're going to feature the two husbands. That might get her hackles up, assuming she has hackles to get up. What's your gut saying, Joe? Is it her and gambling or him and porn, like Maggie said? Or both?"

"I think it's her. She's probably bored out of her mind. Her husband is gone all day. She's not getting any younger. She feels like she doesn't fit in or blend in with the other wives of the justices. Maybe she hates the whole deal. Like she's rudderless. Hey, maybe she's the one into the porn, and the justice is the gambler! Think about that!"

"Nah. When Maggie has a gut feeling, I've never known her to be wrong. I think she's on the money this time. And do not forget for one minute that the justice is the one who called Cosmo Cricket. That ties in gambling right there. Good friend that Cricket said he was, Leonard lied to him. A justice of the Supreme Court lying to his friend. I find that unconscionable," Ted said virtuously.

"Yeah," Espinosa said as he sopped up the last of his pancakes in the heavy syrup. "I think we should have one more cup of coffee before we tackle Mrs. Florence Leonard."

"Spoken like a true reporter slash photographer," Ted said, holding up his cup for a refill.

Thirty-five minutes later the driver of the Diamond Cab that Ted and Espinosa had flagged down pulled as close to the snowbanked curb as he could get outside the Leonard home on Connecticut Avenue. Ted paid him, pocketed the receipt, and eyed the imposing snowbank, all at the same time. "Either we hop it or we walk all the way down to the corner. Your call, Joe."

Espinosa was already on the other side of the snowbank before Ted stopped speaking.

"Looks like all the other houses," Ted said as he picked his way up the walkway, which had not been shoveled.

"Winter maintenance doesn't seem to be a priority here at the Leonard abode," Espinosa grumbled.

The six steps leading to the front porch hadn't been shoveled, either, and held thick ice and globs of snow. It did look like someone had tossed handfuls of rock salt here and there. The porch was clear of snow and ice and held two caned rockers that looked as old as the historic house. A bedraggled artificial Christmas wreath hung on the door. Above the wreath was an old-fashioned bellpull. Ted gave it a hard yank and was rewarded with a two-note bong-bong sound from within.

"Why do I feel like I'm in a time warp, Joe?"

Espinosa grinned. "I think the best is yet to come." He cackled at his own wit just as the door opened.

"Whatever it is you're selling, I have no need of. My religion is my own, so don't try to sell me yours."

"Oh, no, ma'am, we're not here to sell you anything. Mrs. Leonard, I'm Ted Robinson from the *Post,* and this is my partner, Joseph Espinosa."

Both men held out their credentials as the woman peered at them through the ratty screen on the door.

"We're here to ask you to take part in a series we're working on for the Sunday paper. It will feature all the wives and the two husbands of the Supreme Court justices. We came here first since your husband seems to be the most influential justice, aside from the chief justice," Ted said, lying through his teeth. "Possibly an hour of your time, perhaps less. May we come in? If you feel more comfortable calling the paper to check us out, we can wait right out here until you do that."

Florence Leonard was a stick of a woman,

wearing layers and layers of clothes. Her face was made up of angles and planes and jutting bones, but she had piercing blue eyes the color of bluebells. Her hair was unfashionably long and secured on top of her head with a tortoise-shell comb of some sort. She wore no jewelry, not even a wedding ring.

She moved and held open the squeaky screen door for the two men to enter her home. "That won't be necessary. Come in."

Ted looked around, and the only word that came to his mind was "cavernous." He wondered what this beautiful old house would look like with furniture. His footsteps echoed off the dull pine floors as he followed his hostess in her many layers of clothing to a small room shut off from the rest of the house with pocket doors. A fire blazed in the hearth, but the room was still cold. Ted found himself shivering.

Coming up behind him, Espinosa hissed, "It's colder in here than it is outside. And she looks like Nanook of the North. What the hell is going on here, Ted?"

"Like I know," Ted hissed back.

"Take a seat," the woman said.

Ted looked around. There were only two chairs, with a table in between that held a reading lamp.

"I like to sit on the hearth," she added.

Ted sat down, pulled out his portable recorder, and announced the date, the names of the players present, and the reason for the recording. Espinosa discreetly clicked away.

"This is a lovely old house. How long have you lived here?" Ted asked.

"I hate it. It's cold and drafty. I hate Washington. We've been here for the last fifteen years. I try to go home as often as I can. Vermont is home. We were there for Christmas. We . . . I had planned on staying longer, but Justice Leonard said we had to be back here for the New Year. We're freezing to death in this house."

"Doesn't your heat work?" Espinosa asked.

"Of course it works, but you have to be a millionaire to afford to heat it," Florence Leonard revealed. "We use this fireplace when we sit in here. We have one in the kitchen, one in the bedroom, and one in Justice Leonard's office."

Espinosa appeared to be dumbfounded. "Don't your pipes freeze?"

"They did the day we got back. Justice Leonard said that's why they make duct tape. He fixed them. Now, what is it you want to know for your article?"

Ted babbled on, asking question after question. Florence Leonard jabbered about everything and anything that, as far as Ted was concerned, meant absolutely nothing.

"Would a tour of the house be possible?" Ted asked.

"If you like," Florence said, getting up from the hearth. "Follow me."

"The house has a temporary feel to it," Ted said as they passed through one empty room after another.

"It does, doesn't it?" Florence said. "We brought all our lovely antiques with us when we came here, but when I saw how humid it is here in the summers, we moved all our fine things back to Vermont. Neither Justice Leonard nor I can abide air-conditioning. This is Justice Leonard's home office." She stepped aside so Ted and Espinosa could look inside the tidy room with wall-to-wall bookshelves. A computer sat on a Chippendale desk, and a fire was lit in the fireplace.

Espinosa rolled his eyes as he captured the room on his digital camera.

"I never come in here. Actually, Justice Leonard forbids me to enter this room," Florence confessed. "I don't mind. I find the law and politics in general very boring. I have my own interests."

"And what would they be, ma'am?" Ted asked, rising to the bait.

"Reading, TV, maneuvering around on the computer. I have my own, you know. And it is password protected. I needed to do that, considering Justice Leonard's position," said Florence.

"Do you socialize with or entertain the other justices' wives and husbands?" Ted asked.

"I'm sorry to say I don't. They're a bunch of old biddies, and they're all jealous of my husband and me. One of the husbands, I can't even remember his name, likes to think he's important and is always trying to get his name in the paper. I think it's disgraceful."

"Uh-huh," Ted said.

"When do you think you'll be going back to Vermont?" Espinosa asked.

"As soon as possible. I just get on a plane and go. I have my books and TV there and another computer," said Florence.

"I guess when you go home, it feels like a vacation, doesn't it?" Ted asked.

"It does, young man."

"I'm getting ready to go on vacation myself with my girlfriend. We're going to Las Vegas. Neither one of us has ever been there. She can't wait to see all the shows and shop in those high-end stores. We got a package deal for six nights. They said food is very inexpensive, and you get free drinks when you gamble. Have you ever been?" Ted said all in one breath.

Ted didn't think it was his imagination that the woman standing next to him stiffened when she said, "Once, a very long time ago, before Justice Leonard was appointed to the court. Actually, Justice Leonard has a very good friend who lives out there. I can't think of his name right now, but it's some kind of bug. His name, I mean."

"Well, I think that about covers all my questions," said Ted. "Is there anything you would like to add, Mrs. Leonard? Something of human interest."

"I don't think you should put down that I hate Washington. I probably shouldn't have said that. Can you just say I prefer Vermont to this fishbowl life?"

"I can do that, certainly." Ted slapped at his forehead. "I almost forgot. Do you see your husband retiring anytime soon? I know that justices have life tenure, but sometimes they opt out early."

"Good Lord, no. Justice Leonard said he was going to die in the court. I don't even bother to mention it anymore. Neither do our children. We're stuck here, much to my dismay. When did you say this would be in the paper?"

"In one of the Sunday editions," Ted replied. "It depends on how cooperative the other wives and those husbands are. Don't forget, I'm going to *Las Vegas*. Everyone I know has given me twenty dollars to play the slots for them. My vacation might delay things a week or so. I can call you when we're ready to run it."

"That would be lovely, Mr. Robinson. Just out of curiosity, how much did you have to pay for your package deal to Las Vegas?" Florence asked.

"My girlfriend handled all of that, but I think she said it was seven hundred dollars a person, and that included airfare. It's not one of the top hotels, but she said it would do, and wherever it is, you get a free breakfast," Ted said, making things up as he went along.

"That does sound reasonable. Well, I hope you have a lovely time and win lots of money."

"I'm pretty lucky," Ted said, getting into it. "I always win when I gamble. My girlfriend is even luckier than I am. She won one hundred fifty thousand dollars on one of those scratch-off tickets you buy at gas stations. Just like that she won one hundred fifty thousand dollars! She's buying a house with it. Well, a down payment actually."

Florence Leonard's eyes sparkled like Christmas lights. "Scratch-off tickets, and she won that much? That's amazing."

Ted held out his hand. "I enjoyed our interview. I hope you enjoy the article when it makes the paper. Thank you for talking to us without an appointment."

"The pleasure is all mine, gentlemen. I don't get many visitors. Good-bye," Florence Leonard said as she closed the door behind her guests.

The moment the door closed, Ted said, "Maggie was right. Five will get you ten, she hotfoots it to the nearest gas station within ten minutes."

Espinosa guffawed. "That's a sucker bet. She fell right into it. Here's a bet for you, Ted. I bet she sold off all the antiques she arrived with. Wanna bet?"

"Hell, no! *That* is a sucker bet for sure. Let's find a place to be invisible so we can watch and see if she does go to a gas station."

Ted and Espinosa walked down the street, looking for an evergreen to hide behind. When they found one, they turned sideways so they weren't visible from the Leonard residence. Thirteen minutes later the front door opened. They watched as Florence Leonard practically galloped down the steps and across the walkway.

"Now, that's what I call a gambler. But she

might be going to a gas station to buy a quart of milk," Espinosa said.

"Well, we have to check it out, or Maggie will have our hides. So, let's cross the street, keep our eyes peeled, and see what she does."

Forty-five minutes later Ted sent Maggie a text that said, She bgt 150$ of scratch-off tickets. I had 2 give the kid 50$ 2 confirm the trans. U were rt. She said Just L. has no plans 2 retire in the near future & plans to die on the court. Will u marry me?

The reply came back at the speed of light. Yes. Head for Dulles. I have u booked on a flight to VT. Check in on your arrival.

"Hey, Ted, what's wrong? You sick? Come on, what's wrong?"

"We have to go to Vermont. Hail a cab. Maggie said yes."

"About what? The expense account?"

"Hell, no!" Ted said, jumping up and down and waving his arms every which way. "Maggie said yes! I'm getting married!"

Chapter 12

The decision to pack up early and head home was an easy one to make for Lizzie since she was working pro bono and her desk was clear. Nothing urgent was pending; the remaining work could wait another day. Or two, even three days. She packed up her briefcase, reached for her jacket, slipped it on, and turned off the lights. It was three thirty.

What she would do when she got home, she had no idea. Maybe cook or bake something, take a bubble bath, call Cricket and talk for a few hours if he wasn't busy. Or . . .

Lizzie whipped out her cell phone the minute she settled herself in her car. She scrolled down and hit the number she wanted. She smiled when she heard the cranky voice of retired judge Cornelia Easter Cummings, Nellie to those near and dear to her heart.

"Nellie, I know this is late notice, but I was wondering if . . . *you* would like to have dinner with me. I was thinking of our favorite little

135

Italian restaurant," Lizzie said, without mentioning the name.

"Oh, you dear sweet child, there is nothing I would like more. Elias is in bed with the flu, and I simply cannot consume even one more drop of chicken soup. That's a myth, you know. I have never seen a more cantankerous curmudgeon than my husband. I'll tell you what else is a myth. Men say they want to be left alone when they're sick so they can suffer in silence. Actually, my dear, that's a bald-faced, outright lie. This man, this relatively new husband of mine, is running me ragged, and he hasn't even peaked yet. What time?"

Lizzie laughed, but Nellie picked up on the strain in the young lawyer's voice. "Whatever works for you, Nellie."

It was Nellie's turn to laugh. "It will take me a little while to get Elias settled, fluff up his pillows, lay out this and that so he doesn't exert himself, fix him a thermos of chicken soup and one of hot tea. Strap the remote to his wrist so he doesn't have to move too much. You know the drill. *Sixish* works for me if it works for you. Casual, right?"

"Absolutely casual. *Sixish* works for me, too. It's been raining all day here in the District, so wear your boots. The temperature went way up today, and it's water and slush everywhere. I'll see you at six, Nellie. Give Elias my regards. You might want to tie a string of garlic around his neck, or is that a myth, too?"

"Yes, Mother. I'll give it a shot." Nellie cackled. "I moved to the spare room, so the garlic won't bother me." She let loose with another boisterous laugh before she broke the connection.

Lizzie let her mind wander on the drive home. She wondered how Cosmo would be if he got the flu and was confined to bed. She would love to wait on him hand and foot and for him to look at her with his big brown eyes, knowing she was going to make him all better with her undying devotion. She knew, just knew, in her heart that Cosmo Cricket would blow his last breath into her body if he thought she was in danger. When she had a headache, he wanted to call the paramedics for her. God in heaven, how she loved that man, even if he had kept a secret from her.

Lizzie parked her car, gathered up her purse and briefcase. She was still smiling as she made her way into her house. She turned off the alarm, locked the door behind her, then turned up the heat. She headed straight for the kitchen, where she made a pot of coffee before heading upstairs to change her clothes. On her return trip to the kitchen, she made a fire in the living-room fireplace that would be blazing when she returned to chill out with her coffee. First, she would make a few personal calls; then she'd call Cosmo.

Ever mindful of the time, Lizzie called the mountain, spoke via speakerphone with everyone, then called Maggie, who sounded harried and out of sorts. That call was short and concise.

Lizzie shrugged and called Jack, who said he was pumping water out of the basement and would call her back. Harry's voice mail said he was either in the middle of a class or was unavailable, and to leave her number and he'd return her call. That left Bert and his voice mail. There was only one name left on her mental to-call list aside from Cosmo. The person she should probably have called first: ex-Justice Pearl Barnes.

Then again, maybe she shouldn't even be thinking about calling Pearl. Pearl was way out there, running her underground railroad to help save mothers and children. She didn't need Lizzie and her problems. In the end, after several moments of indecision, she talked herself out of making the call.

A smile on her face and in her voice, Lizzie hit the speed dial that would connect her with her husband. She wanted to cry when the call went to his voice mail. Her shoulders slumped, Lizzie made her way back to the kitchen to refill her coffee cup. She was back in front of the fire within minutes. She had half an hour to think before it would be time to leave for Morellie's, where she was to meet up with Nellie.

She should be on top of the world, but she wasn't. She wished she knew the why of it all. Was it because she and Cosmo each had a secret from the other? Yes, she realized, that was part of it, but there was something else, which she couldn't quite pin down. Maybe talking to Nellie would help.

The fine hairs on the back of Lizzie's neck

moved, signaling something was amiss. She blinked. Pearl Barnes. Pearl was the one she needed to talk to. Absolutely, she needed to talk to Pearl. Why had she talked herself out of the phone call? Stupid, stupid, stupid.

Lizzie looked down at the diamond-studded watch on her wrist. She had to leave to meet Nellie in fifteen minutes. Assuming she was successful in connecting with Pearl, would it be a long or short call? She would prefer a long one, but Pearl might not be able to oblige. Maybe she should call and set up a time that would be convenient for both of them. Before she could talk herself out of the call, Lizzie used the special encrypted phone Charles had given to all of them. Even Pearl, who just worked on the periphery for the vigilantes, had one. She was stunned when Pearl picked up on the first ring. Her voice was cautious as always, and Lizzie knew better than to mention names, or even places, for that matter. She said hello, hoping Pearl would recognize her voice. She did.

Lizzie cut to the chase. "When would be a convenient time to speak? I'll need, or I should say I'd like, at least thirty minutes of your time."

"This phone needs to be charged. I'm in the same time zone. Will after ten work for you? Crucial, deadly, urgent?"

"Probably all of the above. My side, not yours."

"Later," was Pearl's response before the connection was broken.

Lizzie sighed as she got to her feet. She finished her coffee in one long gulp, banked the fire, and closed the glass doors to the fireplace before she headed to the kitchen. She rinsed out the coffeepot, prepared a new one because she knew she would need some strong brew when she made contact with Pearl later in the evening.

It was rush-hour traffic when Lizzie exited her house, but she had to go only six blocks. It was still raining. On a nice day she would have opted to walk to her favorite Italian restaurant. Tonight, though, with all the flooding, walking wasn't even a consideration.

The minuscule parking lot behind the tiny restaurant held thirteen parking spaces and woe to anyone who parked there who did not belong. Two spots were reserved for the owners, Rosalie and Rocco Morellie, and had their names. The spot next to Rocco's simply said SG, which meant "special guest" in this case, Nellie Easter Cummings. The remaining ten spots were for the diners. It was early, so Lizzie had no problem parking.

Morellie's was your typical Italian restaurant, right down to the red-checkered tablecloths and curtains. Chianti bottles were on all the tables. Everything sparkled. But it was the wonderful aromatic smell of the different cheeses that hung from the rafters in the kitchen, the roasted garlic, the heady aroma of the sauce that bubbled 24-7 that drew you in and wouldn't let you go. There were only ten tables, and on a weeknight the Morellies turned the tables over twice before they called it a night. On weekends they turned the tables over four times at night. If they had wanted to, they could have stayed past eleven and worked through the nights, and the tables would have remained full, but plump little Rosalie had declared early on that she had a life beyond the eatery during the week. Weekends, she said, she had to defer to the almighty dollar. Rocco wholeheartedly agreed.

When the bell over the door tinkled, the little lady bounded out of the kitchen to embrace Lizzie in a bear hug. Rocco was hot on her heels and almost crushed Lizzie. Husband and wife gibbered in Italian, then finally settled for English as they led Lizzie to her favorite table just as the bell tinkled again and the Morellies rushed to greet Judge Easter.

The bell over the door continued to tinkle until all the tables were full. Then Rocco Morellie flipped the sign that said the next seating wasn't until eight thirty.

No one, however, got the greeting that Lizzie and Judge Easter had received.

Wine appeared, along with a basket of garlic twists, which had both women drooling. Everything was made from scratch. Rosalie made the sauce and the garlic twists, and Rocco made the pasta. No one was sure, but it was speculated that Rocco also made the wine in his basement wherever it was he lived. It was tart, robust, and flavorful. Lizzie and Nellie clinked glasses as they eyed one another over the rims of their goblets.

Small talk first was always essential, and there was no need to order. Both women always had the same thing. Lizzie had the baked ziti, and Nellie had the lasagna. Before they left the restaurant, the Morellies would hand them each a shopping bag with enough spaghetti and meatballs to last them a whole week. They always included bottles of their *special* wine and Ziploc bags of the garlic twists, which only had to be heated. It was a ritual. And at the end of the evening there was never a bill, because, as Rocco put it, Lizzie and Nellie had saved their fat hides when a crooked landlord had tried to demolish the neighborhood. Lizzie had taken the case pro bono, and Judge Easter had heard the case. The Morellies now owned their own building, as did all the other store owners on the block.

"So, how is Elias?" Lizzie asked.

"He thinks he's going to die, but he isn't. I assured him when I put the garlic necklace around him before I left that he'd be better by the time I got home. He believed me. He wanted me to set the heat at ninety. I just dumped all the cats on the bed to keep him warm and turned the heat down to seventy-five. The cats were licking at the garlic, so who knows how that's going to go."

"That's certainly one for YouTube." Lizzie laughed.

"I told Elias the garlic necklace was your idea, and you know how Elias thinks you can do no wrong, so he will be better before I get home. I guarantee it."

"Let's cut to the chase, Nellie. Just so you know, I can eat and talk at the same time. Tell me what you know about the nine justices on the Supreme Court."

"I'll be happy to tell you what I know, which isn't all that much. You really should talk to Pearl Barnes, if you can manage to locate her. For sure, she would be a wealth of information, since she served on the court for more years than I can remember. Can I ask why you want to know, Lizzie?"

"It's personal, Nellie. Right now I'm not comfortable confiding in you or anyone else, and please don't take that the wrong way. If you aren't comfortable talking about the justices, that's okay, too. And their spouses, assuming you know anything about them."

"Actually, Lizzie, Elias, as the former director of the FBI, probably knows more than I do. All of them are qualified, or they wouldn't be sitting there. Personally, I wouldn't have voted for Regions or Taylor, but that's just me. I've never heard a whisper of any kind of negative gossip. For all intents and purposes, they're clean as the driven snow, which is pretty hard to believe, but there you have it. The wives . . . they're all older, grandmothers and mothers. None of them are into publicity. Actually, they shun it. They're normal and dealing with the aging process, like the rest of us. Once in a while they poke their heads out for one charity or another. I remember hearing not that long ago that they all meet for a United Way luncheon or something like that. It's held once a year. Can you be a little more specific, Lizzie? A question might trigger something I know and can't quite remember."

"Have you heard anything about one of them retiring anytime soon?"

"Lizzie, dear, no one retires from that court unless he's dying, and according to the last report I heard, they all passed their medicals with flying colors. No one leaves. They have life tenure. Except for Pearl, and we all know why Pearl packed it in."

Lizzie nibbled on her lower lip. "What about their spouses? What if one of them was sick, like in the case of Sandra Day O'Connor's husband?"

"That, Lizzie, was an exception to the rule. O'Connor was one of a kind. As far as I know, all the wives and husbands are in good health. Is there some kind of rumor going around about one of them wanting off the court?"

Instead of answering Nellie's question, Lizzie asked another one. "Hypothetically, if one were to leave, who do you think it would be and why?"

Nellie closed her eyes for a few moments. When she opened them, she shook her head in bewilderment. "I have no clue. You and I both know sitting on the Supreme Court is every lawyer's dream. Just the nomination alone is something to aspire toward. Once you reach that exalted position, you aren't going to leave unless something catastrophic happens. I'm sorry I'm not more help. You really should think about calling Pearl. I know she keeps up with what's going on with the justices and the court. Back in the day, she was very friendly with one of the other justices, but I can't remember which one."

Lizzie moved slightly so the waiter could set her plate in front of her. She closed her eyes and sniffed. She knew she was going to eat every bite of the food in front of her, even though she'd already had four garlic twists.

"This certainly beats chicken soup for five straight days," Nellie said, digging into her lasagna.

As if by some unheard signal, both women switched their conversation to mundane things, the weather, the rising temperatures, the flooding, when precisely spring would arrive, and plans for the summer.

"Elias wants to go on a cruise. I do not. All you do is eat on cruises and play shuffleboard. I'd rather go to Wyoming and some ranch. We'll argue it out, I'm sure. What about you, Lizzie? Do you and Cosmo have plans?"

"Not really. I hope to be out of the White House by the end of June. I gave the president only six months. I don't even know why I agreed to do it to begin with." Lizzie dropped her voice, her fork poised in midair as she leaned forward. "I have this sick feeling in the pit of my stomach that Martine is not going to honor her promise to the vigilantes."

Nellie stopped chewing and said, "Please tell me you didn't just say what you just said."

"I wish I could, Nellie, but it's out there. I spoke to her COS late this morning, and he said she was like a cat on a hot griddle. She's at war with her advisors. I played it cool and didn't ask any questions, but I'm certain that's what it's all about."

"I don't think I want to go there right now with this," Nellie said. "And suddenly I've lost my appetite."

Lizzie laid down her fork. "I don't know what to do, Nellie."

"When I don't know what to do, dear, I do nothing and watch it play out."

"Would you do that if it involved the vigilantes, Nellie?"

Two words exploded from Nellie's mouth like gunshots. "Hell, no!"

The other diners raised their heads and looked around, then went back to their meals.

"My point exactly," Lizzie said.

Just as Ted Robinson and Joe Espinosa were unbuckling their seat belts and waiting to disembark, Maggie Spritzer was on the phone with Charles Martin to bring him up to date on Abner Tookus's latest reports and Ted and Espinosa's visit to interview Florence Leonard. She signed off by saying, "See ya in a few hours."

Charles peered over his glasses at the women, who were arguing loudly among themselves. Even from where he was standing, he could see the hackles rising on the backs of Murphy and Grady. Annie was sputtering now; Myra, trying her best to defuse whatever was going on.

Charles let loose with a sharp whistle. The dogs looked at him, then lay down, their coats smooth once more. The girls looked embarrassed, even Annie, who started to apologize for what she called her "attitude."

"Everyone needs to calm down," Charles said soothingly. "I have a small amount of news to share, compliments of Maggie." He ran through the report quickly.

"So that just confirms what Yoko and Harry said earlier. I'm not liking this at all. How could the president do that to Lizzie and to us after all we've done for her? How? Someone tell me how?" Nikki bellowed.

"Dear, it isn't going to do any good to get agitated," Myra said quietly.

Annie felt like beating her breast in frustration. She eyed Myra and said, "Nikki has the right to express her displeasure over all of this. I'm about to express my own. But since you are so calm and collected, Myra, tell us right now what you would have us do to correct this . . . this shitful problem."

"Yeah, Myra, tell us," Kathryn snarled. "She promised the pardons. She's going to kick Lizzie in the gut? There's something wrong

147

here. She used us, and that is totally unacceptable."

Myra fingered the ever-present pearls at her neck; then she sat upright and looked around the table. "I thought it was obvious, girls. We will have to invade the White House and snatch our pardons right from under the eyes of everyone present."

"Myra, you damn well rock!" Annie chortled happily. She clapped Myra so hard on the back, Myra's chair lurched forward, and she almost fell off.

"All we need is a plan," Isabelle said, excitement ringing in her voice.

"I think Harry has a plan. He's going to talk to us this evening, when he gets here. I think we can do it!" Yoko said.

Charles, his mouth open, stared at his chicks, as he thought of them. "No! You are out of your minds. You cannot just march into the White House and . . . and steal your pardons. No!"

"Why not, Charles? The pardons belong to us. If your intel is correct, they are signed. Technically, that means they now belong to us. And while we're on such a roll, we'll make sure that Justice Leonard really does retire and Lizzie steps into his place, providing that's what she wants. We can do this," Nikki said.

Charles replied, "I'd like to see you get that past the sniff test in a court of law. *No!*"

"Yes," the Sisters chorused in unison.

Both dogs slithered on their bellies closer to

the Sisters and as far from Charles as they could get without being obvious.

"Traitors," Charles grumbled as he made his way back to his workstation. He knew without seeing them that the Sisters were high-fiving one another. There was no doubt in his mind, none at all, that the Sisters could come up with something that would indeed gain them access to the most powerful address in the world. But would they be able to leave, pardons in hand?

Charles closed his eyes. He hated to admit it, but he simply didn't know the answer to that question.

Chapter 13

Ted strained to see the mailbox numbers in the waning light. He was glad he'd chosen a Toyota SUV at the car rental agency to travel the country lanes he'd been driving for the past two hours.

"I hate this place," Espinosa said as he struggled to see if there was any sign of a mailbox in the high drifts of snow. "The Leonards must be the only people who live on this godforsaken road."

"It's not a road. It's a lane. Lanes are quaint, which means no traffic. Roads carry cars, and there is always traffic on a road," Ted said.

"Shut up, Ted. There are no mailboxes. You know what I'm thinking? Maybe they have to go into town to pick up their mail, like at a post office. This is rural, as in *rural*. What is the GPS saying?"

"That we're right on top of it. When we started down this lane, the GPS said it was three and three-tenths of a mile. So that has to mean we're here, wherever the hell *here* is. Look! There's a house!"

"Yippeeeee!" Espinosa shouted. "Damn, would you look at all that snow! Guess it snowed since the Leonards left to go back to Washington. Looks like over a foot to me. What do you think, Ted?"

"Easily a foot." Ted turned off the ignition and climbed out of the truck. "I hope to hell we don't get stuck. There's no shovel in this vehicle. You waiting for a bus, Espinosa? Chop-chop. It's almost dark out."

"Is that your way of telling me we have to do a little breaking and entering?"

"Unless you can think of another way to find out if the antiques were moved back here, like old Florence said. The only good thing about all this is, there are no neighbors who might get a little too curious."

"Have you given any thought to a possible alarm system?" Espinosa asked as he struggled through the thigh-high snow.

"And that would be hooked up to . . . what? A tree? I didn't see any electrical wires. They use generators out here. In case you haven't noticed, this is *rustic*."

"Maybe this isn't the real house. Maybe this is the vacation home. Would people of the Leonards' stature live like this? Jesus, the guy is a justice of the Supreme Court, Ted."

"Maybe they like to commune with nature. Maybe they're simple people. The guy is really brainy, so maybe he lives in his own world, that

152

kind of thing, and old Flo had to fend for herself, hence the gambling. I'm making this up as I go along," Ted said.

"I already figured that out. Now what, *Kemo Sabe?*" Espinosa asked as they both stomped snow off their boots on the plank front porch.

"Now we pick the lock. It's not a good one, so it shouldn't be a problem."

Ted whipped out one of his credit cards and went to work. Three minutes later the huge pine door groaned inward. A blast of cold air hit both men when they stepped indoors.

"Look for a thermostat, and crank that baby up, or we'll freeze in here. I'll look for a light switch. Well, shit, they must use twenty-five-watt bulbs!" Espinosa said when he clicked on the lamp, which cast a dim yellow pool of light over a maple end table.

"They probably think they're being frugal. Nice place, though," Ted said, looking around.

"I don't see any antiques," Espinosa said fretfully as he pushed the dial on the thermostat to high. "I'm no decorator, but this looks like flea market junk to me."

Ted upended a cushion on the sofa and grunted. "I knew it. Sears, Roebuck. Maggie and I did an exposé about five years ago on bogus antiques dealers. I learned a few things along the way. Even at first glance, I can tell that none of this stuff is even remotely an antique. Check out the upstairs while I look in the rest of the rooms," he said.

"Nothing up here but four bedrooms, all

sparsely furnished. No antiques that I can see. Just regulation maple furniture. There is an old computer up here in one of the bedrooms, but that's it," Espinosa called from the second floor. "It's like Iceland up here."

"Nothing down here, either," Ted said as he bounded up the steps to join Espinosa. "Dining-room furniture is just six chairs, a table, a credenza of some kind. There's a sunroom with wicker furniture, but that's it. The appliances in the kitchen are old, but they work."

"I think this computer is frozen. Nothing is happening. Maybe we should take it with us and get Maggie's guy to pore over it."

Ted looked properly outraged for all of five seconds. "That's stealing. Yeah, pack it up. In for a nickel, out for a nickel, or whatever that phrase is. You taking pictures, Joe?"

"Out the wazoo. It is forever captured on film. We might have a little difficulty in explaining how we got all this. You realize that, right?"

"That's Maggie's problem. We just do what we're told. *Capisce?*"

"Yeah, well, I hope that will hold up when our asses are behind bars," Espinosa said as he snapped several pictures of the outdated computer before unplugging it and carrying it down to the first floor.

"Let me voice a question here. Who are you more afraid of? Maggie or the cops? What's wrong, Joe? I don't like that look I'm seeing on your face."

"Stop being so damn stupid. I'm more afraid

of Maggie, just like you. On top of that, you're marrying her. What's wrong is that this is all wrong. It's not computing. Leonard is a justice on the Supreme Court. And yet he lives like this! You need to look at those papers again. Is there a mortgage on this house? What about the one on Connecticut Avenue? I'm all for comfort and casual, but I think a justice should have some class, for want of a better word. This is not computing for me, Ted. You know what Judge Judy says. 'If it doesn't compute, then it's a lie.' "

Ted sat down on a burgundy plaid couch that had seen years of wear and tear. It was a little warmer than when they first entered the house, but not by much. He riffled through the papers Maggie had given him. "This property consists of sixty-seven acres and is paid in full, no mortgage. The last assessment was seven years ago, and it assessed at nine hundred thousand dollars. Justice Leonard inherited it. He was an only child. The house on Connecticut Avenue is valued at one million seven hundred fifty thousand dollars, and there is no mortgage. Real-estate-wise, the Leonards are solvent. The justice drives a ten-year-old Audi, and Flo drives an eight-year-old Volvo. Both are ultraconservative cars. They have ninety grand in a money market account at Wachovia Securities. That's all they have, plus the justice's salary. So, in summary, yeah, I'd say the justice could be ripe for a little bribe by someone in the White House."

"Now what?" Espinosa said, settling down on the couch, next to Ted. "I guess we could bunk here and head out in the morning to grab the first flight, or we could head back to town and go to a hotel. Makes no never mind to me either way, but I am tired, Ted. I say we build a fire and sleep here. We can get up around five and head out. There should be a seven o'clock flight to somewhere. What do you think?"

"Food. We didn't think to bring any, but I did see some canned stuff in the pantry and a box of unopened cornflakes. We won't starve if we stay. Let's figure out fair and square what this stay costs so we can leave the money on the table. What's that stupid computer worth?"

"You kidding me! You couldn't *give* this hunk of junk away. Five bucks, tops."

"I say we leave a hundred bucks. We're using the heat. We're going to eat whatever we can find and burn a few logs. We're not messing anything up, and we didn't break anything."

"No, you said fair and square, so make it two hundred. You can't get a hotel room for under two hundred," Espinosa said.

In the end they pooled their money and left three hundred dollars on the kitchen table. Ted plopped a salt shaker on top of the bills to hold them in place. Espinosa snapped a picture of the fanned-out hundred-dollar bills.

Fifteen minutes later both men were snuggled into the two ratty-looking chairs by the fire and wrapped in quilts they'd found on the second floor. It was warm, and the fire was burning down, but they didn't want to add any logs, so that when they left in the morning, the fire would be completely out.

"I'm getting married, Joe. Do you believe that?"

"Not till I see you standing at the altar. You sound funny, Ted. Somehow I expected something a little more romantic where you're concerned. A text? What really boggles my mind is that Maggie said yes."

Ted sat upright, his eyes wild. "Yeah, I know. You're going to be my best man, right?"

Espinosa thought about the question for a minute. "I thought Jack Emery was your best friend."

"No more a best friend than you are, Joe. I've known you longer. I want you. So, will you do it?"

"Well, yeah, since you put it like that. You sure you're ready to get married, Ted?"

"I thought I was. The minute I saw that Maggie said yes, I kind of put it out of my mind. I have to think about it now. Marrying your sweetheart is one thing. That kind of makes you . . . you know, even somehow. But I'm going to be marrying my boss. Our boss, Joe. What if she carries that relationship over into the marriage?"

"You can back out right up until it's time to say 'I do.' "

"Jesus, we'll have to buy a house. And get a car. A van, you know, the kind that has sliding doors so you can pile the kids and animals in it before you take off for . . . wherever the hell married people take off for. I'm not the van type. I'd like a sporty car, maybe a convertible."

"Uh-huh," Espinosa said.

"She makes more money than I do. That means she'll want to make all the financial decisions. I might have a problem with that. And Maggie doesn't cook. Wherever we end up, there might not be take-out joints. I'm not a soup-and-sandwich kind of guy. Another thing. Who is going to do all that grocery shopping? You know how Maggie eats. Nonstop."

"That could be a problem," Espinosa muttered.

"And because she's my boss, she could fire me if I do something in our married life that she doesn't like. I'm not going to like living in fear."

"Yeah, that could really be a problem," Espinosa muttered again.

"Now I have the pressure of thinking about and paying for an engagement ring. Christmas was a walk in the park compared to picking out an engagement ring. Listen, Joe, I don't think I'm ready to get married. Help me out here, buddy. How can I get out of it gracefully? Come on, Joe, say something. I'm dying here, can't you tell?"

Espinosa stirred; then a deep snore permeated the room.

"Shit!"

* * *

While Ted was cursing and Espinosa was snoring, Lizzie Fox was taking several deep, calming breaths before she dialed the number that would connect her with ex-Justice Pearl Barnes.

Pearl picked up on the first ring, almost like she was waiting for the call, which came through precisely at ten o'clock. Her greeting was cursory. "Talk to me, dear."

Lizzie took another deep breath. "I need to ask you some questions, but I can't tell you at this time why I need the answers. Will it suffice to say that it involves a lot of our mutual friends?"

"It will. Ask away."

"Tell me what you know about Justice Leonard."

"He was, of course, a colleague, but you know that. If ever a person was born to the court, it was Douglas Leonard. His world is the law. The man could never converse on mundane things or contribute to a conversation. But if it was a matter of law or a discussion on something pending before the court, you couldn't shut him up. He is brilliant, and I thought he had the makings of a chief justice, and I thought when they appointed Notola to that exalted position instead of Leonard, it was because the man has absolutely no personality. In secret we used to refer to him as the DF. Meaning 'dead fish.' I neither liked nor disliked him, and I feel safe in saying the other justices felt the same way."

"The others say you keep up with what's going on in your old bailiwick. Have you heard any rumors, anything at all out of the ordinary?"

"Not a thing, dear. Perhaps if you give me a clue, I might come up with something."

"Do you think he might be retiring anytime soon?"

"Douglas? That man will have to be wheeled out on a stretcher. He's there for life, and he's only sixty-nine. He's got a good many years left to serve on the bench. I think he would die if he had to leave for whatever reason. I mean that."

"What about his wife? If she was ill and needed care, would he retire?"

"Never! He'd hire round-the-clock care for her and pitch a tent somewhere. I never had the impression he was much of a family man. The law and the court are his family. That man is going nowhere. Now you have whetted my curiosity. What have you heard?"

"That his wife has Alzheimer's, and he's going to step down and take care of her."

Pearl Barnes let loose with a loud guffaw, so loud, Lizzie had to hold the phone away from her ear. "Florence with Alzheimer's! That's an absolute riot. First of all, the woman is sharp as a tack. She never quite fit in, always appeared uncomfortable around the other wives. Not that we socialized much on a personal level, but the few times I was in her company, it was like pulling teeth to get her to talk. I do know she's a numbers person. I can't even tell you how I know that. Someone once said her life was reduced to numbers. I'm sorry I can't clarify that any better.

"Florence doesn't really like living in Washington. I think they have a farm or something in New England. Douglas inherited it a long time ago. Maple syrup comes to mind, but it's fallow now. There are several children. Very successful, I seem to recall. Grandchildren, too. I always had the impression that the extended family was not close. Is it a rumor, or is there some juice to what you're hearing, dear?"

"I don't know. That's why I'm calling you. People in very high places, actually the highest in the land, might be responsible for letting it leak. My . . . uh . . . friends are trying to sort through it."

"To what end, dear?" Pearl asked.

"Perhaps to cover up for a promise that isn't going to be kept. It was a well-planned leak that was meant to find its way to me. I'm concerned. My friends are more than a little concerned."

"I see."

"I'm going to throw out something to you, and I want you to tell me your knee-jerk reaction when I voice it, okay?"

"Shoot!"

"Is it even remotely possible that Mrs. Leonard could have a secret gambling problem?"

Her answer came back bullet fast. "Without a doubt. I told you, she's a numbers person. If you mean, does she hang out at gambling casinos, I'd have to say no. It wouldn't surprise me to know she does it online. You can do that, you know? Did you check the financials?"

"Not personally, but I heard their brokerage account is very anemic, where it was once very robust."

Lizzie waited out the silence on the other end of the phone. "Let me be sure I understand where this is all going. Possibly Florence has a gambling problem and may have depleted their savings. And possibly someone is blackmailing Douglas and wants him off the bench, and that's why they're blackmailing him. Is that right?"

"More or less," Lizzie said.

"Then you do not know Douglas Leonard. He has so insulated himself from the real world, it wouldn't bother him one bit. He'd consider it Florence's problem, not his. And do not forget for one minute that he has life tenure. Even if Florence turned out to be an ax murderer, he would still keep his job. I always wondered how the man found his way home at night. If you knew Douglas Leonard, you would never believe any of these what-ifs as even a possibility. Anything else, dear?"

"Then why would he agree to such a thing?"

"If you want my opinion, and it's just my opinion, dear, someone is using him, and he hasn't figured it out yet. Of course, if *he* dies, that's a whole other ball game. Now, if Florence died, it wouldn't cause even a ripple in his life, sad to say."

Lizzie digested all the information, thanked Pearl, and hung up.

"I knew it was too good to be true," Lizzie mumbled to herself as she drained the last of her coffee. "I feel sorry for you, Madam President. No, that's a lie. I don't feel one bit sorry for you. Whatever they decide to do, you deserve it."

Ted's eyes snapped open at five o'clock on the dot. He hadn't slept a wink, even though his eyes had been closed. He'd lived nightmare scenarios all night, one after the other. He was doomed. He brightened for a nanosecond when he thought Espinosa might have the answer to his *doomness*. Not.

"Shake it, Joe. It's five o'clock. We have to tidy up and get going."

Espinosa struggled with the mound of quilts he was wrapped in. He slid to the floor and started to complain that he was stiff all over. "No shower and shave for me in this dump. I'll take care of the quilts and fire, and you warm up the truck. How'd you sleep?"

"Like shit, that's how. I'm doomed, Joe. Listen, I don't want to get married. I mean I do, but not right now. Maggie is going to kill me. First, she'll fire me, and then she'll stalk me and kill me. Then she'll take Mickey and Minnie."

"Yeah," Espinosa said cheerfully. "Get moving. I'm not getting in that truck unless it's warm."

"You don't really give a shit about my life, do you?"

"Nope."

Ted slammed his way through the house and out to the SUV. He cursed long and ripely when he saw the three inches of new snow that had fallen through the night. He slammed his way back into the house, yelling at the top of his lungs. "It snowed. We have to shovel. Did you see a shovel anywhere?"

"Yeah. On the back porch. The truck is your deal. I'm doing the fire and quilts."

Thirty minutes later Ted had the SUV backed up and was heading down the lane and out to the main road. "I'm never coming back to Vermont," he said.

"Uh-oh, here's a text from Maggie. Did you turn off your phone last night?"

"Well, yeah. If you were me, wouldn't you have turned yours off? What . . . what does she want?" Ted asked.

"Yeah, I would have turned it off, but she's pissed now. She wants to know where you are and what you're doing and what went wrong. What do you want me to tell her? Oh, she changed our flight. We're not going to Washington. We're going to North Carolina. She reserved a rental for us on arrival. We're to head up to Big Pine Mountain. Everyone is there. She isn't saying who 'everyone' is. So, what should I say?"

"Say the roads are precarious, and I'm driving. She wants to announce to everyone that we're getting married. She sure works quick." Ted groaned.

"Do you think it will be a festive time?" Espinosa grinned. "Balloons, confetti, streamers?"

Ted winced. "Probably all of the above."

"I'm starved," Espinosa said, hoping to drive the hopeless look from his friend's face. "Those canned string beans and dry cornflakes didn't do it for me last night. I want a robust everything breakfast."

"How the hell can you think about food when I'm suffering like this?"

"My stomach doesn't care about your misery. Look, there's a diner up ahead. If you don't want to eat, I'll eat yours for you."

"Did Maggie respond to your text?"

"No, she did not." Glee rang in Espinosa's voice.

"Already she's pissed," Ted said as he steered the SUV into the nearly deserted parking lot.

"Yeah, I think she was pissed." Espinosa guffawed as he climbed out of the truck.

Ted offered up a single-digit salute as he followed his buddy into the diner.

Chapter 14

It was midafternoon when Ted Robinson and Joe Espinosa stepped from the cable car. There was no one waiting to greet them or show them the way to the main building. Even the dogs were absent.

"I'm taking this as a personal affront, Ted. They could have sent the dogs out to greet us and escort us to the building. Doncha think?"

"What? And spoil the surprise! Remember the balloons, the confetti, and let's not forget the bells and whistles and all that backslapping and hugging that's coming. I can see all those women now, just waiting for another lamb to be led to the slaughter. That lamb would be me."

"Oh, yeah, I forgot about that. You have about one minute to paste a smile on that puss of yours. Remember now, throw your hands in the air, do a little dance, and look like you're happy. If you don't, Maggie will kill you. In other words, perform, Ted, or your ass is grass."

The duo slogged across the slushy compound

in wet snow and ice that was up to their ankles. It was hard, but Ted worked up a smile, had his arms half in the air when they galloped up the steps to the porch and opened the door. His smile disappeared when he didn't hear joyous shouts of "Surprise!" He waited for the bells and whistles to sound and the confetti to fall, but it didn't happen. Maggie didn't rush to him with outstretched arms. Murphy gave a halfhearted bark of welcome, but that was it. Even Espinosa was nonplussed at these strange goings-on.

"What took you so long?" Jack shouted from the recliner, where he was leafing through a magazine.

"Eat me! Vermont is not exactly around the corner from this place. Besides, we had to walk the last fifty miles, then climb this godforsaken mountain, while you're sitting on your ass, reading a magazine," Ted snarled as he peeled off his sodden shoes and socks. "Fetch, Emery! I need something warm, or I'm going to croak."

"Yeah," Espinosa said as he, too, peeled off his wet, ice-cold socks and shoes.

A voice erupted from behind Jack's chair. "Who is that uncouth person speaking? Ah, the Hardy Boys. You're late, so that means you don't get to know anything." Harry Wong rolled over and extracted himself from his pretzel position.

"Eat me!" Ted snarled again.

"Not in your condition. I can smell you all the way over here," Harry said.

"I'm going to give you that one, you terrorist, but if you'd been where we were, you'd smell, too. Anybody have any extra clothes we can borrow while we wash ours?" Ted asked.

"Yeah, brown bag, second bedroom. Did you guys get anything?" Jack said.

"Oh, yeah. But you ain't gettin' it till we brush our teeth, shave, and shower. By the way, where's Maggie?" Ted inquired.

"In the dining room. They're cooking," Jack said.

On the way down the hall, Espinosa hissed. "That's where they're going to do it. Jack and Harry being here is a red herring to throw you off. C'mon, buddy, we have to hustle."

"Why?" asked Ted.

"Because the girls are planning something. That means if we're late, it's either going to get cold or melt. And, the best reason in the world is that Maggie has no patience."

Resigned to whatever was coming his way, Ted stripped down and hit the shower, while Espinosa brushed and flossed, then brushed and flossed a second time. Then he shaved. Twice. He stepped into the shower just as Ted stepped out.

"I'm feeling sick to my stomach," Ted said as the foursome bundled up for the trek across the compound to the dining hall.

"Must be that heavy breakfast you ate," Espinosa volunteered.

"Don't you mean the heavy breakfast that *you* ate, Joe? I just had coffee," Ted replied.

"Guess it's prewedding jitters, then." Espinosa guffawed. "You got it together, Ted? I'm going to open the door now. Remember, sparkle, sparkle. Be happy. This is your crowning moment!"

Smile in place, arms raised, Ted walked through the open door that Espinosa was holding for him. He blinked. No confetti, no streamers, no bells, no whistles, and no shouts of "Surprise!" This time Grady was the one who offered up a halfhearted bark. Delicious aromas were everywhere. The girls, busy, shouted out a greeting and went back to what they were doing. Ted didn't know if he should laugh or cry. He risked a glance at his partner, who was grinning like an idiot.

Maggie appeared out of nowhere. "You guys get good stuff?"

"You know it," Ted said through clenched teeth.

Espinosa was still grinning as he poured himself a cup of coffee from the sideboard.

"Ted, can I talk to you a minute? In private, if you don't mind. Like out on the porch," Maggie asked.

Oh, shit. Here it comes, Ted thought as he pulled on his jacket and followed Maggie out to the front porch. He waited, his insides shaking like a tub of half-set Jell-O.

"Listen, Ted, the last thing I want to do is hurt your feelings. I love you. You know that. I'm just . . . what I mean is . . . I said yes when I meant to say no. Well, that's not true. I did mean yes, wanted to mean yes, but not now. I'm not ready for the house in the sticks, the van with sliding doors, and cooked meals every night. What we have is working for us right now. You know what they say. If it ain't broke, don't fix it. You and I, we don't need that piece of paper. I am yours forever and ever. I hope you feel the same way. Did all of that make sense?" Maggie asked fretfully.

Sweet Jesus, he was off the hook! Somehow or other he managed to let his face crumple into a look of pure misery. "Yeah, I guess so. I was so . . . I couldn't sleep all night. I couldn't wait to get here." *Liar, liar, pants on fire.* "So your yes is now no."

"Yeah, for now it's no. That can change at any time, though."

Please, God, not anytime soon. Play the game would be Jack Emery's advice. Still looking miserable, he said, "I guess I'll have to cancel the ring and wait until you're ready to say yes. I was going to pick it up on Monday."

"No! I'll take the ring."

Ted forgot about being miserable and thought about his bank account and how high his credit-card bill was. "You still want the ring?" he all but screamed.

Mistaking Ted's outburst for excitement, Maggie replied, "I said, 'Yes, I'll take the ring.' What I really said was, 'No! I'll take the ring,' but 'no' meant 'yes.' Oh, I can hardly wait. I know it must be beautiful, because you have such good taste. I'm going to stop chewing my nails so the ring will look even more beautiful on my hand. Oh, I am so excited! Tonight I am going to screw your brains out, so be prepared."

A moment later Ted was left standing alone on the front porch. The guys joined him just as he said, "Fuck! I'm now engaged."

"Oooh, oooh, what happened?" Espinosa asked. "Why aren't you looking happy, Ted? You're among friends here, buddy. I told the guys about your dilemma. They understand. Talk to us, buddy. It will make you feel better."

"She said yes but said yes meant no, and she doesn't want to get married now but maybe soon, like in someday, and she loves me," Ted revealed. "I should have left it there, but I wanted to make it look good, so I said I would have to cancel the ring or pick it up on Monday, or something like that, and she said no, but no meant yes and she'll take the ring. I do not have a fucking ring! She is expecting a fucking ring on Monday. Then she said she is going to screw my brains out tonight."

Jack whistled. "That's heavy!"

"What's that translate to in the way of condoms?" Harry asked curiously.

Espinosa laughed, the sound bouncing off the mountain.

"I have the answer for you, Ted. Call our saviors, Miss Jill and Miss Patsy at Dorchester Jewelers," Jack said. "Don't go too heavy on the explanations. Ask them to send you an emerald-cut diamond, platinum, size six, and to put it in a snazzy velvet box and overnight it to you at my address. You come by on Monday and pick it up, and your problem is solved, and Maggie will probably screw your brains out that night, too. I wouldn't tell that to the ladies, though. Their number is on my speed dial. You want me to call them for you?"

"How much is it going to cost?" Ted asked.

Jack huffed and puffed. "How would I know something like that? Everyone, even a fool, knows you can't put a price on love. Maybe you should be asking yourself what your life is worth if you don't follow through. If you have to ask the price, then you can't afford to get engaged. Just do it, asshole."

Ted did it. "Miss Jill promised delivery for midmorning on Monday. Miss Patsy said she would personally pick out the diamond and knows I won't be disappointed. I promised to send a picture of my betrothed wiggling her finger for the camera."

Jack reached for his phone. "See how easy that was!"

"Man, I'm glad I'm not you," Harry said.

Espinosa stared off into space as he envisioned the day he might be in Ted's place, planning his own engagement to Alexis.

Ted sat down on the top step, not caring if his ass got wet from the melted snow, and cried.

The tantalizing aromas once again greeted the guys as they trooped into the dining room.

Nikki was pouring fresh coffee from the urn

on the sideboard. "What's wrong with Ted?" she whispered in Jack's ear. "His eyes are all blood-shot."

"He's catching a cold. Isn't that what you said, Ted?" said Jack.

"Yeah. Got my feet wet too many times. My mother always said when your feet get wet and cold, you get sick." Ted reached for his cup of coffee and downed it in two quick gulps.

"Yeah, my mother always said that, too," Jack said cheerfully.

Maggie looked horrified. "Teddy, you're getting sick! Why didn't you say something? I'll make you a hot toddy. Go over by the fire and wait for me. I don't want you getting sick on me now that we just got engaged."

Ted managed to offer up a tortured groan as he did what his beloved ordered. Jack grinned, and Espinosa eyed Alexis, his mind racing. Harry, a strange look on his face that could best be described as sappy, cringed as Yoko tweaked his ear, then whispered something to him. Later, Jack described Harry's look to Nikki as one of alarm.

Then they were all seated at the table, looking at one another, with the exception of Charles, who was working in the command center. The questions came fast and furious.

It was Myra who held up her hand for silence. "One at a time, boys and girls."

"I have an idea," Annie said, jumping up, her eyes sparking. No one missed the jittery tone. "I saw it online yesterday, when I was reading the morning paper, and I've been thinking about it ever since. Listen to this, and tell me what all of you think. The White House, and I assume this was Martine Connor's idea, is planning a patriotic affair in three weeks. Lincoln, Washington, all the presidents. All the guests are to come as famous figures from past administrations. Even the ladies. Dolley Madison, Betsy Ross, Bess Truman. It's our own personal invitation to the affair, without the invitation. Are you all following me here?"

"I certainly am, dear," Myra said. "We simply arrive in whatever attire Alexis dresses us in, stroll up to the White House with no invitation in hand, then march to the Oval Office, confiscate our pardons, and leave, presumably by the back door. Is that what you're saying, Annie?"

Annie nodded. "Exactly. You are so astute, Myra. And you are not clutching your pearls for dear life, and that alone tells me you think this will work."

"It could work," Nikki said thoughtfully.

"The invitations can be copied, right down to the grade of paper," Isabelle said. "I can do them myself."

"The costumes will be no problem. Three weeks is plenty of time for me to research it all," Alexis said.

"I can play it up really well and give it a lot of press," Maggie said.

"Harry's people can be security once we come up with something that will work," Yoko said.

"What else did the article say, Annie?" Kathryn asked.

"Three hundred guests. A buffet dinner. Music. The article was skimpy on the details," said Annie.

"That means security out the wazoo. The White House takes priority, so that means the District will have very poor security that night. I wonder if that guy Hank Jellicoe will be called in. If so, Harry's people can suddenly become *his* people. No questions asked," Jack said.

"Forewarned is forearmed," Bert said as he mentally tried to figure out how many of his people would be called in to assist the Secret Service. "A lot will depend on the checkpoints that lead to the Oval Office and who is manning them. The FBI hates these pissant affairs they throw at the White House."

"I almost forgot. The article said some anonymous donor was paying for the shindig, so taxpayers shouldn't get upset," Annie said.

"I wonder who that anonymous donor could be?" Myra asked.

"When and if you find out, dear, let us all know," Annie said sweetly.

"Well, that's one problem solved. We just have to arrange the details," Nikki said.

"Which then brings us to Lizzie and what, if anything, we should do about that."

"I want to know whose side Hank Jellicoe is really on," Kathryn said. "How do we know we can trust him?"

The door to the dining hall opened, and

Charles appeared in time to hear Kathryn's last comment. His comment before taking his place at the table was, "It smells wonderful in here. I can't wait to sit down to dinner, one that I didn't prepare. But to answer Kathryn's question, he can be trusted. That's all I'm going to say. Right now we have another problem. I just got off the phone with Pearl Barnes. She said Lizzie called her last night to ask her some questions but said she couldn't tell her why she was asking. Pearl said she told Lizzie what she could, but she thought about the call all night and into today and decided she better call us just to be on the safe side."

Myra reached for her pearls. "What . . . what did Lizzie want to know, Charles?"

"Everything there is to know about Justice Leonard and his wife," replied Charles.

Nikki jumped up, her arms waving wildly. "I knew it! I knew this would happen! We never should have kept Lizzie out of the loop. She figured it out on her own. Now she's going to think . . . God only knows what she's thinking right now."

"She's thinking what we thought . . . think . . . that it was all a setup to get out of giving us our pardons and making a fool out of Lizzie. If I were Lizzie, that's what I would be thinking," Myra said.

"And Myra is right," Kathryn said glumly.

"Not if we beat Connor to the punch," Maggie said. "And we're well on our way to doing just that. We have the resources to make Leonard step down, whether he likes it or not. We also have the ability and the chutzpah to get Lizzie nominated and sworn in, if that's what she wants. If not, we hone in on some other deserving candidate and make it happen for her—or him. We can do this!"

The dining hall rocked with the women's cheers.

Charles excused himself and returned with two bottles of champagne. "This, ladies and gentlemen, deserves a toast." He poured generously into wine flutes sitting on the sideboard. "To the next new justice of the Supreme Court, Elizabeth Fox de Silva Cricket!"

"Hear! Hear!" the group cried.

Charles poured a second time. "To the vigilantes' upcoming pardons!"

The dining hall rocked with the deafening sounds of "Hear! Hear!"

"I think we're on a roll here, Myra. Let go of those damn pearls, or I'm going to stuff them in one ear and pull them out the other!" Annie hissed.

Myra let go of the pearls and smiled weakly. Nevertheless, it was a smile that everyone saw. Their leader was happy with their toasts.

"Oops, one last toast. I heard just this minute that Maggie and Ted are now engaged. Bottoms up, boys and girls!" Charles said as he poured out the last of the champagne.

Maggie beamed. Ted would have fallen over, but Jack and Harry braced him up.

The women oohed and cooed at Maggie,

while the guys slapped Ted on the back and said things like, "You lucky son of a gun," "Name your first after me," and, "Life is just going to get better."

All lies, but as Harry said later, it sounded good at the time, and they really had to say what they said for Ted's own sanity.

Chapter 15

It was totally dark outside, but there were stars in the sky when the group left the dining hall, stuffed to the gills, as Jack put it. They chattered among themselves as they walked through the melting snow to the command center.

Inside, they shed their outerwear and their rubber boots. The men knew the drill and stayed in the main room, while the women followed Charles to the command center to plot strategy.

"Gather round, boys. A little five-card stud." Bert whipped out a deck of cards from a drawer in the coffee table.

Ted removed the candy bowl and a stack of magazines and books. They all sat down crosslegged and watched as Bert shuffled the deck.

A box of elbow macaroni was plopped in the middle of the table by Espinosa. "Because," he said virtuously, "gambling is illegal."

The others hooted and hollered at this over-the-top declaration.

Still miffed with his current financial situation, Ted started to grumble. "This is pissing me off, gentlemen. We're members of the vigilantes, and yet we can't sit in on the strategy-planning meetings. Why the hell is that?" Not waiting for a reply, he rumbled on. "We do the legwork, put our asses on the line, but we have to sit out here."

"Shut up, Robinson. You're whining," Harry said. "I think they think we couldn't handle it. They're wrong, of course, but then again, they're women."

Jack smacked his friend on the back. "Jesus, Harry, that was profound."

"Deal," Espinosa said as he counted out the elbow macaroni. Each player received ten pieces of pasta.

Around the corner, in the hallway that led to the command center, Nikki poked her head out. Satisfied the guys were indeed playing cards, she whispered to Kathryn, "None of them have a clue about gambling. And not one of them has a poker face. I bet if we sat down with them, we could clean them out in minutes just by watching their expressions."

Kathryn giggled as she watched Bert try to come to terms with his hand.

"Annie and Myra, excellent poker players that they are, could wipe up the floor with all of them," Nikki whispered.

The moment Nikki and Kathryn took their seats at the table, Charles called the meeting to order, and Myra took the floor. "Lizzie is our first order of business. We need to decide right now how we want to handle all of this. Maggie?"

"Why don't we set up the webcam and talk to her face-to-face? Let's let her make the decision for us," Maggie suggested. "She has got to be sick to her soul that Martine Connor would abuse their friendship after all Lizzie and the rest of us did for her. To play Lizzie like that is unforgivable. But we have to bear in mind that Lizzie is not supposed to know any of this. It is entirely possible that the president has some game plan in mind, and we aren't reading it right. It's a slim possibility, but it nonetheless exists."

"We can put a plan in place to ensure that Lizzie gets the nomination, if that's what she wants. Didn't someone say Cosmo said it was going to be announced the following day, or did I hear that wrong?" Annie asked.

"No, you heard it right, Annie, but Cricket corrected what he said later on by saying he was in shock and got it all wrong. No announcement was going to be made anytime in the near future. That's what threw him into such a state of flux," Charles said. "So far, it's still all secret, and the reason it's secret is that it is all bogus."

"That's just another way of saying it's all a bunch of crap, which is what all of us have been saying since we first heard about it," the outspoken Kathryn said.

"Ah . . . yes," Charles responded.

"I've taken the first steps," Maggie said. "Ted and Espinosa interviewed Mrs. Leonard. I sent them to Vermont to check on whether the antiques she spoke of were indeed there or sold off. When they return with me tomorrow, I'll have them work around the clock to interview all the other Supreme Court wives and husbands, and we'll run the article in the Sunday edition. My idea is to run a second article the following Sunday with interviews from the justices themselves. It's going to be boring as hell, but it gives credibility. Now, if someone wants to really go for the gusto where Justice Leonard is concerned, I'm all for that. Maybe if he sees his future going down the drain, he'll give it all up. But is that what we want?"

"Why did he do it in the first place?" Isabelle asked.

"Probably money. But ask yourself this, if the elected leader of the nation came and asked a favor of you, as well as promising you some untold sum of money, what would you do? Especially if he's aware of his wife's . . . problem," Nikki said.

"But from what we've read and heard about Justice Leonard, the man is above the fray. He lives for the law, and he lives in a bubble. I'm almost certain the man didn't think for one nanosecond there would be any blowback. He was just helping the president out," Yoko said.

"That sounds suspiciously like you want the man to skate on this," Annie said testily.

"Oh, no!" Kathryn exploded. "That was dirty pool. The man called Cosmo Cricket. Who in his right mind would think a husband wouldn't tell his wife that kind of news? He knew exactly what he was doing when he made that call. I say we go after him and make him pay for leading Lizzie down the garden path."

"But, dear, Cosmo is that kind of man. He did not tell his wife. And Lizzie was not supposed to know," Myra said.

"Bullshit!" Kathryn shrieked. "Leonard fully expected Cosmo to tell his wife, and so did Martine Connor."

"Kathryn's right," the others agreed in unison.

"Why?" Alexis asked.

"Because, dear, Martine thought Lizzie would be so overwhelmed, so ecstatic that she might be going to the Supreme Court that she would be lax and perhaps even try to talk us into being more patient, buying the president more time with the pardons," Myra said. "I guess she does not know Lizzie as well as she thinks she does. Lizzie figured it out for herself. If left to her own devices, and we agreed not to intervene, I think Lizzie could still make it happen, some way or somehow."

The women agreed with this assessment, too.

"So, that leaves us exactly where?" Nikki asked.

"Sweetie, weren't you listening in the dining room? We're going to invade the White House. We're still on for that little caper. All we have to do is figure out who is going to go into the Oval Office and steal the pardons, which are rightfully ours since they've been signed. Oh, and we have to figure out if they're still in the desk drawer or the file cabinet," Annie said airily.

"That's probably life in the federal pen," Kathryn said sourly.

"Only if we get caught. I, for one, do not plan on getting caught, dear. I think we just need a foolproof plan. Charles is in charge of that little item. With input from us, of course. You *can* do this, can't you, Charles?" Annie's tone of voice clearly said his response had better be affirmative.

Charles smiled. "As long as you don't mind a new member to our little organization. We're going to need his help to pull this off. I am, of course, speaking of Hank Jellicoe. Decide now, so I can put him on alert."

The Sisters looked at one another. The conversation was heated for the first five minutes, then tapered off until it yielded a solid vote of yes. Charles nodded and got up to go to his computer.

He was back in minutes. "Hank said we have incredibly bad timing. He is at the White House as we speak. He will be delighted to become an honorary member of the vigilantes and wants to know if he gets a badge or a decoder ring at his initiation."

"And you think that's funny?" Kathryn grumbled. "What's he doing at the White House at this time of night?"

Before Charles could reply, Annie said, "I don't think we want or need to know why he's there. Or, do we, Charles?"

"Hank has always been a bit of a rogue, albeit a nice one. That's not to say he hasn't been a cad a time or two. Women, for some reason, seem to find him irresistible. He's the best at what he does."

"And that would be . . . spying, charming the president, joining up with the vigilantes?" Yoko said.

Charles chuckled. "All of the above, I'd say."

"So by tomorrow we should know if our pardons are still in the desk drawer or the file cabinet? He should be able to furnish us with a floor plan of the White House, not that we couldn't get that on our own, and details for the upcoming patriotic party, which is set for a few weeks from now, plus a real-life copy of the invitation and perhaps the guest list. Am I safe in assuming all of the above?" Annie said, a sour tone to her voice.

This time Charles laughed outright. "Assuming he has no other plans for the evening, which I doubt."

Kathryn looked genuinely confused. "How does that work when you're boffing the president? Does someone escort you in? And then what do you do? Ring a bell or something when you're ready to leave? Isn't the president worried about her image being besmirched? Don't they gossip at the White House? Does he stay over for breakfast, or does he leave before it gets light out? Another thing. How long has she, the president, known this guy? She hasn't been in office that long. Or are you telling me our first lady president is a loosey-goosey?" Kathryn said all in one breath.

The Sisters were stunned when Myra said spiritedly, "Yes, Charles, I'd like to know the answers to Kathryn's questions myself."

Charles looked acutely uncomfortable. "I'm sorry to say I do not know the answers, but if you like, I can call Hank back and ask him."

"Do that, Charles," Maggie said.

The others picked up the gauntlet.

"Yes, we need to know the answers before we agree to induct him into our little circle," Annie said.

Charles rose to the challenge regretfully and stomped his way to the computer station, where he picked up his satellite phone and pressed a number. He turned his back to the Sisters and spoke in a hushed tone.

When Charles returned to the table, he had a slip of paper in hand, which he read from. "Mr. Jellicoe has carte blanche at the White House, which carries over from past administrations. Boffing the president has nothing to do with his entrance to and exit from Sixteen Hundred Pennsylvania Avenue. No one escorts him. He simply calls ahead. The president is not worried about her image being besmirched. Yes, people do gossip at the White House. Then they get fired and write tell-all books. Sometimes he stays for breakfast. He has known this president for a little over seven months. There was an instant attraction between the two of them, and she made the first move, not that you asked that question, but he volunteered the information.

"No, the president is not a loosey-goosey, but she is uptight, because she carries the weight of this nation on her creamy white shoulders. And he volunteered something else you didn't ask for. He . . . uh . . . he said to tell you all the sex is spectacular even when she's uptight. He also said pillow talk will give him all the answers he needs, and he will relay them to us tomorrow. Then he said, 'Do not call me again this evening.' I hope, ladies, that answers all your questions."

Speechless with Charles's disclosure, the Sisters gaped at him.

Kathryn looked absolutely flabbergasted. "Just like that, she's going to spill her guts to her lover. Our president has loose lips! Oh, my God! Now I'm sorry I asked."

"Don't be, dear. It's better to know . . . certain things now rather than later," Myra said, tongue in cheek.

Annie was doing her best not to laugh, not at Charles's disclosure but at Myra, who was trying her best not to appear naive.

"Do any of you have any idea what I could do with all that information?" Maggie grinned.

"Save it, dear. We might be telling you in a few weeks to run with it," Annie said. "Do you have it committed to memory?"

"I do. And I know all the right adjectives to use to bounce it up a little, too," said Maggie.

"Ladies, can we now get back to the matters at hand?" Charles asked. "I believe we were trying to decide what to do about Justice Leonard. We also need to talk about Lizzie and set up a meeting to decide what she wants us to do."

Fifteen minutes of very heated dialogue later, it was decided that Maggie would go to Justice Leonard's home, ostensibly to interview him after Ted's initial interview, and break the news to him that on a date to be decided, he would be announcing his decision to leave public service and work in the private sector when the term ended in June.

"Most likely," Maggie said, "the announcement will come the day after the patriotic party. That will give him time to get his affairs in order, so to speak."

"What if he kicks up a fuss? What if he refuses to resign?" Alexis asked.

"Trust me, he'll resign," said Maggie. "He won't like it, but he'll do it. Just let me worry about Justice Leonard."

The Sisters nodded. Maggie always came through for them.

"Time to call Lizzie," Nikki said. "Is the webcam set up, Charles?"

"We're ready to go," Charles said.

"It's her voice mail," Nikki whispered. "I'll leave a message for her to call us back."

Annie looked at the clock and said, "With the time difference, Lizzie is probably talking to her husband, the way she does every evening. She allows nothing to interfere with her calls, and that's the way it should be. The Capitol could burn down, and she wouldn't pay attention. We'll try again in another hour."

Outside the command center, the poker game was in high gear. Harry had a mountain of elbow macaroni in front of him, clearly winning.

"I thought you said Wong didn't know how to play poker?" Ted snarled at Jack.

"I didn't say he didn't *know* how to play. I said he never plays. There is a difference, Ted," Jack replied.

"Since I've cleaned you all out, pay up," Harry said cheerfully.

Bert slid fifty bucks across the table. Ted signed an IOU for seventy dollars, explaining that he and Espinosa had left all their ready cash back on the table in Vermont.

Harry looked pointedly at Espinosa, who signed his own IOU for eighty-five bucks. Jack was the last to pony up, with forty-eight dollars.

Bert looked at his watch. "Looks like they're going to be in there for a little longer," he said, jerking his head in the direction of the command center. "Let's head over to the dining room and guzzle a few beers."

No one needed any urging as they beat a path to the door.

"I have a great idea. We can plan Ted's bachelor party while we toast him," Jack said. "I think we should do it in Vegas, because you know what they say about Vegas. What happens in Vegas stays in Vegas, and we're definitely going to want whatever we plan to stay there. What do you say, Ted? Vegas?"

Ted nodded. "Why the hell not."

"Once you put that ring on Maggie's finger, she's going to like the way it looks, and then she's going to start having second thoughts, and I betcha that inside of a month she's picking a wedding date," Espinosa said.

"Who died and appointed you Mr. Bridal Consultant with all the answers?" Ted snarled.

"I have a lot of sisters, and that's the way it works. So, okay, don't believe me. See if I care," Espinosa returned.

Ted wanted to cry all over again.

Chapter 16

It wasn't that there was no activity at the White House; there was. Behind the scenes, people still moved about, seeing to things. The Secret Service moved a little slower, possibly a little quieter, because it was the middle of the night. Phones still rang; computers and printers were being utilized by a skeleton staff. The kitchen wasn't exactly a beehive of activity, but chefs were moving about, seeing that things were ready the moment the president woke.

No matter how hard the kitchen staff worked to anticipate this new president's culinary desires, they failed. One day the president wanted dry toast with elderberry jam, and the next day, peach-and-honey yogurt. On still another day she requested a grilled cheese sandwich on sourdough bread, for breakfast no less. Taking her requests as personal affronts, the head chef had scoured the District for elderberry jam, and now the pantry had a whole case of it, but the president had never asked for it again. The peach-and-honey yogurt expired before she could request it a second time. The sourdough bread grew healthy mold before she ever asked for it again.

The absolute bottom line for the head chef and all his staff was that coffee was to be ready at all times, even in the middle of the night. Freshly brewed when the request came in and five minutes to get it to her. The beans had to be freshly ground, and the president wanted only recycled filters used to filter the strong coffee. Under no circumstances was she ever, as in ever, to be served anything other than 100 percent Colombian coffee. The pantry held six burlap bags of the fragrant beans.

The president had been what the kitchen staff called uptight for the past week. She'd found fault with everything they prepared for her. Even the coffee. She'd made a special trip to the kitchen to ask the chef and his staff what *their* problem was. Then she had raided the pantry and the larder right under their noses and had had one of the staff carry everything up to her own personal kitchen, where she said she would cook for herself since they couldn't get it right.

There was turmoil among the Secret Service agents, who grumbled to their superiors, who told them just to do their jobs, and they knew that women were difficult to deal with at certain times of the month. They would try to share the burden fairly among those assigned to the president's personal detail.

The only person who appeared unaffected by the recent turmoil was the new chief White House counsel, Elizabeth Fox Cricket.

The scuttlebutt was that there was an internal war going on in the White House, and bets were being laid down as to who would win, the president or the people who worked for her. The current score was zip to zip.

The latest rumor to circulate was that heads were going to roll. But probably not till after the president's cockamamy patriotic party in February.

The night chef looked at one of four clocks he kept in his kitchen, four clocks so no matter if he was standing north, south, east, or west, he could see the time. Right now it was shy of five minutes to four in the morning. He anticipated a call any minute, because the president had a guest, who would undoubtedly be leaving soon. He was almost certain a call would come down for coffee, juice, and possibly bagels. He'd just made a batch, and they were still warm. He looked over at one of his assistants, pointed to a bowl of oranges, and said, "Squeeze them. Be sure there are no seeds left, and leave the pulp. The president likes pulp."

Sad to say, the president and her guest would not be partaking of the chef's efforts on this particular morning.

Martine Connor rolled out of bed, took one look at the mangled sheets, then at the man sleeping peacefully on the left side of the bed. She pulled on her favorite robe to cover her naked body and ran to the kitchen. She felt like a giddy schoolgirl as she made coffee, squeezed six oranges, and sliced several stale bagels. When they were toasted, no one could tell that they weren't fresh, she told herself. She quickly set the table for two. Then she leaned against the counter to stare at her reflection in the black glass on the microwave's door. Considering the wild night she'd just had, she didn't look all that bad.

Where this relationship was going with Hank Jellicoe, she had no idea. She did admit to herself that she would like to see it go *somewhere,* though. She let a smile tug at her lips. Here she was, the leader of the free world, wondering where this particular relationship was going and worrying about her messy hair.

She heard him before she saw him. He was fully dressed in jeans, a flannel shirt, and sturdy boots. His hair was slicked back, and he smelled minty and manly when he took her in his arms. They both laughed when he nuzzled her neck and whispered, "Was it as good for you as it was for me?"

Then they both laughed out loud when she responded, "Better."

The toaster oven pinged. Martine extricated herself from Jellicoe's embrace and proceeded to serve him breakfast.

"This is one for the books. The president of these United States is serving this lowly peon breakfast in the White House. I like it," Hank said, chomping down on a bagel. "These are stale. You know that, right?"

"I was hoping you wouldn't notice. I like extra crunch."

"I do, too, as long as it doesn't crack my teeth. Look at me, Marti. What's wrong? You're with me, but you're not. I'm a good listener, and you know I will never divulge anything you tell me. My clearance is at the top of the ladder."

"I'm not trying to be evasive, Hank. It's personal, and I have to work it out in my own way and deal with it. I'm just not ready to talk about it to anyone."

Hank finished his coffee in one long gulp and handed her the cup. The president hustled to fill it. Hank was chauvinist enough to appreciate the president hustling to please him.

"Don't you have any friends you can talk to? Women do that, I hear."

"You can't have friends, living here. I used to have friends. I suppose you could say Lizzie Fox, my new chief White House counsel, is a close friend. At least she used to be. That's why I fought so hard to get her to take the job. I felt like I needed an ally in here. The only problem is, I don't have time to spend with her. I made a lot of concessions to get her to come on board, which means she's either eight to five or nine to five. She makes her own hours, and I think it's safe to say, she makes her own rules, too. I live in fear that she's going to bail on me."

"Why would she do that?"

The president got up and pulled the belt of her robe so tight, she actually winced. "I didn't say she would. I said I live in fear that she might. She just got married, and her first loyalty is to her new husband. If her husband needed her, and she was in the middle of some earth-shattering crisis, she would flip me the bird, and off she would go. That's Lizzie, and there is no one in this whole wide world that I admire more than her."

Jellicoe appeared thoughtful. "Does she feel the same way about you?"

"She used to. I don't see the harm in telling you I owe her a debt, and I made a promise to her, but I am having a hard time honoring that debt and honoring that promise. I want to so badly, I can taste it, but . . . other people are standing in my way. That's part of my problem."

Jellicoe leaned in closer to the table. "Then get rid of those people, Marti. A person is only as good as her word. I personally want to believe that I am solid gold when it comes to my word or promises that I make. How else do you think I managed to survive in this business? I want you to think about that. Lizzie Fox is someone you never want to make an enemy of."

Martine Connor's eyes popped wide. "Just like that? Get rid of them? Where do I find their replacements? I seem to be batting zip here with staff. Do you know Lizzie?"

"All you have to do is call me, and I can have your replacements on board within hours. People who will be loyal to you, people who have no agenda other than to serve at your command, people you will be comfortable with. *People you can trust.* Of course I know Lizzie. I know Cosmo, too. They're at the top of my short list of friends."

"You never told me you knew Lizzie."

The president's voice was so accusatory, Hank reared back in his chair. He looked at his breakfast partner and saw the panic on her face. "I know a lot of people, Marti. Why would you think I should mention the names of my friends to you? I didn't see you mentioning any of yours first crack off the bat. What difference does it make, anyway, if I know Lizzie and Cosmo Cricket?"

"That's because I don't have any friends. I did mention Lizzie when you asked. I just find it strange that you know Lizzie and didn't see fit to mention that you knew her and that she now works here. How . . . how well do you *know* Lizzie?"

Hank laughed. "Well enough that I sent a smashing wedding present and well enough to get ticked off that I wasn't asked to be Cosmo's best man, but I understand the serendipitous decision to get married, and I wasn't around at the time. Actually, I was in Angola at the time, but I would have done my best to get back if I had been asked. Lizzie and I used to have dinner when I was in town. I can't think of a more perfect couple than Cosmo Cricket and Lizzie. Listen, honey, I have to leave now. It's getting late. I guess I should say early. So, do I get to see you sitting behind your desk in the Oval Office before I go, or are you going to weasel out on me? I'd kind of like to take that particular memory with me when I leave."

Martine Connor bit down on her lower lip. "Why does that sound to me like you aren't coming back? But as you like to say, a promise is a promise. How's that memory going to look, me in my bathrobe, my hair all messy?"

Jellicoe smiled. "Why would you think I won't be coming back? I will if you want me to. But to address your question, that's the beauty of a memory, Marti. The real you. I want to see the real you behind that desk. I want to see where you live and work so when I think of you, I can visualize it. That's why I love memories. They can be so real at times when you don't have anything else. So, is it a go or not?"

Martine slipped into presidential mode. "Come along. Don't look at anyone or make eye contact, okay?"

"Got it! I know the drill, Marti."

"Why are we doing this, Hank? I think you know this building better than I do. Off the top of your head, how many times have you been here?"

Hank stopped in his tracks so abruptly, the president smashed into him. "Thousands. I told you why. But I wasn't sleeping with my commander in chief then. Therein lies the difference. If I wanted to, which I don't, I could sketch this out for you right down to the tiles and the wormholes in the wood on the floor. Like I said, I just want to see you sitting behind your desk in your bathrobe. Humor me. Or, I can leave now and let you get back to running the world. Your call, Marti."

"Don't be silly. We're here. I have to take a deep breath each and every time I walk into this room. I don't know if I will ever get used to it. So, you just want me to sit behind my desk and look presidential in my ratty old bathrobe?"

"Exactly!" He grinned. "Now, lean forward and look straight at me." He made a box with his hands, like a photographer framing his next shot. "You are now speaking to the man who is falling in love with you."

"Oh, Hank, really?" She wasn't the president then, even though she was sitting in the president's chair. She was just Martine Connor, who was falling in love with the man staring at her.

"Yep. Now, wink at me like we share a secret. Ah, now, you see? That's the memory I'm going to take with me. My turn now."

"What do you mean, your turn?" Martine asked nervously.

"My turn to sit behind the desk so you can capture my likeness. I want us both to have the same memory. What? Did I say something wrong?"

"Well, no . . . I don't . . . this is . . ."

"Highly irregular?"

"That, too," Martine said, getting up from behind the desk and walking over to where Hank was standing.

Hank did some arm flapping and foot shuffling as he seated himself. The toe of his boot snaked out imperceptibly to open the bottom drawer of the president's desk. He raised his ankle a little higher as he smiled into the make-believe camera the president was holding.

"Do I look handsome and dashing? Do I look like a man you could maybe fall in love with?"

Clearly flustered, Martine smiled weakly. All she could do was nod, because she didn't trust herself to speak. This wasn't right. Some internal something or other was twanging away at her insides.

"Okay, here comes the wink! Did you capture me in all my glory?" Hank asked as he slid the bottom drawer shut, with barely any foot movement at all.

"I did. I have to get back. They'll be bringing me the PDB to look over."

"Ah, yes, the President's Daily Brief. Okay, I'm outta here. Do I get to kiss the president in the Oval Office?"

Hank had a bad moment when Martine jammed her hands into the pockets of her robe and looked him in the eye. "Do you want to?"

"I do, but I can see your heart isn't in it. I guess it's all those cameras. I'm sorry, I've made you uncomfortable by asking you to bring me down here. I know there are a hundred sets of eyes on me, so I can find my way out. Thank you for a wonderful evening, Marti."

The president licked at her lips, turned, and left the room without another word. She turned right, and Hank turned left. Her shoulders slumped, and there were tears in her eyes as she walked down the hall. She felt one of them splash on her hand.

Every pore in her body shrieked that the leader of the free world had been conned, and it had all just been captured on film.

But it wasn't captured on film. Hank Jellicoe had seen to that. The only thing captured on film was the contents of the president's bottom desk drawer.

Hank waved offhandedly to some of the Secret Service agents as he made his way out of the West Wing. Outside it was still dark, and a light rain was falling. He climbed into his specially equipped Humvee, which was outfitted just the way the Secret Service Suburbans that transported the president to various destinations within the District were.

The Humvee seemed to have a mind of its own as Hank drove with one eye on the side of the road for an all-night establishment that served food and coffee. It wasn't the food and coffee that he wanted, but the anonymity of a dark parking lot.

Hank knew this place, had conducted business here on other occasions. It was a mind-your-own-business kind of hole-in-the-wall that drew a certain clientele. Hank had a way of fitting into any group or situation. He whipped out his satellite phone the minute he put the Humvee into park and dialed the number that would put him in contact with Charles Martin. There were no greetings. Hank's words were minimal. "I'm uploading it now." Five seconds later he was out of the Humvee and striding toward the hole-in-the-wall, where he would order a man-size breakfast of pancakes, eggs, sausage, and a double side of bacon, along with toast, juice, and coffee.

Hank settled himself on a ratty stool at the counter so as not to take up a whole booth and looked up to catch the early-morning news.

Another day in the life of Hank Jellicoe.

Chapter 17

Martine Connor entered her quarters and immediately walked over to the window that she'd stood at hundreds of times since moving into the White House. The temperature had risen during the night and had climbed still higher throughout the morning. It was raining out now, a slow, steady rain that was melting the snow even as she stared at it. She turned and looked around as she tried to remember why she'd come up here to her quarters in the first place. Did she come because she couldn't concentrate? Or did she come to cry? Well, she'd never been a crier, so that wasn't it. She swiped at a tear at the corner of her eye.

How could she not have known that Henry Jellicoe knew Lizzie? How? She was the president of the United States and was supposed to know everything. Well, almost everything.

Frustrated with her thoughts and where they were taking her on this dismal morning, Martine walked over to the refrigerator, a stainless-steel monstrosity she had chosen from a catalog and had come to hate. She poured herself a glass of orange juice, which she didn't want, but before she did that, she banged her clenched fists so hard on the countertop, she thought she'd broken some fingers. She gave a very unpresidential snort. If she broke her hand or her fingers, how could she sign her name to all the different things that were put in front of her every day of the week?

Where in the name of God had her backbone gone? The orange juice, which she'd been holding in her hand, spilled over the side of the glass as she plopped it down on the counter. She whirled around, then squared her shoulders before she marched out of her quarters and made her way to the West Wing and the Oval Office.

Martine settled herself behind her desk. She licked at her lips before she bent down to open the bottom desk drawer. Before she could change her mind or think twice, she picked up the folders that contained the presidential pardons for the vigilantes and placed them on her desk. She kicked the drawer shut with her foot. She didn't realize she was holding her breath until she let it out with a long loud *swoosh* of sound.

Her foot inched out, and she pulled open the opposite drawer and withdrew the file on Global Securities, which she had asked Lizzie to pull for her. It had to weigh at least ten pounds. "That would have been the time when you should have told me you knew Henry Jellicoe,

Lizzie," she whispered to herself. "Makes me wonder why you didn't," she continued to whisper.

Martine took another deep breath, then picked up the phone. "Toby, can you come in here for a minute? Bring my schedule for today."

She made a second call to her secretary, Jackie Hollis. "I want you to call Lizzie and invite her for lunch in my quarters. Ask her if she prefers corned beef on rye or pastrami on rye. Some potato salad would be nice and some apple pie for dessert. Call the kitchen and ask them to serve us around one fifteen. Do not take no for an answer where Lizzie is concerned. Thank you, Jackie."

The president looked up to see Toby Daniels standing in the doorway with a sheet of paper in his hand. She motioned for him to come forward. The president scanned the sheet of paper and said, "Reschedule this, this, and this. Then I want you to call all my advisors and have them up here at exactly three o'clock. This is not negotiable."

"Should they ask why, what would you like me to tell them?" Toby asked.

The president laughed. Toby thought it was the strangest sound he'd ever heard in his life. "Now, that depends, Toby, on whether you want me to tell them or you want to tell them yourself that they're all going to be fired. I want security in place to escort them out of the White House the moment they leave this room. You know the drill. I want to see the press release before you send it out. That will be all, Toby. You're smiling, Toby. Why is that?"

"Just wondering what took you so long," he replied, grinning.

"I got a swift kick in the pants this morning that made me see the light. I'm feeling pretty good right now, Toby."

"Replacements?"

"It's being taken care of as we speak. Well, almost. I have to make a phone call. That's why I want to see the press release first. The press will want to know the names of the replacements. I take it you approve?" It was more a question than a statement.

"I do."

Toby gave an airy wave of his hand before he closed the door behind him.

The president walked out to Jackie Hollis's office and said, "I want you to call the head of Global Securities and tell him . . . to . . . tell him I'm ready to take him up on his offer and to have his trusted advisors in my office at eight o'clock tomorrow morning. Tell him to watch the news. The White House will be making an announcement later this afternoon. What did Lizzie say about lunch?"

"I went down to her office, and she seemed in a bit of a daze this morning. She said lunch is fine."

"Lord, she isn't sick, is she? There's so much flu going around."

"Oh, no. I think she was preoccupied, and

she just wasn't being Lizzie. We all have days like that, or maybe it was me, and I didn't read her right, Madam President. And she wants corned beef."

"I'm having one of those days myself today, Jackie." Martine Connor patted herself on the shoulder as she made her way back into the Oval Office, where she plopped down in a very unpresidential sprawl. "And the truth will set you free." That quotation from Jesus' speech to the children of Abraham on the Mount of Olives was right on the money.

The president's gaze went to the impressive stack of pardons sitting on the corner of her desk. The very same pardons she knew Henry Jellicoe was looking for. Did he think for one minute that he had fooled her? Obviously he did. Her face burned at the thought. And all that arm waving and the oversize watch. She'd been wise to that, too. But she had let him get away with it. She'd let him use her. Her face continued to burn. Well, she had no one but herself to blame. She'd allowed herself to be bamboozled by her advisors. And to think it took only a roll in the hay to bring it front and center. The heat in her face and neck grew so intense, she got up and ran to the small private lavatory and doused her face with cold water.

The moment she stepped back into the office, Jackie Hollis rapped on the door. "Madam President, Mr. Jellicoe would like me to put him through to your office."

"I bet he would. Can I trust you to deliver a verbatim message, Jackie?"

"Of course, Madam President. And that message would be . . . what?"

"Tell Mr. Jellicoe that as the leader of the free world, I am contemplating my navel and cannot be disturbed. Verbatim, Jackie."

"Shall I wait for a reply, Madam President?"

"Absolutely not, and if he calls back, tell him I cannot take his call. I also want his clearance rescinded immediately."

Martine Connor dusted her hands dramatically, then walked over to the window the minute Jackie Hollis closed the door behind her.

Her mother had always told her as a child not to cut off her nose to spite her face. At the time she had had no clue what that meant, but she did now. And yet, here she was all those years later, *and* the president of the United States to boot. "*And* what did I just do? I just cut off my nose to spite my face," she mumbled.

Toby Daniels poked his head in the door. "Madam President, we have five minutes to the meeting in the Situation Room, and your press secretary would like five minutes of your time after the meeting. If she runs into overtime, you will still make your luncheon with Lizzie."

The president gathered up her folder and her briefing book and followed her chief of staff out of the office. Before she left, she laid her hand on the stack of pardons sitting on her desk, a move that did not go unnoticed by her COS. He wished he could clap her on the back and say something like, "Good going, Madam President," but that would not be seemly, so he just grinned as he followed the leader of the free world down the hallway.

Lizzie thanked the Secret Service agent for the escort to the president's quarters. Martine Connor opened the door the minute she heard footsteps outside. If she sensed a slight stiffness to Lizzie's slim form, she ignored it as she gave her friend a bone-crushing hug. She linked her arm with Lizzie's as she led her into the kitchen, where lunch was already laid out under gleaming silver domes.

"Remember now, we're Marti and Lizzie in here. I have so much to tell you. I have things to apologize for and some things I think you might congratulate me for, but first, let's eat and talk about nothing serious. Are you settling in? How's your husband? What do you think of this awful weather?"

"I am settling in, but I have to tell you, this is a very boring job. I have to be honest. I don't think I could ever get used to it." Lizzie chomped down on a briny pickle and rolled her eyes. "I haven't had a pickle like this since I was a kid."

"I'll send you a barrelful. The chef puts them on every plate, no matter what he serves me. And your new husband?"

"He's fine, but he misses me. As for the weather, spring can't get here soon enough for me."

The small talk continued, talk of Christmas,

New Year's Eve, and the latest Washington gossip. And then it was like some invisible alarm went off that only Martine could hear. She pushed her plate aside and leaned toward Lizzie, her voice low but not a whisper. "We need to talk, Lizzie. I want you to listen to me very carefully, and I don't want you to say a word until I'm finished. Agreed?"

Lizzie nodded, then watched as Martine got up and started rummaging in the kitchen drawers. When she sat back down, she opened her clenched hand. Coins dropped on the table. "Sixty-seven cents. Your retainer. Do you accept it?"

Puzzled, Lizzie nodded.

Martine Connor took a deep breath and let it out slowly. Lizzie thought she saw a fine sheen of perspiration bead up on the president's forehead. "In my zeal to honor my promise to you and the vigilantes, I may have . . . No, that's wrong. I made a mistake. At least I *think* I might have made a mistake. Quite by accident, I overheard one of my senior advisors talking on his cell. I didn't mean to eavesdrop, and I gave no indication that I had heard his end of the conversation. It would seem he and Justice Douglas Leonard are friends. Justice Leonard is gravely ill. He'll be leaving the court when it goes into recess. No one knows this, Lizzie, except for a few people. I anguished over that information before I acted on it. I used my office to . . . to try and make it work for me, for you, and for the vigilantes. When I spoke to Justice Leonard and explained the situation, he agreed to help me. Quite willingly, I might add. It was Justice Leonard who came up with the scenario that . . . that we used in my attempt to resolve my problem. And it is . . . was a problem. I hope this is making sense to you, Lizzie." Martine held up her hand. "No, no, don't say anything yet."

Lizzie shifted in her chair, her eyes glued to the woman opposite her, her ears tuned to every word the president was saying.

"So what I did was hatch this plan. Then I threw it out there, to your husband, who assured me he wouldn't mention my plan to you. Did he, Lizzie?"

"No, Martine, he didn't mention it to me."

"I hated asking him to keep something like that secret from you."

Lizzie almost smiled. "What secret? Maybe you should tell me what this particular secret is so I know what you're talking about."

Martine Connor smiled, but it was a weary smile. "Lizzie, why don't I believe that you don't know what I'm talking about? Never mind. Don't answer that. My plan, Lizzie, was to nominate you to fill the vacancy on the Supreme Court. Justice Leonard agreed with me and said you would make an excellent nominee. I was so relieved when he agreed with me. We all understand the vetting process, but I truly, truly believe we can make it happen.

"Did I have an ulterior motive? Of course I did. I thought I was buying time with the pardons and that you would somehow be so caught up in the process, you'd cut me some slack where the vigilantes were concerned. What that means to you, Lizzie, is, I was being a coward. And I was using you. I have it all in hand now. I stood tall, just the way you used to tell me to do. I'm not excusing myself, but I am trying to do the right thing now. I am doing it. You need to believe me, Lizzie. Please, I need you to say you forgive me."

"What will my forgiveness do for you, Marti?"

"It will let me look in the mirror without loathing myself."

"When will you pardon the vigilantes?"

"You do have a one-track mind, don't you, Lizzie? The pardons are on my desk. Ready to go. My advisors . . . you know . . . That's not even important anymore. Those advisors will be gone by three fifteen this afternoon. Henry has . . . He agreed to help me. By eight o'clock tomorrow morning, my new advisors will be on board. Everyone will step up to the plate, and we won't be missing a beat. That's what I most regret, that I allowed them to browbeat me, that I listened to them. So, in that sense I failed you and the Sisters. But, I'm making it right now, and whatever the fallout is, I'll handle it."

Lizzie's eyes narrowed. "You didn't answer my question, Marti. When are you going to go public with the pardons?"

"Lizzie! You aren't getting it! They're ready on my desk. That means anytime the vigilantes want to stop by and pick them up, they're theirs. Why else do you think I'm having that silly pa-

triotic party? I don't mean it's silly to be patriotic. I sort of thought the ladies would . . . you
know . . . stop by and pick them up. Like during
the party."

Lizzie was stunned at the president's declaration. "You're serious, aren't you? Why do you
want to set yourself up like that? The press will
crucify you."

"The *Post* won't. Lizzie, I know the score.
Henry just tried to put one over on me. Now,
that one hurt. I'm not going to worry about anything until I hear the word *impeachment.* Even
then I don't know if I'll worry about it."

"That's a pretty gutsy attitude, even if you are
the president."

Martine Connor shrugged. "So, how do you
feel about taking the bench on the Supreme
Court? I know you know, Lizzie."

Lizzie smiled. "It's true, I do know, but
Cosmo didn't tell me. He enlisted the aid of a
few friends, and word got back to Maggie
Spritzer, who in turn told me. At first I thought
it was a dream come true. As you know, every
lawyer worth his or her salt aspires to sit on that
particular court, and I'm no exception. I was
stunned, ecstatic, over the moon, all of the
above. Just to be nominated was enough. I don't
think I got as far in my thinking that it might actually happen. The vetting process is a killer.
Everyone knows that."

"What is it you're trying to say, Lizzie?"

"What I'm saying is, no thanks!"

"Lizzie, it's a sure shot. We can get you the appointment. Is it your husband? Why? I don't understand."

"It is a dream come true, and I do thank you, but I can't accept. I'm pregnant, Marti. My doctor just called this morning to tell me my test came back positive. You're the first to know. I haven't even told Cosmo yet. I can't believe it. Me! I'm going to be a mother! Me, of all people. Cosmo is . . . God, I don't know what Cosmo is going to do or say."

"Oh, Lizzie, how wonderful! You are going to be such a good mother. I'm sure your husband is going to . . . to go over the moon." Tears filled the president's eyes. "I am so happy for you and Cosmo. I understand completely. The Supreme Court wanes in light of motherhood."

"It does, doesn't it?" Lizzie giggled. "I want you to be my baby's godmother, Marti."

Tears rolled down the president's cheeks. "Even after . . . ?"

Lizzie nodded. "I'm going to pack up and take the red-eye tonight. This is something I want to tell Cosmo face-to-face, not over the phone. I'll be back in a few days."

Martine was suddenly all business. "So, I want to be sure I understand what we've said here. It's okay for the vigilantes to attend the patriotic party and pick up their pardons in person?"

Lizzie laughed. "The only thing you have to decide is this. Do you want to see them invade the White House, which is what they threatened to do, and you said would never happen, or do you want to pave the way for them and make it easy?"

"I think I'll flip a coin. Call it, Lizzie." The president picked up a quarter from the table. "Heads, the vigilantes invade the White House under their own power. Tails, I pave the way for it to happen."

Lizzie laughed. "Heads!"

After Martine flipped the coin, it rolled around for what seemed an eternity, finally coming to a stop in front of Lizzie, with the American eagle grinning up at her.

"Tails," Lizzie said, sounding disappointed. "Too bad. I guess you get to help in the invasion of the White House."

Martine leaned close and hugged her old friend. "I'll start looking for your replacement. I want you to enjoy every moment of your pregnancy. Truly, Lizzie, I am so happy for you. Can I plan a baby shower here at the White House?"

"Well, yeah, Marti. I want my baby to have that memory. Are you sure you want to do that?"

"Oh, Lizzie, I do. We could have it this summer in the Rose Garden." The president looked at her watch. "Oh, God, I'm late. I have to go, Lizzie."

Arms linked, the two women walked to the door. They hugged one last time before the president opened the door. She shed her personal persona like a chameleon and turned into the president of the United States. She winked at Lizzie and said, "Fly safe."

"You know it, Madam President."

Lizzie tripped down the hall behind the Secret Service agent. Her eyes sparkled as she started to hum under her breath.

She was pregnant.

She was going to be a mother.

How awesome was that?

Pretty damn awesome, she thought.

Chapter 18

Cosmo Cricket shifted in the oversize bed and sniffed Elizabeth's scent on the pillow. He rolled over, the huge custom bed shaking with his weight. He could still smell her perfume, more so now. Was he dreaming? If he was dreaming, then how could he be aware of his wife's perfume? He sniffed again, savoring the sweet, musky scent of her. He cracked one eye to see the red numerals on the digital clock. Way too early to get up. He sensed movement on the floor. He didn't have a dog or a cat, so what was moving?

He reached out to snap on the bedside light as both eyes snapped open. "Elizabeth! What are you doing here? Why are you sitting on the floor? How long have you been sitting there?"

Lizzie smiled. "I came to see you. I'm sitting here because I didn't want to wake you. I've been here for more than an hour. I like watching you sleep. You look so peaceful."

Cosmo's mind raced. Then his heart started to pound. She knew. He felt fear then, fear unlike anything he'd ever known. She knew about the possible nomination and that he'd kept it from her. She'd come here to ax him, to tell him she couldn't abide a liar. They'd promised each other there would be no secrets between them. But . . . her tone of voice was light . . . truthful sounding. She looked so . . . ethereal sitting there on the floor. He shook his big head like a wet, shaggy dog getting a bath to try and clear his thoughts.

"Are you hungry?" he asked. He shook his head again. Of all the stupid things to have said, that had to be the stupidest.

"Only for you," Lizzie said.

Cosmo's heart continued to pound. Well, that didn't sound like she was there to give him the kiss of death. Throwing caution to the winds, he leaned over and reached for her hand. Leaning over the way he was, he could see her beautiful face more clearly. She looked, for want of a better word, dreamy. Her eyes, which usually sparkled, appeared glazed to him. He could feel panic start to rise in him. In the time it took his heart to beat twice, he was out of the bed and sitting in front of her, his long legs outstretched. He reached for her and tried to pull her close. She resisted. Then she stiff-armed him. The panic was engulfing him now as he stared at the woman he loved more than life itself.

"Cricket, I have something to tell you."

Lizzie called him Cricket when things were

right and Cosmo when she meant business. His panic did not subside.

"Look at me, Cricket." Like he could do anything but look at her. "I'm pregnant. I just found out this morning. That's why I'm here. We're going to have a baby! We're going to be parents."

"We're having a baby?" Cosmo said as his eyes rolled back in his head.

"Well, technically, we made a baby, and I'm the one who is going to have it, but, yeah, we're having a baby."

Cosmo felt his eyeballs settle back into place. "I feel like you just gave me the whole world with a big red bow on it. A baby! I'm going to be a father! A real honest-to-God father! Jesus, Elizabeth, why are you sitting on the floor?" Without waiting for her answer, he somehow managed to get to his knees, then his feet. He scooped her up in his arms and set her gingerly on the side of the bed. Now he was on his knees as he stared up at her. "You're okay, right? We'll get a nurse to follow you around, a housekeeper to wait on you. We'll even get a dog to keep you company. I'll quit my job and we'll—"

"Do none of the above. I'm fine. I don't want a nurse or a housekeeper, and no, you will not quit your job. I'll go for the dog, but that's it."

"But—"

"No buts, Cricket. I want your promise."

Like he could deny her anything. He promised. "Pickles, ice cream, watermelon. I'll make sure we never run out, okay?"

"Okay." Lizzie giggled.

"I thought . . . Christ, I thought all kinds of things when I woke and saw you sitting there on the floor. I was so sure you—"

"Found out about the Supreme Court nomination? I did. I understand, Cricket. I had lunch with the president today. I turned it down. Not that it was actually offered, but I told her thanks but no thanks. I did tell her I was pregnant. I'm sorry she was the first to know, but I had no other choice. She cried, Cricket. It's such a long story, and I don't want to go down that road right now. But she did say she would start looking for a replacement, because she knew I'd want to spend these months with you. You know what, Cricket? I am hungry. I think I'll take you up on your offer of breakfast."

Once again, Lizzie found herself scooped up and trundled out to the kitchen, where Cosmo settled her into one of the padded chairs.

"This is it, you know. From here on in you do not get to carry me around like a baby doll."

Hands on his hips, Cosmo glared at his wife. "What if you trip and fall? We should get you one of those button things to wear around your neck that will summon the paramedics. I'll do that at nine o'clock, when business opens. Absolutely I am going to do that."

"Okay, this is where we have our first fight, *Cosmo*. No button! I am not going to trip and fall. I am not going to gain a ton of weight. That means I will not be top heavy. Honey, millions of women have babies every day. Somehow or other, they make it through the nine months, carrying on normal lives. I appreciate your concern, truly I do, but I do not want to be smothered. Are you listening, *Cosmo?*"

The use of his given name convinced Cosmo that Lizzie meant business. He hung his big head and nodded. "What would you like for breakfast?"

"Everything. Eggs, pancakes, waffles, bacon, sausage, juice, coffee, the works. Today we celebrate. Tomorrow I will start to eat healthy. Try not to use every pot and pan in the house, okay?"

Cosmo's laugh shook the house as he lumbered from the refrigerator to the stove and back to the table. "Are you going to have that test that will tell us if it's a boy or a girl?"

"We have to discuss it, Cricket. That's not a decision I want to make on my own. We have six months to decide." Lizzie giggled then. "It's not like we can give him or her back."

Cosmo was smiling like a lunatic as he rattled his pots and pans. The heady aroma of frying bacon spitting on the grill almost made Lizzie swoon. She was sooo hungry.

"Anything else new in the nation's capital?" Cosmo asked.

"Hank Jellicoe is having an affair with the president. But something went awry this morning. Maggie and Ted are getting engaged. I'm saving the best for last. I'll tell you all about it when we watch the sun come up. I love sitting out on the deck, all bundled up, with you. I think about it all the time, Cricket. I don't know what I like most, watching the sun come up or watching the sun set. For some reason, watching the sun come up or set in Washington does nothing for me."

One eye on the grill and one eye on his wife, Cosmo said, "Who told you? I thought I could trust those guys. I needed input, Elizabeth. I wanted to do the right thing by you."

"The boys didn't tell me. Somehow Maggie wormed it out of Ted, and she told me. Swore me to secrecy, of course. It really isn't important, Cricket. You all did what you did for the right reasons."

"What about the house? Are you upset over that?"

"What house?"

"Crap! I just assumed they would have told you about that. I bought a house in Old Town in Alexandria. I had it gutted and redone. I didn't decorate it, though," he added hastily, a look of pure panic on his face. "We can sell it if you don't like it. I need more space, more room to move around, Elizabeth. I don't expect you to sell your little house. I know how much you love it. I want to always keep this one, too. I thought I would surprise you. The guys loved the house, but they all warned me not even to think about decorating. It has a fenced-in yard, Elizabeth. Beautifully landscaped. A really nice place, to my way of thinking, for raising a family. We could even get a dog or a cat. It was supposed to be a surprise."

"Well, it worked, honey. I am surprised. I like Old Town. Do you have any pictures you can show me?"

"I have before and after. The contractor was good about that. It's like a brand-new house in an old neighborhood. You know, the kind where there are big trees, green grass yards, and in the fall you rake the leaves and jump in them. We'll have neighbors to be friendly with. We'll be parents soon—God, how easy those words just rolled off my lips—so we'll meet other parents."

"Do you think we'll make good parents, Cricket?" Lizzie asked anxiously.

"I *know* we will."

"So what do you think about Hank and the president?"

"Is it serious? I got a memo yesterday that Hank will be in town the day after tomorrow. The casino owners have a proposition to present to him and asked me to sit in. I haven't seen him in a while. Are you going to ask me to fish around for details on his romance?"

"Cricket!" Lizzie said indignantly. "Of course." She grinned.

Cosmo laughed. "So Maggie and Ted are going to take the plunge. I'm happy for them."

"Well, I'm not sure about the plunge, but Ted did get a ring. No wedding date has been set. Maggie says she's in no hurry. At first she said she was going to get artificial nails, because she's a nail biter. You know, to show off the ring. Then she said she's going to let her nails grow, and when they do grow and she gets her first manicure is when she's going to okay that walk down the aisle. She hasn't explained all of that yet to Ted. You aren't getting it, are you, honey?"

Cosmo stared at his wife as he tried to comprehend what she was saying. Finally, he said, "All you wanted was a pair of rhinestone cowgirl boots for someone else and a plain gold wedding band. Whatever." He threw his hands in the air. "I'd rather talk about Hank."

Lizzie just laughed.

A few days before the scheduled liberation of the pardons was to take place, Hank Jellicoe pulled his SUV to the curb in front of the Hoover Building just as Bert Navarro exited the Federal Bureau of Investigation and walked to the waiting SUV. He climbed in, and the truck shot away from the curb almost before the door was closed and the director could buckle up.

"You want to share what this cloak-and-dagger is all about, Hank?"

"Do you think you can wait for my pearls of wisdom until we have a big, juicy steak in front of us?"

"I guess that's your way of telling me you aren't talking until you eat. How's business?"

"Ah, now, that's something I can talk about. In a word, booming."

"Too many bad guys out there, eh?" Bert chuckled.

"Being in the same business, guess you know they never slow down. You lock them up, and a new crop pops up without missing a beat. I wasn't sure you'd agree to meet with me, since I just snagged three of your best agents."

"We both know money talks and bullshit walks. The Bureau can't match the kind of money you pay your people. I understand the cost of college is going up. The economy sucks. Who can blame a guy, no matter how good he is, if he's struggling to take care of his family and wants to make more money? It's called taking care of business, Hank."

"So, no hard feelings, kid?"

Kid? Compared to Jellicoe, maybe he was a kid. "No, Hank, no hard feelings. Where are we going?"

"Benito's. I got a voice mail last night from Benny himself, who said he got a shipment of Kobe beef, and a dozen steaks have my name on them. I'm a sharing kind of guy, so I thought to myself, who better to share them with than the director of the FBI?"

Even the skimpiest of Kobe steaks at Benito's started out at a thousand bucks, or so Bert had heard. Benito's was definitely out of his league. "You are so full of shit, Hank, your eyes are turning brown." Bert laughed.

"Tell me that again after you sink your teeth into one of those steaks. Ah, we're here! Loosen your belt so you don't embarrass me when you start chowing down on that melt-in-your-mouth beef."

Bert climbed out of the SUV and looked around. There was absolutely nothing about

Benito's that might lead anyone to think he was going someplace special. There were no neon signs. The parking lot was run of the mill. Regulation. The front door was just a heavy-duty front door, with credit-card stickers, which alerted diners Benny took every credit card known to man.

Inside, Bert looked around again. Again, nothing to make him think he was anywhere special. It was clean, though. And it had tablecloths, and they probably used cloth napkins. The tables and chairs were wood. The bar was small, with only eight stools. The mirrors sparkled. Polished wood floor. Windows that looked out over a courtyard barren of trees and shrubbery. He supposed the place could be called intimate, with only twelve tables, none occupied at the moment.

A man appeared out of nowhere. Bert assumed it was Benny himself by the way he hugged Jellicoe and quickly ushered them to a table. Within seconds a bottle of Japanese beer was set in front of Hank. Benny was introduced, and the men shook hands. Bert winced at the man's grip.

"What'll it be, Mr. Director?" Benny asked.

"Tonic water," said Bert.

"That's the only thing you get to order, Bert. You come here for steak, you get steak. Benny doesn't mess around with medium rare, well done, or fried. He does it one way, and it's his way. He's been known to throw people out of here just for asking for something. You get a salad that no one eats and a five-times baked potato. That's all there is."

All Bert could think of to say was, "Uh-huh."

Hank cut right to the chase the moment Bert's tonic water was set in front of him. "Listen, kid, I asked you here for two reasons, the first being to share the steak with you and to offer you a job. In case you don't know this, things are coming to a boil. The vigilantes will have their presidential pardons in a matter of days.

"I'm aware of your relationship with Kathryn Lucas. Once the women are cut loose, it isn't going to be the picnic everyone thinks it is going to be. The moment the media picks up the scent of your relationship, you're dead meat. That goes for Jack Emery, too. Someone is going to put two and two together and come up with four. I'm looking to retire, and I want to have you step in. I don't expect you to give me your answer over this lunch, but I do want an answer by the end of the day. That means six o'clock. You'll have to have your resignation ready to go if you accept my offer. When this lunch is over, I'm heading to Emery's office to present an offer to him. Say something, kid."

"I don't know what to say."

"Did I make sense? Did you understand what I said? More to the point, do you see the pitfalls that await you if you stay at the Bureau?"

"Yes to all three questions. Why me? Why

Emery? How . . . how certain are you that the president is going to pardon the girls?"

"You're good. I've followed your career. Elias Cummings, your predecessor, and I were great friends. Still are. He said I couldn't do better than you. Emery for the same reason. Plus you're all tied to the vigilantes. As to how certain I am that the president is going to pardon the vigilantes . . . I saw the pardons with my own eyes. Forewarned is forearmed."

Bert's head was reeling. Jellicoe made sense. It all sounded right. He wished he knew what Jack was going to say. He wanted to call Kathryn so bad, he had to clench his fists so he wouldn't pull his cell phone out of his pocket. "Where would I be based?"

Hank finished his beer, held out the bottle. A fresh bottle was placed in his hand. Bert had yet to sample his tonic water.

"Wherever you want to be based. The one place you don't want to be is here in the District."

Bert's mouth was so dry, he couldn't swallow. He finally took a slug of the tonic water. "Salary?"

"I know you know everything there is to know about my company. Tell me what you think you're worth."

Bert squared his shoulders. "Five hundred thousand. Stock options. Unlimited expense account. Not to be abused. Thirty days' sick leave, six weeks' vacation. Moving fees."

"Agreed."

"Shit! I sold myself short, didn't I?"

"Yeah, kid, you did, but to show you my heart's in the right place, I'm not going to hold that against you. I was prepared to offer a cool million a year. It's yours. You also get to use our chalet in Vail. We have a rather nice estate in Maui, which is yours to use anytime you can get away. We issue you a company car, and we pay all tax and insurance. And after a complete physical and drug test, we insure you for ten million dollars. You need to know there is going to be some extensive travel involved, but you and Emery, if he comes on board, can divvy that up to make it work for you both. And one last thing. No one, and I mean absolutely no one, can know about this. If Jack comes on board, then you and he can talk about it to your heart's content. Are you with me on this?"

Bert nodded once. He felt so light-headed, he thought he was going to pass out. He knew he should be saying something, but he didn't know what to say.

Huge platters, the kind wives served Thanksgiving turkeys on, arrived. Hank laughed at the expression on Bert's face. "Think of this as a one-of-a-kind meal, just like the one-of-a-kind job I just offered."

Bert picked up the steak knife, which was as big as a butcher knife, and sliced into the steak in front of him. He sampled the succulent Kobe beef, rolled his eyes, then smiled. "I don't have to wait till six o'clock. I accept your offer, Hank." He laid down his fork. His right hand shot forward. Hank grasped it, and they shook heartily.

"You made the right decision, kid. Welcome to Global Securities."

Chapter 19

Hank Jellicoe kept one eye on his SUV, parked smack in front of the courthouse, and the other eye on the door from which he knew Jack Emery would emerge. He pulled the hood of his Windbreaker a little more snugly around his head to avoid getting wetter than he already was. If it wasn't snowing, it was raining. Damn weatherman never got it right. Just that morning he'd predicted milder than normal temperatures, with no mention of rain.

Jellicoe watched as yet another beat cop stopped at the SUV, looked at the impressive decal on the windshield. He looked around to see if he could pick out the owner as people rushed by. He shrugged and moved off. Jellicoe grunted something that could have been obscene and turned back to watching the door.

Jack Emery finally emerged from the courthouse ten minutes later and after still another police inspection of the SUV.

Jellicoe stepped forward and said, "Mr. Emery,

Hank Jellicoe. I wonder if I might have a word with you. My vehicle is there at the curb. We can sit inside to get out of this pissy rain."

Jack blinked. He'd seen pictures of the man standing in front of him, heard about him via the girls and Charles. He nodded, followed Jellicoe to the SUV, and climbed inside. "You mind telling me what this is all about?"

"That's why I'm here. How about we head to the nearest watering hole, grab a beer or some hot coffee, and I'll tell you all about it? You have to be anywhere in particular? I can drop you off."

"Just home, for another fun evening of watching television by my lonesome." Then he remembered that Harry, Bert, Ted, and Espinosa were supposed to come over to watch a game on TV. Or was it poker night? He couldn't remember. But that wasn't until later. "Unless you want to give me a lift home. I was running late this morning, so I took a cab. I have both coffee and beer. I live—"

"I know where you live. Georgetown it is."

They drove in silence, Jack marveling at the man's driving expertise. Finally, when he couldn't stand the silence any longer, he said, "Are you just a man of few words, or are you contemplating something sinister here? What the hell is going on?"

"I don't talk a lot unless the person I'm talking to is stupid. You don't look stupid to me, Mr. Emery. Mind if I call you Jack?"

"Hell, no. Call me whatever you want. I'd just like to know why I'm here in this spiffy set of wheels, which sort of, kind of reminds me of those Chevy Suburbans the president tools around in."

Jellicoe made a sound that could have been laughter. "Actually, this set of wheels has things in it those Suburbans don't. And, to answer the second part of your question, life is sinister. It's how you deal with it that takes the bad out of good."

"Is that supposed to be profound?"

"Uh-huh."

They drove for another ten minutes of silence before Jellicoe parked directly in front of Jack and Nikki's house. "Out," was all he said.

"Hey, you can't park here. They'll tow you away in five minutes," Jack said.

"Yeah, I can park here. No one is going to tow me away. I can leave this baby here for ten days, and the guy parked across from me will be stuck for those ten days. You sure do talk a lot, Emery."

"Suit yourself, but when you leave my house, your wheels will be in the impound lot. This is Georgetown, Mr. Jellicoe. We don't do shit like that here."

"You worry too much, Mr. Emery. Can we just get the hell in the house so I can dry out?"

Jack shrugged, marched up the four steps to the front door, which had been replaced since that memorable night when Harry had kicked it in, opened it, and turned off the alarm. He turned the heat up and started a fire. "Coffee, beer, or me?" he quipped.

"Coffee with a big slug of brandy. This is nice," Jellicoe said, looking around.

"Yeah, it is, but it isn't mine. Belongs to Nikki Quinn. She's letting me stay here to keep it maintained. But I assume you already know that."

"I do. Let's have our coffee here in front of the fire. I like cozy."

"You could have fooled me," Jack said as he measured out coffee. He opened one cabinet after the other until he found the brandy bottle. "You look like a half-and-half kind of guy to me?" It was a question.

Jellicoe nodded.

"You want me to throw your clothes in the dryer? There's a robe in the laundry room. Are your feet wet?"

"Sounds like your mother knew my mother. If your feet are cold and wet, you're gonna get sick. She had another little ditty," Jellicoe called over his shoulder on the way to the laundry room. "Always wear your good underwear, in case you're in an accident."

Jack guffawed as he watched the coffee drip into the pot. Suddenly he was liking this guy.

Settled in front of the fire, Jellicoe got right to the point. "I'm here to offer you a job." He leaned forward and gave Jack the same spiel he'd given Bert, adding only the information about the deal he had made with Bert.

The only difference between Jack and Bert

was that Jack's eyes didn't glaze over. He eye-balled Jellicoe and said, "How much?"

Jellicoe laughed. "What do you think you're worth? More than Navarro?"

"A million should do it. Same perks you're giving Bert, and he doesn't get top billing. We're equals, or it's no deal."

"Done. You have to hand in your resignation by tomorrow morning at nine. Now, what should we talk about?"

Jack started to laugh and couldn't stop. He slid off his chair and rolled across the floor, choking and sputtering.

"What's so damn funny?" Jellicoe demanded.

"I'm just realizing how professional you look in that silly-looking orange and brown bath-robe. And I can see your wee-wee."

"It's *your* robe, you dumb cluck."

"Actually, no, it isn't my robe. It belongs to Harry Wong. He was staying with me a while back and forgot to take it with him. On him it looks good." Jack rolled over, sat up, and hugged his knees. "Let's get serious here. Who else knows about this magnificent offer you just made to Bert and me?"

"Absolutely no one. The contracts will be ready in the morning, right after you tender your resignation. Why are you asking?"

"Because of the guys. We're a team, Jellicoe. We're all going to be facing the same problem in a few days, once the vigilantes receive their pardons. We can't stay here, that's for sure."

Jellicoe pretended to think. He had predicted that this exact conversation would occur and was prepared. "Okay," he said agreeably. "I can use all of you, but you have to go to boot camp."

"Whoa. Whoa. No one said anything about boot camp."

"I'm saying it now. I have rules and regs. I do not, let me repeat, I do not run a Mickey Mouse operation. You'll ace it. Not to worry. What time are the guys due?"

Jack looked at his watch. "Actually, they're ten minutes late. I thought you knew everything."

"Almost everything."

Jack leaned forward. "Swear to me on your mother that the Sisters are, honest to God, going to receive pardons. No bullshit, Jellicoe."

"They are, honest to God, going to walk away from that stupid patriotic party a few days from now with their pardons in hand."

Jack let out a sigh so loud, Jellicoe reared back. Then he smiled. He so loved happy endings. He hoped his own was going to be just as good.

The doorbell rang just as the dryer in the laundry room pinged. Jellicoe got up to get his dry clothing while Jack went to the door.

The guys had arrived.

"No poker tonight, boys, but I do have some entertainment scheduled. Settle in, and I'll bring us refreshments. But first, let me introduce our leading entertainer to those of you who do not already know him. Fellows, meet

Henry Jellicoe, also known as Hank. Hank is the head and sole owner of Global Securities. Harry, Espinosa, Ted, meet Hank Jellicoe. He's going to entertain you while I gather up our refreshments. Bert, why don't you join me in the kitchen?"

"I'll be with you in a second, Jack. First I need to make a pit stop," said Bert.

In the kitchen Jack leaned up against the back door and squeezed his eyes shut. Had he just done what he thought he had? Was Jellicoe the answer to all his prayers? Was he finally, after all these years, going to be able to get married to Nikki? A lone tear rolled down his cheek. He brushed at it with shaking fingers. He felt like he'd just stepped into a patch of four-leaf clovers.

Jack looked around the tidy kitchen. He loved Nikki's house, but without her in it, it was just a house. Where would they all end up? Jellicoe hadn't said, but then again, he hadn't asked. His mind raced. Who in the media would put it all together once they made a mass exodus from the District? How long would it take for those in authority to put two and two together? *Not long,* he thought. Maybe that was why he sensed such urgency in Jellicoe. He couldn't even begin to imagine the fallout that would engulf the White House when the pardons became public.

Maybe now was the time to start thinking about Hank Jellicoe as his guardian angel. Yeah, yeah, that sounded good.

Jack opened the refrigerator, hauled out his

twelve-pack of Heineken, and set the bottles on a tray. Since Bert hadn't joined him yet, he put one bag of pretzels between his teeth and two bags of chips under his arms before he shouldered his way through the swinging door of the kitchen.

His buddies were staring into the flames. It looked like they were all in a trance. Hank Jellicoe was on his feet, doing stretches.

Jellicoe eyed the tray, then the guys, just as Bert walked into the room. "They're on board. Right now they're in a state of shock. It's safe to say, your team is ready to go. Listen, if you don't mind, I have to leave. I've got things to do and places to go."

Jack was still holding the tray in his hands, still had the pretzel bag between his teeth and the chips under his arms.

"Here," said Bert. "Let me help you with that."

Jack was like a robot when he handed the tray and munchies to Bert and followed his new benefactor to the door. Jellicoe stuck out his hand, and Jack grabbed it. "I feel like I should say something, but I don't know the words. Thanks? It hardly seems enough. Just tell me why?"

"Thanks will do. Will it help you if I told you I am in love with the president of the United States, and this is what she wants for the people who put her into office?"

Jack tried to wrap his mind around the words Jellicoe had just uttered. "No."

"Well, there you go. Guess you'll have to make up your own happy ending, then." Jellicoe dug his hand into his pocket and pulled out a wrinkled card. "Crap, I forgot to mention something. Well, that's okay. You can tell the guys. You all need to be at this address at ten tomorrow morning. When you put your John Hancocks on the contracts, you'll get a signing bonus. A quarter mil each. That should give everyone sweet dreams tonight." Jellicoe winked at Jack, punched him in the arm, and was gone without another word.

Jack watched as the head of Global Securities walked down the steps and out to his SUV, which was still in the same spot it was two hours ago. "Son of a bitch!"

Back in the family room, the guys were still in the same trance. Jack tossed two huge logs onto the fire, watched the sparks shoot upward, then shouted at the top of his lungs, "Campfire time, guys. I have additional information. Listen up." He ripped open the munchie bags and handed out the beer once he had everyone's attention.

Ted was the first to speak. "What the hell did we all just agree to?"

"Where are we going?" Espinosa asked.

"Who's heading up this team?" Harry asked.

Bert and Jack raised their hands.

"Oh, shit!" Ted said.

"Ha! Listen, I said I had further news. Tomorrow morning we all report to this address to sign our contracts," said Jack. "What Hank forgot to tell us, and what he told me to tell you all, is that there's a signing bonus. You're going to like this. It's two hundred fifty thousand dollars."

His eyes as round as saucers, Espinosa said, "That's a quarter of a million dollars!"

"You do understand we're signing on to Global Securities for five years, right?" Jack asked.

The others nodded that they understood.

Ted's eyes were so glassy, Jack thought he could see himself in them. "I can repay the loan I took out to pay for that engagement ring and not sweat it," Ted murmured.

The five of them sat down and started to talk. They spoke of their worries, of the future, which now seemed assured, of their hopes and dreams and the loves of their lives as they munched, drank, and stared at the dancing flames, which seemed to mesmerize them. When someone asked why Jellicoe had made them the offer, Jack told them what Jellicoe had told him.

"And to think Hank Jellicoe was someone we never knew but only heard about on the news or read about. And now he's saved all of us. What do you guys think? Is he really in love with the president? Or was he bullshitting me?" Jack asked.

As one, the guys shrugged.

"He didn't strike me as the kind of guy to make up a story like that. When we were on the mountain, Charles did say Hank goes in and out of the White House like it is his summer home. I guess it is possible. The president isn't married. She's attractive, so maybe he was telling the truth. The more important question would seem to be, do we care about his personal life?" Jack asked.

His eyes on the flickering fire, Bert responded, "Only in how it affects us. I have to be honest, I had my doubts about the pardons ever coming through. I've had more than one hairy nightmare over this. Jellicoe is leaving it up to us as to where we want to set up shop. I think we all need to sleep on it, talk it over with the girls. Then all of us can make a decision."

"Jellicoe was pretty firm, Bert, on not talking to anyone, and he stressed *anyone,* about this until he gave the okay. Since Ted's the one with the loose lips, I think we need to agree we do as he says," Jack said.

"You give it up, you're dead," Harry said.

Ted took one look at Harry's serene expression and knew he meant every word. He nodded.

Jack's cell rang. He reached for it automatically and clicked it on to hear Lizzie identify herself. "What's up, counselor?" He mouthed Lizzie's name for the benefit of the others.

"Jack, I . . . I wanted you to be the first to know. Well, actually, you're third, but when I tell you, you'll understand. By the way, I'm in Vegas. Cricket is right here next to me. I just . . . what I wanted . . . if it wasn't for you . . . I . . . uh . . ."

Alarm bells rang in Jack's head as he looked down to see that somehow or other he'd clicked on the speaker, and the others could hear Lizzie. "What's wrong, Lizzie? Talk to me."

Everyone else in the room turned rigid, their eyes glued to Jack and their ears tuned to the voice talking to Jack.

"Nothing's wrong, Jack. In fact everything is so right, I am beside myself. I just wanted to thank you for saving my life that night at the cemetery. If you hadn't had the foresight to read me the way you did, I wouldn't be sitting here, calling you to tell you I'm going to have a baby. Me! I'm pregnant. I'm going to be a mother. It's taken me a few weeks to get used to the idea before I could begin telling everyone about it. Cosmo and I have been spending a lot of time making plans for the house in Old Town, the one no one told me about. Say something, Jack."

Jack's eyes started to burn. He tried squinting as the others clustered around him, and he saw they were having the same problem he was, even stone-faced Harry. "That's . . . that is probably the most wonderful thing I've ever heard, Lizzie. Congratulations. I don't think there will be a better mother than you in the whole wide world. I'm so happy for you, beyond happy. The guys are here. We just had a meeting, but that's for another time." He held the phone aloft, so the others could shout out their congratulations.

"Thanks, Jack. I wanted you to . . . You understand, right?"

"I do, Lizzie. Just be happy. Tell Cosmo we'll wait for the cigar until he comes East next time."

"I'll tell him, Jack. Night."

"Good night, Lizzie. Well, boys, it's been a hell of an evening. All good. Let's have another beer and call it a night. Unless you want to have a sleepover, and we all go together to the meeting in the morning."

In the end, after some discussion, it was decided everyone wanted to go home to *think*. Jack felt only relief, because he, too, wanted to do some heavy-duty thinking.

When they made their last toast of the evening, it wasn't to the vigilantes, upcoming pardons, or their new jobs; it was to Lizzie and the new baby she would deliver in the coming months.

There wasn't a dry eye in the house.

Chapter 20

Ted Robinson breezed through the doors of the *Post* building just as it was turning light outside. He hadn't slept at all and felt both elated and depressed. He wondered how that was possible. He stopped at the kiosk that sold sundries, magazines, and the paper. He dropped some coins on the counter, picked up the paper, then headed to the café across the lobby.

Since it was so early, he had the café to himself, but only for a few seconds. He looked up as a waitress and Joe Espinosa appeared at the same moment.

"Couldn't sleep," Espinosa mumbled as he sat down, his copy of the paper on top of Ted's. They both ordered egg-and-bacon sandwiches, coffee, and juice.

Ted pointed to the dark headline on the front page of the morning paper. "Man, that guy moves at the speed of light."

"FBI director resigns!" Espinosa mumbled.

Ted looked down at the article, written by

Maggie herself, which said in part that the director had made the difficult decision to move into the private sector to head up the worldwide firm of Global Securities.

The rest of the article dealt with Bert's successes and his few failures, his high recommendation from former director Elias Cummings, and his general background and years he spent as a special agent in the Bureau. The article went on to promise an in-depth personal interview with ex-Director Navarro for the next edition.

"That's a pretty snappy picture of old Bert," Espinosa said. "I didn't know this was going to run, did you, Ted?"

Ted shrugged, which meant no. "I haven't talked to Maggie. I fired off my resignation via e-mail, just like Jellicoe instructed. Don't know if Maggie's seen it yet. I am not looking forward to handing over the paper resignation. How about you?"

Ted's voice sounded so jittery, Espinosa winced. "I don't have a problem with it, but then again, I'm not sleeping with Maggie, like you are. Are you having second thoughts?"

"I didn't close my eyes once last night. I spent the whole night worrying and spending all that new money we're going to get. And when I wasn't doing that, I was trying to straighten my backbone for the inevitable when Maggie gets hold of us. I am *not* looking forward to seeing her this morning."

"You better not screw up like the last time,"

Espinosa said ominously. "You have to stop letting Maggie walk all over you."

"Yeah, I know. I'll hold it together. C'mon, finish up here, so we can get our resignations on her desk before she shows up. It's going to take me five minutes to clear out my workstation. Then I'm outta here. How long is it going to take you?"

"Just long enough to pick up my dental floss, my toothbrush, and my sunglasses. Five seconds maybe." Everyone at the paper knew how anal Espinosa was about brushing and flossing.

"Then let's do it," Ted said, getting up from the table. He dropped some bills and said, "Lunch is on you, buddy."

The newsroom was starting to come alive when Ted and Espinosa stepped out of the elevator. Seeing no lights on in Maggie's office, they raced across the room, resignations in hand. Like two errant children, they dropped the two envelopes on Maggie's desk and raced to their workstations, where they cleaned out their cubicles. They made it safely to the lobby and were almost outside when Maggie whistled sharply as she pointed to the café they had just left.

"You screw this up, Ted, and I'm going to kick your ass all the way to the Mexican border. You hear me?" Espinosa asked.

"Yeah."

Inside and seated at the same table they had just vacated, Maggie looked at them with a piercing gaze. "You two have some explaining to do."

Ted squared his shoulders. "About what?"

"Where were you last night?" Maggie quizzed. "I tried calling you all night. How come I had to get the headline from Bert and not you? How come I, the EIC, had to do the interview, and not my star reporter? Well?"

"Well what?" Ted asked.

Maggie glared at both men.

"I had personal business last night," Ted said. "It was poker night. You knew that. I told you in the morning. You weren't listening. You never listen to me, Maggie. I'm getting a little sick and tired of it, too. I do have a life outside this god-damn paper."

"You're up to something. I can tell," said Maggie. "You might as well spit it out right now, instead of making me work for it. Give it up. *Now.*"

Ted's eyes narrowed. Espinosa was impressed with how his friend was standing up to their boss. "Or what?" Ted asked coldly.

"Or else you're fired, that's what."

"No problem, Miss EIC. I quit. I tendered my resignation via e-mail in the wee hours of the morning. Joe's is there, too. There are hard copies on your desk." Ted slid off his chair and headed for the door, Espinosa right behind him.

Ted's voice was so shaky, Espinosa had a hard time understanding what he was saying, which was, "I thought that went rather well, considering that we left her speechless."

"Are we expecting her to grovel? Beg us to return? Come running after us?"

"None of the above."

"You feeling pretty powerful right now, Ted?"

"No. I feel like shit. Were we supposed to make our resignations effective immediately? No one said."

"Too late now. We're technically . . . no, officially unemployed. What the hell are we going to do till ten o'clock?"

"Let's go to Harry's dojo. We can hang out there and all go together. Unless you have a better idea."

"That'll work," Espinosa said.

"Just in case you're interested," Ted said, "Maggie is calling my cell. I have it on vibrate. You wait. She's going to rip me a new one."

"You are such a chicken, Ted. She can do that only if you let her. How the hell did you let her get such power over you? I'm almost ashamed to be seen with you. You are such a *wuss,* and you are pathetic in the bargain."

"I know."

Espinosa stepped to the curb and hailed a taxi. Both men stepped in, Ted taking the right corner, Espinosa the left. Three people could have sat between them. Espinosa rattled off Harry's address, then leaned back and closed his eyes. They didn't speak again until the taxi pulled to the curb outside Harry's dojo.

"Look, I'm not back watering here, but what the hell is the point to all of this?" Ted asked.

"The point, you dumb cluck, is Jellicoe does not want Maggie running with this until everyone is on board and everything is signed, sealed, and delivered. Bert was . . . I guess he wanted that out there right away. Maggie would have a special edition ready to go in ten minutes with the mass exodus. I'm thinking, and I say I am thinking, he wants us all far away from here when the stuff hits the fan. Makes sense to me. You need to stop thinking with your dick, Ted."

"That was a low blow, Joe."

"It was meant to be a low blow. You deserve it."

The dojo was empty, which was surprising, because Harry always scheduled early-morning classes for the local precincts. What was even more surprising was that Harry was dressed in a sport jacket, a pristine white shirt, and sharply creased trousers. His tie shrieked *power*.

"Did someone die?" Ted asked, knowing Harry's aversion to getting dressed up.

"No, someone did not die. At least no one I know. I am dressed this way because when someone is about to hand me a check for a quarter of a million dollars, the least I can do is look *nice*. You two should be ashamed. You look like rag-pickers," Harry snorted. "When one walks into a bank to deposit a check in that amount, it garners respect. When you two walk in, they're going to call the cops."

"What's wrong with the way we look?" Espinosa asked defensively. "I showered and shaved. My clothes are clean. I'm a working stiff."

Harry went back to his green tea and the paper he had spread out in front of him. "I know you guys saw the paper, but did you see what's on page three?"

"Why don't you just tell us, Mr. Fashion Plate?" Ted retorted, angry with himself that whatever Harry was seeing he'd missed.

Obviously, Espinosa had missed it, too, because he was leaning over Harry's shoulder.

"These two little boxed questions," said Harry. "Right at the top of the page. The first box asks the question of the reader as to which Supreme Court justice is retiring in June. The second boxed question asks if the vigilantes should be pardoned. Readers are asked to e-mail the *Post* with their responses.

"Just before you got here, I heard on Fox News that the *Post*'s Web site crashed. A few, and they stressed the word *few*, people were interested enough to ask who the retiring judge is. The rest of the people were voting to pardon the vigilantes. The numbers were in the thousands, and all within twenty minutes of the papers hitting the street. Pretty amazing. I guess Maggie will now move the boxes to the front page until she gets a number she's happy with. Pretty damn clever, if you ask me."

"I can't believe you said all that, Harry. You usually just grunt. This is exciting." Espinosa cackled. "By the way, when are your killer friends arriving?"

"Eat me! Day after tomorrow, and you're first on my shit list, so bear that in mind," Harry retorted.

"Why are you always so damn cranky, Harry?" Ted asked curiously.

Harry appeared to give Ted's question some serious thought. "I think it might have something to do with dealing with dumb shits like you two day in and day out. And the fact that you can't keep your lip zipped. You weaseled on Cosmo Cricket. Does that answer your question?" Harry snapped.

"It does!" Ted said, saluting smartly. "However, now that I am about to become financially independent, I have turned over a new leaf. This is the new Ted Robinson, intrepid reporter, saluting here."

"Yeah, right. Maggie snaps her fingers, and you're off and running." Espinosa cackled again.

Ted just looked sheepish.

"Enough of this frivolity," said Harry. "I think we should be heading out for our appointment. May I say one more time how tacky you both look?" Harry shrugged his slim frame under the designer sport jacket, adjusted his power tie, then shot his cuffs. "Stay behind me and pretend you do not know me. Is that clear, gentlemen?"

Espinosa continued to cackle. "Ted, who *is* this guy?"

"Someone Jack Emery introduced us to a lifetime ago. Move it, Espinosa, before this schmuck decides to take a swing at us. Listen," Ted hissed, "we are doing the right thing, aren't we?"

Espinosa stopped cackling long enough to

look worried. "This is a hell of a time to wonder about it, Ted. It sounds good, feels even better, and I sure can use the money. Think in terms of how much cat litter you can now buy by the truckload. You can store it all in your new attached garage, which will be attached to the new house you're going to buy. Which then opens up another can of worms. Once you have a house with an attached garage, complete with designer kitchen, fireplace, and one of those showers with fifty jets to pummel your body, Maggie is going to be on you like white on rice. There's no way she's going to wait for her fingernails to grow out. So, yeah, this is the right thing we're doing."

"Shut the hell up, Espinosa," Ted said. He was starting to feel sick to his stomach.

Thirty minutes later the cab they were in rolled to the curb outside a two-story brick building in Georgetown—Nikki Quinn's all-female law firm.

"I should have known when I saw the address on the card. It seemed familiar, but I missed it," Ted said, slapping at his forehead.

"That's because you're stupid," Harry said, getting out of the cab and leaving Ted or Espinosa to pay the driver.

"Pony up, boys. The fare was twenty bucks, and I gave him a five-dollar tip. I no longer have an expense account." Ted stood still, his hand out until Harry and Espinosa each slapped eight dollars into it. "See, now we're getting along. Did I say one word about putting in the extra dollar? No, I did not. I could have asked for thirty-three cents from each of you, but I didn't. Fair is fair."

Harry turned around, his serene countenance scaring the hell out of Ted, who backed up three steps.

"I like being generous," Ted said.

Inside, the receptionist hustled the trio down a hall to a conference room, which held trays of pastries, fresh fruit, an urn of coffee, and crystal pitchers of orange juice. Bert and Jack were munching on Danish. Their meaningless conversation came to a halt as Ted and Espinosa sat down.

The five of them looked at each other, but no one said a word. Their expressions, however, clearly questioned why they were all there.

"See you made the headlines, Bert," Ted said.

"Yeah," the ex-director said. "Kind of gave me a jolt when I saw it in black and white."

"You guys see the boxes on page three?" When Bert and Jack just stared at Harry, he elaborated.

"Maggie is on it, eh?"

"And," Espinosa said quietly, "he did not cave in to Maggie this morning, so our secret that isn't a secret is still safe. What about you, Jack?"

"I walked out with my bag of M&M's, my Montblanc pen, and didn't look back," Jack reported. "Took me ten minutes to assign my caseload, another ten minutes listening to my boss harangue me, and I am now a free agent. I have to admit I felt crappy about not giving notice, but when they fire someone, it's on the spot without notice, so I managed to stifle my guilt. I'm looking forward to that trip to the bank. Unemployed with a quarter of a million dollars in the bank. Works for me, gentlemen."

"The best part is we have a month off before we show up for . . . uh . . . boot camp. Then thirty days later we take over Global Securities. Elias Cummings asked if we could use an old codger as a consultant, and I said yes. Just for the record, he knows the Mideast like the back of his hand. I think, boys, we just had ourselves one hell of a coup," Bert said.

"How come you guys are so quiet?" Jack asked as he fixed his gaze on Ted, Harry, and Espinosa.

"How about fear of the unknown, opposed to the tried, true, and familiar?" Ted said.

"Nothing ventured, nothing gained, I always say," Jack said.

"Yeah, I say that, too." Bert guffawed.

The door to the conference room opened, and Hank Jellicoe, followed by a dumpy older lady in a bright red suit, entered the room. "Time is money, boys, so let's get right to it. Olive, meet my new boys, Bert Navarro, Jack Emery, Harry Wong, Ted Robinson, and Joe Espinosa. Boys, this is Olive Kramer. She comes highly recommended by Lizzie Fox. Lizzie, however, will be overseeing the final details of our little venture. I think it's safe to say, you're all in good hands. Olive is going to give you your contracts. Jack, Bert, you're both lawyers. Read over the contracts. Make sure you're happy with them. Any questions, ring the buzzer there on the wall. Olive and I have some other business to take care of. Your signing bonuses are in the envelopes attached to the last page of the contracts. When you're finished, give two short buzzes, and we'll do the cleanup."

"Sixty fucking pages!" Jack said. "What the hell kind of contracts are these?"

"The kind where you sign your life away," Bert said. "I'll take the first thirty pages. You take the last thirty. You know what to look for, and so do I."

Ted, Harry, and Espinosa flipped through the thick contract, their eyes glazing over at the legalese in front of them. No one opened the envelope stapled to the last page. With nothing else to do, they all reached for the food in the middle of the conference table. Espinosa poured coffee for everyone, even Harry, who actually drank it.

An hour later, Bert looked at Jack and Jack looked at Bert. Both nodded.

"It's fair. No surprises. Flex your fingers, gentlemen, and sign your name to the last page," Bert directed. "I think once you sign your name, it will be okay to open the envelope. However, do not sign the check until you are at the bank, with a bank officer."

The only sound to be heard in the room was the faint scratching sound of pens as they flew across the pages. The sound of the envelopes ripping was thunderclap loud. The sound of five indrawn breaths was even louder.

"I never, ever saw a check made out for this amount of money," Harry said. "Particularly one with my name on it."

Bert reached out and pressed the buzzer on the wall twice. Olive what's-her-name and Jellicoe entered within seconds.

Olive scanned the back pages of all five contracts, nodded, and left the room, the five torn envelopes in her hand.

The men shook hands all around. There was no conversation, but Jellicoe pointed to a young woman carrying five very large manila envelopes. "Your insurance packets, car insurance info, life insurance, etc. I'll be e-mailing all of you thirty days from now. See ya," he said, striding out of the room.

"I guess it's official, guys. We're now employees of Global Securities," Jack said.

"Should we celebrate?" Espinosa asked.

"Yeah, we should, but not till *after* we hit the bank," Ted said.

"How about this?" Jack asked. "We each go to our respective banks, then meet up at my house. I'll pick up some Chinese. How's that sound?"

The others agreed that it worked for them.

Outside, the boys separated, sappy grins on their faces.

Chapter 21

Jack Emery, duffel bag slung over his shoulder, parked his car outside Harry Wong's dojo. He walked around to the back of the building and let himself in. He felt tense, uncertain as to why Harry had called him. Then again, Harry never did anything without a reason. It was way too quiet for midmorning. Maybe Harry was meditating. Jack tried to make as little noise as possible, just in case. He didn't call out but entered the workout room as though he belonged or, at the very least, was coming for instruction.

Jack gaped, then he gawked, and then he swallowed hard as he tried to focus on what he was seeing, which was ten men of indeterminate age, all dressed in white martial arts garb, each with a wide black belt at the waist. Harry was dressed the same way.

He remembered what his mother used to say. *Jack, does the cat have your tongue?* In this case, the cat definitely did have his tongue. Instead of offering up a greeting, Jack bowed low. The men in front of him bowed, too, even Harry. Jack felt light-headed.

"What's up, *Kemo Sabe?*"

Jack finally found his tongue. "Not much, Harry. Just trying to acclimate myself to my new position in life. You going to introduce me or what?"

Harry grinned. "Jack, I want you to meet the ten deadliest men in the world."

Jack nodded, his heart kicking up an extra beat as Harry rattled off names with too many *x*'s, which Jack would never remember or be able to pronounce. When he was finished, everyone bowed low.

One of the men, who looked to be about sixty years of age but was probably a hundred and ten, jabbered something as he jerked his head in Jack's direction. Harry jabbered back, then said in English, "He's my brother." The men looked comically skeptical but nodded. Some of the men even smiled. They laughed outright when Harry told them that "his brother," Jack, had a black belt, and that he himself had trained him, and that they were evenly matched. Show-off that he was, Jack bowed once more.

More jabbering at the speed of light.

"It's not polite to speak a foreign language in front of someone, especially when the person under discussion doesn't understand what's being said," Jack huffed.

The old guy, whose skinny arms were like ropes, eyed Jack and said quietly, "Harry-san did not want to embarrass you, Jack-san. He told us you are his brother, that he would trust his life to you, that if he had to, he would die for you, even though you are not of his blood. He told us you are a learned man, versed in the law of your land, and that you do not take shit from anyone." This was all said in impeccable English.

"You happy now, Jack?" Harry asked, a strange look on his face.

"Funny you should say that, Harry. I feel the same way about you." To the others' delight, Jack bent down and kissed Harry on the cheek. He was airborne a second later, then landed with a thump on the mat.

The others crowded around, murmuring strange words. The old man held out a hand to pull Jack to his feet.

"You know I let him do that, right?" Jack said.

Solemn nods.

Jack turned to Harry. "I'm meeting up with the guys and heading to the mountain. Dress rehearsal for the big party. You coming, staying, what? I've been trying to call you, but you turned your cell off. That's why I'm really here. Plus, you called when I was in the shower, and when I tried to call you back, you weren't answering."

Harry shrugged. "What do you want from me, Jack? I have ten of the most important people in the world right here. At least to me, they are. The last I heard, the rehearsal was two days away. I wanted to brief these guys on my own."

"That makes sense, but how are *you* going to do that if *you* aren't briefed? Maybe you can set up a webcam or something if you're planning on staying here."

"Surely you jest," Harry said, favoring Jack with one of his ominous expressions.

"Yeah, I'm jesting. I don't know what to tell you, then. Jellicoe is going to be on the mountain, and he's got pictures of everything, maps, and he's in on the security that's going to be in place. I don't know how your guests are going to figure in on it."

"We're all very adaptable. They're smart enough to figure out the good guys from the bad guys. I'll be there to point the way," Harry said.

"What about Yoko?" Harry never missed a chance to be with his beloved.

"Yoko will understand."

"So, where's everyone staying? You cooking, or do they live off weeds and that other crap you eat?"

Harry pointed to a neat pile of bedrolls in the far corner of the room. "Takeout," he said. "And before you can ask, these guys came on their own dime, under their own power. You know that old Michael Jackson song 'I'll Be There'? That's all it took, me calling their name, and here they are. By the same token, if they ever need me, I drop things on a dime, and I'm there. I'm just telling you this for future reference."

A Brazilian by the name of Jaoa stepped forward and let loose with a string of something it was impossible to follow, but Harry seemed to be getting it all. "He wants to know if we want *el presidente* kidnapped. He would be honored, as would his colleagues, to do that for us."

"Uh . . . maybe another time. Tell him I appreciate the offer, though."

Another one of the ten stepped forward. He, too, rattled off a long question.

"Bomani stands for 'mighty warrior'," said Harry. "He's from Malawi, and he wants to know what they're supposed to do with all the dead bodies."

"Jesus Christ, Harry, what the hell did you tell those guys?" asked Jack.

The ten men standing in front of Jack burst out laughing.

"I told them you were a dumb shit and to yank your chain," Harry replied. "They know exactly what's going on. They know what to do and how to do it. No one will be left standing, but that doesn't mean they won't rise to walk again. They will, but with difficulty. Anything else?"

Jack decided to quit while he was ahead. He bowed low and started toward the door.

Harry caught up with him and handed him a little enamel box. "Will you give this to Yoko?"

"Sure. No problem. Listen, Harry, about those guys back there. Which one can catch a bullet?" Jack asked fretfully.

His face more serious than Jack had ever seen it, Harry replied, "All of them."

"You're full of shit, Harry."

Harry's face grew even more serious. "No, Jack, I'm not."

Jack believed him. "Listen, Harry, how about if I send over a guy I know who can set up a computer and webcam? I really want you to sit in on the meeting. This is just way too important to leave anything to chance. What do you say?"

"Okay, Jack. Make it for late this afternoon, though. Do not look inside the box. If you do, I'll have to kill you."

"If you tell me what's in it, I won't have to peek."

"It's a perfect pearl. It's what I want to have set into a ring for Yoko's engagement ring. I want her approval before I do it. My friend back there, Chin-Haex, whose name means 'truth in the ocean depth', is from Korea. He goes all over the world to dive for pearls when he isn't practicing his art. He brought me the pearl. There is not another one like it in the whole world. Don't lose it, Jack."

"I'll guard it with my life, Harry. And I won't open it. Who knew you were such a romantic, you dumb shit?"

Harry laughed and gave Jack a formal bow, which Jack returned.

"See ya," said Jack.

"Yeah, see ya."

Less than a mile away, Martine Connor was sitting down to a luncheon with five East Coast governors. After the luncheon, they would discuss highway issues for forty minutes, until she had to scurry to the West Wing to meet with the chairman of the Federal Reserve. She chatted, holding up her end of the conversation, but her mind was elsewhere. She thought about how quickly she'd reinstated Henry Jellicoe's clearance, which she'd ordered canceled. Her mind was also on Lizzie and what was going to go down on the premises three days from now.

The president was not unmindful of the morning headlines. She was also going to personally track all the reports pouring into the *Post* on possible pardons for the vigilantes. The *Post* predicted that if it were to happen, her approval rating would skyrocket to 85 percent. The thought made her giddy, especially since Henry Jellicoe had predicted the same thing, but his estimate had been that her approval rating would reach 90 percent.

So much for all those advisors she'd knuckled under to. Well, they were gone now, and there had been barely a mention of the mass exodus in the *Post*. In fact, the only thing she could find was on page seventeen. Her new advisors' names and résumés had been on page four, and as yet, she'd seen barely a ripple in the media. It was business as usual. At least for now.

Somehow she managed to smile and make appropriate comments to the governor of New York, who was sitting on her left. Later, she couldn't remember a thing that was said by anyone at the table. She shrugged. She could always go online to find out what she herself had said and, of course, to read through her guests' comments. Assuming that she cared enough to do so, of course. Since she didn't, this particular luncheon conversation would forever be a mystery.

In three days she would see Henry Jellicoe. Seventy-two hours. She turned to the right, to listen to the governor of New Jersey. She nodded to show she agreed that snowplows did indeed dig up the roads during the winter months.

The president looked down at the pink mess on her plate. *Why do they always serve poached salmon at these luncheons?* she wondered. She was relieved when her plate was taken away and a dessert of chocolate mousse in the shape of the Capitol was set in front of her. Coffee appeared. Once coffee was poured, she would have another fifteen minutes before the luncheon was over. She risked a quick glance at her watch. Knowing how she hated these luncheons, Martine knew that her press secretary would give her a signal, which meant she would stand up and say something like, "I hope you enjoyed this luncheon as much as I did." Blah, blah, blah.

Two hours later the forty-fourth president of the United States made her way to her personal quarters, where she mixed herself a stiff drink. She debated a full minute before firing up a cigarette. As she puffed away, she made a promise to herself. *As soon as the vigilantes are safely on the road to getting on with their lives, I am going to quit smoking.* Henry Jellicoe had told her he would help her quit, because he had gone cold turkey and knew how hard it was to kick the nicotine habit. That was then; this was now. Still, she *was* going to quit whether Jellicoe was in her life or not.

Martine Connor's stomach clenched into a tight knot when she thought about what was going to go down in less than seventy-two hours. Perspiration beaded on her brow. How was it she could deal with a worldwide crisis and not break a sweat, but a simple matter of honoring a promise she'd made could throw her into such a state of panic? How?

She finished her drink in one long gulp. Her eyes started to water, and her throat burned, proof that she'd never be a serious drinker. She crushed out the cigarette, which she'd barely smoked, because of the guilt she felt. Finally, she couldn't stand it a moment longer. A second later she pulled her personal cell phone out of the pocket of her suit jacket. No calls. Her shoulders slumped. "Well, what did you expect?" she asked herself. "You refused to take Henry's calls, a dozen or more."

She tried pep-talking herself out of acting like a sophomoric teenager instead of the president of the United States. Why didn't you just ask me to help you? I would have. But would I really have? And even if I would have, how could Hank have known that I would? I was prepared to betray Lizzie's trust, even if in the end she would gain from it, to avoid having to do what I had promised. The thought popped up from that wellspring of conscience, where she could not hide from herself, from the place that had finally enabled her to break with her advisors and do the right and honorable thing. And it softened the blow when she could not help thinking, instead, *You used me, made a fool out of me.*

"Even presidents fall in love," she whispered to herself.

Chapter 22

The sun was dipping behind the horizon as the guests from the last full cable car walked across the compound to the main building, where the Sisters and Charles waited.

Lizzie, fresh from her flight from Vegas, was the center of attention as the Sisters oohed and aahed over her condition. There were hugs, squeezes, giggles, and misty eyes as Lizzie beamed and sparkled.

The men stood to the side, and Charles said, "This is not something we're invited to observe, much less participate in. The women have a lock on it, as you can see."

And the guys could see and hear scattered exclamations of boy versus girl, pink versus blue, white baby furniture, rainbow-colored mobiles, and hand-painted murals. When the chattering women switched up to breast-feeding versus bottle-feeding, Charles led the parade of men closer to the fire, where they hunkered down to listen to Hank Jellicoe expound on the expertise of the Secret Service versus "my own people" and how there was simply no contest.

Jack tried his best to hide his skepticism. He had a healthy respect for, if not an ongoing love-hate relationship with, the Secret Service. He tempered that respect with the thought that he'd never seen *Jellicoe's people* in action. He listened with half an ear to what his new boss was saying. Wrong. Jellicoe had turned over the reins of the company to him and Bert and the others, so he wasn't his boss. Jack was his own boss. He felt a head rush at the thought.

Jack turned to look at the chattering women, his gaze locking with Lizzie's. Without stopping to think, he got up and went over to Lizzie and hugged her before he kissed her on the cheek. "I don't have the words to tell you how happy I am for you and Cosmo, Lizzie. I hope you'll always be as happy as you are right this moment."

"Jack . . . I—"

"Shhh. Leave the past where it belongs, in the past," Jack said. "This is today, and tomorrow isn't here yet."

Nikki beamed as she winked at Jack. He felt warm all over. In a matter of hours, albeit more than a few, he would be able to spend every waking moment with her. They could make plans, not worry about schedules, not worry about looking over their shoulders. They could plan a wedding, actually have a wedding. They could go to the cabin in Montana or to some exotic beach and just love and adore each other. For three weeks. Three weeks that he knew would go as fast as a lightning strike.

A chill ran down Jack's spine when he realized that Nikki didn't know about his resignation, his signing a contract to take over Global Securities. He had honored his word and hadn't spoken of the deal to anyone. And as far as he knew, none of the others, not even Ted, who with his weak backbone hadn't caved to Maggie, had told anyone. That was when he realized Maggie wasn't standing in the group of chattering women. He asked where she was.

"She said she could do more by staying at the paper," Annie told him. "She's putting out a special edition dealing solely with the vigilantes. She's running chapter and verse from day one and urging everyone all over the country, the world, too, to vote for a pardon for us. She's been twittering and blogging twenty-four-seven. She said the response has been phenomenal. The three major news channels are giving her hours of coverage. She knows what she's doing. And she's doing it herself. She said Ted and Joseph resigned, saying they were moving on to greener pastures. She's very perturbed over that. Would you happen to know anything about those resignations, Jack?"

Before Jack moved back to the fireplace, where his colleagues were standing around and staring at him, he countered the question with several questions of his own. "Me? Shouldn't you be asking Ted and Espinosa that question?

I'm not their keeper, nor do they confide in me about their personal decisions."

The baby chatter wound down, and the Sisters were on maternity fashion when Charles clapped his hands for everyone's attention. "The command center or the dining room?"

Since it was approaching the dinner hour, it was decided to adjourn to the dining hall, where within minutes a cold and hot buffet would be laid out. The kitchen that very afternoon had been a beehive of activity, with Alexis making real Southern fried chicken, black-eyed peas, and johnnycake. Nikki had baked a ham, while Isabelle and Kathryn had prepared a thick, hearty vegetable soup and a pot of chili. Yoko had fixed the garden salad, several cold pasta salads, and dessert, while Myra and Annie had overseen the table setting and the canapés.

The reason for the buffet was, as Myra put it, "The less time we have to spend worrying about cooking and eating, the more time we can devote to the most important mission of our lives."

Dinner and the cleanup all went smoothly as the Sisters worked in tandem. Finally, fresh coffee was poured, and Hank Jellicoe took the floor. He cleared his throat, then said, "It was not, nor is it, my intention to upset any of you by keeping secrets from you. I have one way of working, and the moment I deviate, all hell breaks loose. I say this so you will all understand what I am about to tell you." Hank looked around the table, with its extra chairs to accommodate everyone, and was satisfied that he had everyone's attention.

"I specifically asked Charles to dismantle the computers so none of you would be able to read the papers online. Bert resigned as director of the FBI yesterday afternoon, and Jack resigned his position as assistant district attorney late last evening. Both resignations went into effect immediately. Ted and Joe Espinosa also tendered their resignations to Maggie early this morning. Harry Wong has agreed to come on board and will be closing his dojo sometime during the next month. I'm retiring once this gig at the White House comes to a close. Bert and Jack will be taking over Global Securities. As yet, we have not decided on a base of operations.

"It is imperative that all of you leave here once your pardons are in place. I'm sure all of you have given a great deal of thought to how and what you will do once you are free. There will be a free-for-all when the media get wind of Bert and Kathryn and Nikki and Jack. The same goes for Ted and Joe. Since Harry trains FBI, CIA, and local law enforcement, he would be in some serious trouble should anyone link him to Yoko. Are you all following me here?"

Heads bobbed up and down.

Jellicoe went on. "Good. I will remain at the helm for the next month, a figurehead only. That means you all have thirty days to do whatever you want to do until the guys have to report to boot camp. I'd like to see all of you settled somewhere safe, away from the media's prying eyes. Things will settle down in time, and we can hope that at that point in time you can all resume your old lives, if that's what you want."

"In this country or out of the country?" Nikki asked quietly.

"That's what you all have to decide among yourselves," said Jellicoe.

"If we go out of the country, we won't be here to see Lizzie through her pregnancy and the birth of her baby," Kathryn said.

Isabelle looked like she was about to cry. "Listen, I just . . . I was hoping . . ."

Jellicoe smiled. "This might be a good time to tell you, Isabelle, that Stu Franklin works for me. He always has. So does Fish," he said, his gaze going to Annie. "How else do you think you were able to have such a successful mission in Vegas? He's my top instructor at our boot camp. Fish, of course, does things his way, but his way, for some reason, always works. Couldn't do it without Stu and Fish. Does that answer your question?"

Isabelle's eyes sparkled. "It does!"

Annie just stared off into space. But she did nod to show she understood.

"The pardons are a sure thing, then?" Myra asked.

Charles got up and went into the kitchen. He came back with a large manila envelope. He opened it and spread the contents on the table. "An hour after this set of pictures of your pardons in the desk drawer was taken, this second set of pictures was taken by . . . an associate of Hank's. As you can see, the pardons are now on top of the president's desk. This picture," he said, where the pardons were fanned out, "have all your names on them. Signed, sealed, and just waiting to be picked up. The rest of the pictures are pretty much a road map for you to follow. It will be up to you to choose someone to . . . uh . . . pick them up."

"And then?" Annie snapped.

"And then you walk out of the White House free women. The president will make an announcement at the end of the party, at which point you will be long gone. Maggie at the *Post* will have her edition ready to go."

"It's all set up, then?" Myra asked.

"A done deal," Jellicoe said.

"What if something goes wrong?" Kathryn asked.

"Like what?" Jellicoe asked. "My people will be all over the place. Harry Wong and his people will be everywhere also."

Kathryn, mulishly stubborn, fixed Jellicoe with a burning gaze. "So what you are telling us is that the Secret Service is going to stand down and let you and *your people* take over at the White House, is that right?"

"Well, not exactly, but close enough that you do not have to worry about it," replied Jellicoe.

"Yeah, right," Kathryn said. "You know what they say about the best-laid plans of mice and men. It just takes one independent thinker to screw things up. What a coup to nail us in the White House!"

The Sisters started to murmur among themselves. It was obvious to the men that the Sisters were leaning more on Kathryn's side and not giving too much credence to Jellicoe and his promises. When it looked like things were going to heat to the boiling point, Charles suggested the men go outside for a cigar and leave the women to their discussion.

The moment the door closed behind them, Kathryn literally exploded. "I'm not buying this. This is just too damn easy. Aren't the rest of you seeing what I'm seeing? I understand wanting the pardons so damn bad you can taste them, but my gut is not happy with all this. Another thing. Don't you find it a little strange that all of a sudden Hank Jellicoe is going to retire and turn over a multibillion-dollar security firm he worked all his life to build to *the boys*?"

"You do make some excellent points, Kathryn. But Charles trusts Hank," Myra said defensively.

Yoko stood up. "Harry and his friends will not let anything happen to us, Kathryn. If Harry weren't involved, I would be just as worried as you are."

The heated argument continued as Kathryn refused to budge an inch in her thinking. All she kept saying over and over was, "Convince me, and I'll go along with it."

When it looked like it might turn into a howling, hair-snatching, stomach-punching event,

Lizzie stood up and banged her coffee cup on the table. "Listen to me, all of you. I'm going to do something I've never done in my life. I'm going to betray a client's confidence. I want it clearly understood right here and now that what I am about to tell you stays with all of you, and you take it to your graves. I want to see everyone's hand *high* in the air."

Seven hands shot upward.

Lizzie continued, "I'm going to tell you what Hank wouldn't tell you. He and the president are in love. That's the bottom line. To be blunt, they're having an affair, which so far no one knows about. He wants to marry her, and that's why he's so willing to turn over his business to the boys. The president told me in confidence that she is not going to run for a second term. Personally, I think she'll change her mind once she and Hank get married. I know no female president ever got married in the White House, so this will be a first. Because," she quipped, "she's our first female president. Right now the two of them are having a little tiff, but that will change. Hank just stepped in to help her keep her promise to all of us. Now, Kathryn, do you understand? If Hank says it will work, then it will work. Yes, the president has her role in all this, and she will carry out that role. You will all walk out of the White House free women.

"No one can accurately predict the aftermath, but I don't think we need to worry about that right now. This is what you all have going for you right now. If you want to back off, say so now. A tremendous amount of time and effort has gone into this mission. It's yours for the taking. It's what you've wanted since we put Marti in office. She's coming through for you, later than expected, but she is doing it. What? I'm not hearing anything here. Five minutes ago you were willing to kill one another, and now you can't think of anything to say. Be quick before those men freeze out there."

Without having to be told, one by one, the Sisters raised their hands.

The bad time was over, and Kathryn was smiling. "Do you think she'll invite us to the wedding?"

"I think you can count on it," Lizzie said.

Yoko scampered over to the door and opened it. "Please, gentlemen, come inside," she said sweetly.

Jack hung back. "Yoko, hold on. Harry asked me to give you this. He said he'd kill me if I opened it. I did not open it."

Yoko looked down at the little enamel box, opened it, and stared down at the perfect pearl, nestled in a fold of black velvet. Tears rolled down her cheeks. "With all of this going on, he is thinking of me. He is just so sweet. Isn't he sweet, Jack? It is so beautiful. I have never seen such luster. Thank you for bringing it to me. Harry would not have killed you. He loves you like his own brother. He does, you know."

"I know," Jack said gruffly.

Yoko slipped the little box into the pocket of

her jeans. "Come. We must sit in on the final details. I am so happy, Jack."

Jack laughed. "I'm just as happy, Yoko."

The *Post* headlines and the top-of-the-hour news for the next three days alternated between the pardon count for the vigilantes and the patriotic party at the White House, with the vigilantes garnering the most publicity. Every Web site and switchboard Maggie set up crashed within hours with the number of people calling, texting, and e-mailing in to vote to pardon the vigilantes. The switchboard at all three news channels went down repeatedly with the high volume of call-ins. One excited commentator likened it to the number of hits people logged hoping to get a ticket to the Michael Jackson funeral. Maggie finally gave up at the end of day two, when the number had just fifty thousand to go to make it a full billion hits. Worldwide. She decided to gild the lily a tad and ran with a headline that was three inches of solid black and said, ONE BILLION! "Numbers don't lie," she mumbled to herself as she turned to watch the television sets in the newsroom, which were tuned to the three major news channels.

One gutsy anchor from CNN, with a very dry, brittle comb-over, said, "This is how you have to look at it readerwise, folks. The vigilantes are on page one of a five-hundred-page book. The White House patriotic party is on page four hundred ninety-nine, and Justice Leonard's impending retirement is on page five hundred. Wake up, all you stiffs at the White House, and do what the people want. The people who voted you into office in the first place. I voted to pardon the ladies!" He ended his commentary by saying, "There's been a run on powdered wigs at every costume shop within a fifty-mile radius."

Maggie giggled, glad she'd sent her secretary out early to get her powdered wig. She walked back to her office to view her costume. She was going to the festivities dressed as Betsy Ross. She checked her backpack, emptied half of it out into one of her desk drawers, and dumped in her three cameras and her press credentials, a banana, and a package of peanut butter cookies. She settled the backpack more firmly inside Betsy's sewing bag, which came with the costume and powdered wig. Now all she had to do was wait until six o'clock, when her driver would pick her up and drop her off at 1600 Pennsylvania Avenue.

Maggie leaned back in her swivel chair. She hated it when she wasn't 100 percent in the loop. She started to nibble at her nails and then stared at the engagement ring, which she'd been wearing for over two weeks. She'd promised to stop chewing her nails, and she was trying. If she squinted, she could almost see some new growth to her nails. The emerald-cut diamond wasn't just beautiful; it was exquisite. She had had no idea that Ted had such good taste.

She turned sideways and looked at Ted's and

Espinosa's resignations, still lying on her desk, where they'd been since they handed them in three days ago. Like she was really going to accept them. If they quit, she was quitting.

Something wasn't computing, and being as smart and as astute as she was, she figured the resignations had something to do with what was going to happen tonight. Tomorrow her star reporter and her star photographer would be back in the saddle, chasing down some new scoop. She wondered why she didn't believe her own scenario. A shiver worked its way up and down her spine, then moved to her arms. She blinked away a tear. She didn't know how she knew, but she knew neither one would be marching into the newsroom tomorrow morning, just as they hadn't for the past two days.

Everything was changing at the speed of light. First, it was Justice Leonard and his upcoming departure from the Supreme Court; then it was Lizzie's possible nomination. And then, just a few hours ago, Lizzie had called to share her unbelievable news. She had turned down the offered nomination a few weeks ago because she had found out that she was pregnant. She apologized for not telling Maggie right away, but she and Cosmo had decided to wait before going public. She hoped that Maggie understood.

Lizzie Fox was going to be a mother. That had to be right up there with getting a Pulitzer. Only better.

If the vigilantes pulled off this last mission,

they were home free. How dull life was going to be. For her, not them. They'd all be happier than a posse of pigs in a mud slide, but what about her? "What am I going to do when they all go off to wherever they're going to live their lives?" She loved the thrill of danger, loved the thrill of outfoxing the opposition with the written word. Her life would become humdrum. Boring to the nth degree.

Maggie bit down on her lower lip. Once she kicked all the bullshit aside and looked at it full in the face, as she was doing right now, right this second, she couldn't deny that it was the thrill of being needed. When everyone rode off into the sunset, she wouldn't be needed anymore. Even Ted had proved he didn't need her by resigning. Suddenly she felt so bad, she wanted to cry. Not being needed had to be the worst feeling in the world. Did her mother feel like that when she sent her off to college? Back then did she even care enough to ask? She simply couldn't remember.

God, how she hated pity parties. She peptalked herself then. *Come on, Maggie. Pull up your big-girl panties and get on with it. Your life is going to be whatever you make out of it. No one is in control of your life but you. Chop-chop!*

Maggie gave her undies an imaginary hitch and said, loud enough for anyone passing by to hear, "What a crock! Everyone needs someone, even those who won't admit it."

Chapter 23

Harry Wong looked at the ten most deadly martial arts experts in the world, who were now attired in spiffy khaki Global Securities uniforms, the logo of the company emblazoned on the pockets in gold thread. To a man, they refused to wear the visored caps and steel-toed boots GS had provided, and Harry wasn't about to argue the point.

"Here's the plan, gentlemen. We ride to the White House in one of GS's security vans, where Mr. Jellicoe himself will meet us. We've gone over the layout, and you all said you have it committed to memory. Mr. J will assign you to your post. Any run-ins with the Secret Service, you simply put them to sleep.

"Jack just called and said there will be pictures of the ladies in their costumes on the closed-circuit TV in the van. In addition to the ladies, there will be another woman separate from them. Her name is Maggie Spritzer, and she will be dressed as Betsy Ross. Shield her, too.

Don't let anyone get to her. She's going to give the ten of you publicity like you only dreamed about. Any questions?"

The old man with the ropy arms stared at Harry. "What? You think we're stupid?"

Harry laughed. "Not one little bit, but in this country they have a saying, and they call it Murphy's Law, which means what can go wrong will go wrong. But," he added hastily, "we all know that doesn't apply to any of you."

"Harry-san, does that friend of yours, the one you refer to as a dumb shit, really think we can catch speeding bullets with our fingers?" one of the ten asked.

Harry laughed again and said, "Yeah, he does. I don't see any need to enlighten him at this point in time, either." Harry looked at his little army and bowed low.

In the van the men looked at everything in amazement.

"Pretty high tech," one of them said. "My country has nothing like this."

The others agreed.

Harry pressed buttons, and picture after picture appeared on the screen. He rattled off the names of the Sisters and gave a little scenario on all of them. "These two," he said, pointing to Annie and Myra, "Mama-sans." He pointed to Jack, Ted, Bert, and Espinosa. "These men are . . ."

"The dumb shits," the old man said with a twinkle in his eye.

Harry grinned. "You guys catch on quick. Okay, here are your credentials. Just slip them into your pocket. If anyone gets overly aggressive, just whip these babies out and go about your business. You got that?"

Heads bobbed up and down.

"Any other questions?" Harry asked. "Okay, then we should get this show on the road. Buckle up, gents."

As Harry tooled along, he was grinning to himself at the conversations wafting toward him. He wondered if his friends would kill him when he wasn't able to produce Sylvester Stallone at the end of this little caper. He wished he hadn't been so rash when he made that particular promise. Nor was he going to be able to produce the Jonas Brothers. He didn't want to think about the other rash promises he'd made to ensure his friends' arrival here in the States. If he had time, maybe he could enlist Jack's help. Yeah, yeah, good old Jack would come to his rescue. Just to be on the safe side, Harry yanked out his phone. One eye on the road, one ear on the conversation behind him, he somehow managed to text Jack to apprise him of his concern. A text came back so quick, Harry almost collided with a Honda Civic carrying a bunch of giggling girls, which was swerving all over the road. He leaned on the horn and was stunned to see the windows go down on the Civic. Four middle fingers saluted him. The text read, Always knew you'd get your dick in a knot. I'll see what I can do.

While Harry bemoaned what he imagined to be his early demise, Jack texted Maggie and asked what she could do for Harry. She in turn texted Abner Tookus, who brought to bear every contact he had in the world. Ten minutes later Jack texted Harry, saying, The best they could do was a webcam meeting with Sylvester and the Jonas Brothers. Just say Stallone is getting married and the Jonas Brothers' flight was delayed. It's the best I can do. Viewing time is 9:06. Be in the van at that time. Take it or leave it, bro. And you owe me for saving your ass, and do not think for one minute that I'm going to forget this, either.

Harry's return text read, Okay. There was grateful, and then there was grateful. You never, as in ever, gave Jack Emery the edge.

As Harry steered the van to where a local cop on horseback was directing traffic, he called out, "We have arrived, gentlemen. I see Mr. Jellicoe. Remember now, you are in charge. Pay no mind to all those cops, the FBI, or anyone else. Tonight, gentlemen, we are golden. On behalf of all those milling about on the grounds and inside the White House, welcome to Sixteen Hundred Pennsylvania Avenue."

"If you ever decide to give up your day job, Harry-san, you can seek employment as a tour guide," the old man said as he hopped out to the ground.

Harry was the last to get out of the van. He pressed the remote on the key chain, locking the doors of the one-of-a-kind security van. He marched up to where Hank Jellicoe was standing and saluted smartly.

"No one likes a smart-ass, Wong," Jellicoe said.

"Takes one to know one," Harry shot back.

Jellicoe eyed Harry for a full minute before he spoke. "You really think those ten guys there, yourself included if you want, can take all my people *and* the Secret Service?"

Harry tilted his head to the side, as though he was pondering the question. "Depends if you mean with one hand tied behind their backs or with both hands tied behind them. In other words, I don't *think* we can do it. I *know* we can do it." Harry waited to see if there was going to be a comeback, and when there wasn't, he knew he'd won the round.

"You're looking rather dashing this evening, Harry," Jack said, coming up to stand next to him. Right behind him were Bert, Ted, and Espinosa, similarly attired. "Did you know these are designer uniforms, Harry? They are. Our new boss just told me that. And they're free when you work for Global Securities. You understand my text? You know, Harry, I put my ass on the line to get those guys to agree to save *your* ass. The magic moment is nine-oh-six. You're one minute late, and it all goes down the tubes."

Harry looked down at his watch. "That's precisely fifty-six minutes from now."

"So it is," Jack said happily.

A devil perched itself on Harry's shoulder. He leaned over and kissed Jack on the cheek. Betsy Ross clicked her camera, and the moment was caught forever.

The ten deadliest men in the world looked at one another. A few rolled their eyes; a few shrugged. It was the old man who quipped, "Who knew?"

Jack started to laugh and couldn't stop.

"What's so damn funny, Emery?" said Harry.

"You, you dumb schmuck. Those guys, *your people*, now think you and I are . . . How should I say this? *A couple*. And Betsy Ross over there got it on film."

What sounded like a ripe discussion suddenly escalated to voices being raised. Jack stepped back as Jellicoe went at it with one of the Secret Service agents, who stopped whatever he was about to say next to talk into his sleeve. Jellicoe pushed forward, Harry and his friends ahead of him. Jack waited a moment to see if a contingent of Secret Service agents would follow. They didn't. "Chalk one up for Global Securities," he muttered.

Inside the White House, Jack closed his eyes for a moment to get a mental fix on where he was supposed to go. Nikki and the girls had arrived fifty minutes ago and were milling around, trying to familiarize themselves with the layout. He saw them then, off to the side, talking to a man dressed like Abraham Lincoln.

Jack smiled at the Sisters' costumes. Annie was Bess Truman and looked more like Bess than Bess had herself. Myra was Lady Bird Johnson. He craned his neck to the right to pick out Jackie Kennedy, aka Isabelle. Because of her height and exceptionally long legs, Alexis had chosen to be Uncle Sam. No one questioned that Uncle Sam was white and this Uncle Sam was black. Yoko wore a tattered garment and had a bandanna tied around her glossy black hair. A small placard around her neck said, CHILD SLAVE. It was Kathryn, however, dressed as Paul Revere, who caught the eye, and it was Kathryn whose duty it was to make it to the Oval Office to pick up the pardons and secure them in her mail pouch.

Betsy Ross, her eye on her watch at all times, maneuvered her way through the crowd, snapping picture after picture. She sidled up to Jack and hissed, "Tell me this is going to work."

"My people tell me it is going to work, Betsy," Jack said out of the corner of his mouth.

"Will you stop with that 'my people' crap already? Do you know what I had to pay out to get Sylvester Stallone to do this? Well, do you?"

"I don't want to know. Where are those guys, anyway?" Jack asked.

"Believe it or not, they're guarding the portals leading to the Oval Office. I heard enough snapping and snarling between Jellicoe and the Secret Service to last me a lifetime. I have to hand it to the president. She stepped up to the plate, and they all backed off. I got a picture of the president kissing Mr. Jellicoe. On the lips!"

"No shit! You gonna run that in the paper?"

"No! But I'm going to send them a copy. The Marine Band is going to play 'Yankee Doodle.' How neat is that?" Maggie said through clenched teeth.

Sensing Maggie's nervousness, Jack said, "How's the food?"

"Food! Food! You're thinking about food at a time like this! They have everything in the world on those buffet tables. And you can't get near them. I have pictures. The president looks like she's headed this way." Maggie looked at her watch and moved away.

Jack scanned the crowd of "patriotic" guests and walked away in the opposite direction. He risked a quick glance at his watch. Time was marching on, just like the music the band was supposed to be playing. Where in the hell was the damn band? He looked over at the Sisters, who had now split up and were in clusters of two and attached to small groups of guests. They looked like they didn't have a care in the world. His eyes raked the room. Nothing stood out, no one appeared anxious, and no one seemed to have a clue that this was anything other than a party. At the White House. No matter how boring the party, just to be able to say you were invited to the White House was a coup in itself.

Security cameras? Where the hell were they? Jack had a moment of panic when he looked around, spotted Hank Jellicoe attired in a nifty tux that looked like it had been made especially for his lean frame. He looked around again to see if anyone else was similarly attired. Nope. And Jellicoe stood out like the white elephant in the room. Jack shrugged. Obviously, he had a reason for the way he was dressed.

The president—now, she was dressed in a

crinoline and looked like she'd just stepped from the pages of *Gone With the Wind*. He wasn't sure, but he thought she was dressed as Dolley Madison.

Jack continued to watch the president as she made her way past the little clusters of guests, and when she stopped to speak to Paul Revere, Jack's breath caught in his throat. He watched as a startled Kathryn straightened her shoulders, tugged at the ponytailed wig she was wearing before bowing and reaching for the president's hand to bring it to her lips. Even from where he was standing, Jack could see the humor in the president's eyes. She was saying something to Kathryn, but he couldn't read her lips, and Kathryn nodded slightly but didn't speak. The president moved off. Jack looked down at his watch again.

Harry tapped Jack on the shoulder. Jack almost jumped out of his skin. "Don't ever do that again. I almost had a heart attack."

"And if I do, what are you going to do about it?" Harry asked, his tone vague as his gaze swept the room. Harry was definitely on duty.

"I'm going to kiss you on the lips, that's what I'm going to do. What do you think of that? Then I'm going to send the picture to all those ninja magazines you subscribe to."

"Eat shit, Jack. We both know you aren't going to do that. I think there is a diversion about to take place. Honest Abe, the really tall, lanky one, is about to have a mishap . . . aaaany second now."

Jack saw it all in slow motion. Two waiters, with heavy platters held high, were advancing to the head buffet table, where the president was talking to Hank Jellicoe and the lanky Abe Lincoln. Abe took a misstep, jostling Jellicoe, who lost his footing and landed across the buffet table. The heavy platters went upward, the contents showering down on the president just as strains of "Yankee Doodle" blasted through the room. Jack blinked as a gauntlet of Secret Service swarmed in to surround the president, who was laughing so hard, she couldn't catch her breath as she sampled the roast duck that was dripping down her face. She went off into another peal of laughter as Betsy Ross clicked away with gay abandonment.

"And there goes Paul Revere, galloping off for her last ride of the evening." Harry cackled.

Harry and Jack continued to watch as Hank Jellicoe slid to the floor to sit next to the president. "I would like it very much, Madam President, if you would accept this engagement ring I have somewhere in my pocket. I just have to find it. As you can see, I even got dressed up for this momentous event."

And that was how the president of the United States and the retiring head of Global Securities announced their engagement to the world. Betsy Ross captured every living moment. She uploaded the pictures, and they were on the way to the *Post* for the special edition that would hit the streets at midnight, just as the patriotic party came to a close. She fired off a quick text to tell her people to hold the press for one more set of pictures, which would be arriving momentarily.

"I guess she said yes?" Jack said, grinning from ear to ear.

"Yeah, I think it was when Jellicoe was licking the duck sauce off her chin. She's sporting a ring that's bigger than the one Ted gave Maggie," Harry said, laughing.

Paul Revere, mail pouch on her shoulder, tripped down the hall, her boots clattering on the polished floor. She sucked in her breath as she visualized the route she had to take to get to the Oval Office. She longed for Paul's trusty steed, which would have had her at the door to the Oval Office within seconds. She wondered if she would get the crazy urge to shout, "The British are coming!" when she reached the door. Probably not, because by that time she would be dead from fear or in chains, being led to a federal prison. Her heart was pounding so hard in her chest, it sounded like a set of bongo drums.

Two more hallways, three more corners. God, what if she made a wrong turn? Her hand went to the ponytail on the wig she was wearing and the tiny transmitter that allowed her to hear Bert whispering in her ear. "You're doing fine, honey."

"I wish I had a horse, Bert," she hissed. "I'd have our pardons in hand, and we'd be home free."

"You should have told me you wanted a horse. I could have delivered Delilah, but she wouldn't have done you much good, since she can't turn left, and you have two lefts to make," Bert quipped. "Uh-oh, here comes an agent. I can see him on the parabolic gizmo. You can do it, Kathryn. One of Harry's guys is coming up fast on his left. Do not panic, honey."

Kathryn's heart pounded hard in her chest. How could she not panic?

The Secret Service agent was big. He looked to Kathryn like he wrestled alligators for a living and ate his winnings. She saw his raised hand, palm outward, which meant to even a stupid person, "Stop in your tracks." She stopped.

"This area of the White House is off-limits to guests. How did you get here?" the agent demanded, his gaze going everywhere.

Kathryn knew the agent wasn't going to be impressed with her panicked humor, but she tried, anyway. "As you can see, I'm Paul Revere. I fell off my horse and got stranded. I didn't know where to go. That means I'm lost."

She saw the swirling puff of smoke behind the agent just as Bert whispered in her ear. "That was good, honey. The smoke will hover around the camera. You need to keep going. Harry's guy, Boris, is coming up fast. Do not hang around to watch the outcome. I'll relay it to you."

Like she was really going to stand around when her freedom lay just around the corner. Sometimes men were so dense.

"I thought I told you to stop!" the agent said ominously.

Kathryn saw Boris coming toward her. She wanted to barrel down the rest of the hallway, to do what Bert said, but if she kept going, the agent was going to turn and see Harry's guy. She stopped and smiled. "Hello, Boris!"

"Good evening!" Boris said pleasantly.

The agent whirled, became aware of the vapor hanging in the air, then of Boris himself. "What the hell . . ."

"Keep going, honey," Bert whispered. "You're going to hear commotion. Ignore it. The bastard alerted his control, and here he comes. Ah, here comes that old guy, the one who can catch bullets with his bare hands. Ooooh, this is good. This is sooo good. Okay, honey, you are at the door. Take a deep breath and open it."

Kathryn took a deep breath. "Oh, Bert," she whispered, "I never thought I would ever, ever be standing here. It's so . . . awesome. The carpet is blue, with the great seal—"

"Kathryn, you aren't there to admire the decor. Get the pardons and get out of there. Kathryn, are you listening to me? Do not, I repeat, do not sit down in the president's chair and pretend."

"Hmm." That was exactly what she was doing.

Suddenly the earpiece in Kathryn's ponytail gave off an earsplitting whistle. "Get out of there, *now!*"

Faster than lightning, Kathryn was on her feet and running for the door.

"The pardons!" Bert's voice shrieked in her ear.

Five seconds later the pardons were in her mail pouch and she was running down the hall, back the way she had come. Puffs of smoke were everywhere as she jumped over prone figures on the floor. Harry's men at work. Kathryn was so breathless from running, she could barely keep going. She stopped and leaned against the wall when she heard Bert's voice tell her to stop, catch her breath, and walk through the door on the right. She clutched at her knees as she struggled to take deep breaths. She could do that.

"Okay, walk through the door, honey," Bert told her. "The girls are waiting for you. Go straight to the exit and follow instructions. I'm proud of you, Kathryn."

Kathryn swallowed hard as she let her gaze rake through the room. A commotion at the buffet table. Was that the president sitting on the floor, with food all over her? She must be hallucinating or on some adrenaline high. Yet another rendition of "Yankee Doodle" was being played by the Marine Band.

"God, if I had a horse, I'd be halfway to New Jersey by now," Kathryn mumbled to herself as she caught up to the Sisters. "I got them. I have them right here in my mail pouch. Oh, God, we're free. Did you all hear me? We're free. The proof is right here in this bag. I didn't have time to look at them, though. That office is awesome. Bert said I had to get out right away. I'm going to faint. Someone hold me up."

"If you faint, Kathryn, we will leave you here," Nikki said. "Get hold of yourself. Five more minutes, and we're outside. You can do it, Kathryn. You're safe! Take a deep breath, and get with the program. Do you hear me?"

"Okay. Okay. I'm okay. I did it. Oh, God, I did it," Kathryn declared.

Nikki nodded. "Yes, you did, and we are all grateful." Kathryn sagged against Nikki, who jerked her upright. "You know, you're right. We should have gotten you a horse."

Kathryn started to giggle and couldn't stop as the Sisters half dragged her to the door that would lead them all outside.

"Where's Paul Revere?" Jack asked.

"On your six o'clock, man. And the Sisters are right behind her. Mail pouch looks to be full."

Jack sucked in his breath. "They're going to do something stupid, right? How the hell many choruses are there to 'Yankee Doodle'? Those Secret Service guys look *pissed.*"

"That they do. It's because all the security cameras went out at the same time. I thought you knew that, Jack. You say you know everything. How'd you mess that one up?"

"I got caught up in the moment. What are *they* going to do?"

"How should I know?" Harry snapped.

Surrounded by Secret Service and Global Securities agents, the president and Hank Jellicoe made their way across the room to cheers and laughter. Instead of leaving by the exit, the president—holding Jellicoe's hand—took a slight detour and went behind the Sisters.

Suddenly powdered wigs flew in all directions; facial latex and other cosmetic prostheses dropped to the floor. Velcro bindings were opened, and costumes slithered everywhere just as the Sisters reached the door.

Gasps and shouts of "It's the vigilantes!" filled the crowded room.

The ten deadliest men in the world surrounded the vigilantes.

"Oh my goodness, so it is!" President Martine Connor could be heard to exclaim.

Betsy Ross clicked and clicked.

Paul Revere held her mail pouch high. Then she shouted, "Yo, Miss Betsy Ross! See this! It's our presidential pardons! See, our names are on here!"

"Got it!" Maggie shouted.

The score of Secret Service agents looked to their boss. President Connor, duck sauce still dripping, shrugged. "I guess I forgot to tell you about that!"

Betsy Ross captured each handshake as the president made her way down the line to each of the vigilantes. She turned to the side and whispered to Lizzie Fox, who was attired in a Mamie Eisenhower getup. "I gotta say, you all put on a hell of a show. And I damn well got engaged in the bargain. Boy, Lizzie, do you have any idea how homely you look in that getup?"

Lizzie laughed as she started ripping at her wig and her own latex cheeks.

Outside, in the brisk night air, with the Secret Service scowling, Global Securities agents beaming, the Sisters looked at one another before they high-fived one another.

"What time is it?" Harry asked anxiously.

"You got three minutes to get to the van. Go!" Jack bellowed as Betsy Ross also looked at the time on her watch. She literally flew to the Global Securities van and waited a nanosecond for Harry to unlock it.

"Come on, you guys. Shake it!" Harry ordered as Maggie pressed button after button.

Gasps filled the van as Sylvester Stallone appeared on camera. It was hard to tell if it was really Sylvester or not with the reception. Whoever it was grinned crookedly, repeated the name of the ten deadly men, and said, "I admire your work. I'm sorry I can't be there to shake your hands."

"Okay, everyone happy with that?" Betsy Ross yelled. "Okay, here come the Jonas Brothers!"

The picture was just as grainy, and whatever the brothers were singing was sketchy and scratchy, but no one cared.

Harry was being pounded and pummeled as the ten men congratulated him for keeping his promise. The old man with the ropy arms and Fu Manchu mustache punched Harry on the shoulder. He looked at Harry and squinted.

Harry blanched. "Listen, I'm not . . . I didn't . . . Yoko!" he bellowed.

Yoko bounded into the van and ran to Harry and kissed him so hard, his teeth rattled. "What?" she said a moment later.

"Nothing. It's not important. I just wanted to see you," said Harry.

The old man pointed to Jack, who was kissing Nikki outside the van, and chortled with laughter. "He is one dumb—"

"No! No, he isn't. He's my brother," said Harry. "And those women out there, they're my Sisters. And we're all free now."

"Ah, so. That means game over, right, Harry-san?" the old man said.

"Maybe yes, maybe no," Harry said.

Epilogue

Alexis walked around the rooms with a box of tissues in her hand, which she offered to her Sisters like bonbons on a plate. Everyone snatched at them as they dabbed at their eyes and blew gustily.

Packed bags sat near the door, waiting to be carried out to the cable car. No matter how hard they tried, the Sisters couldn't take their watery eyes off the bags and each other.

"This should be the happiest day of our lives," Yoko cried as she sniffled into a wad of tissues. "This is the day we said our lives would be complete. I do not feel complete. I do not." Her shoulders shaking, she leaned into Kathryn, who put her arm around the little Asian woman and squeezed her close.

"I feel like someone died. This is how I felt when Julia left us," Isabelle sobbed. "We're a family, we've been a family for years, and now we're going to separate to the four winds. I'm sorry. I promised myself I wouldn't do this, and here I am, falling apart."

Nikki's voice was so choked, she could barely get the words out. "I dreamed almost every night about this day and how happy I would be when I could run to Jack and tell him . . . tell him I was free to get married. For so long it was what kept me going day after day. Now that this day is here, I don't know what to do. I really don't know what to do," she wailed.

Kathryn drew a long, deep breath. "I feel like I did that day so long ago when I didn't think I could go on one more day. I went to Nikki and she brought me to all of you and you gave me my life back. I thought there could never be a life after Alan died. You all proved me wrong. I just want to thank you from the bottom of my heart. I don't know what to do, either, but I think Bert will help me if I falter. We're family. Nothing will ever change that. Nothing!"

Annie and Myra stood clutching each other, their eyes on the girls, who were trying so valiantly not to lose control. Neither trusted herself to speak. Besides, what was there to say? The girls rushed to them, circling them with their arms as they cried out their thanks and their misery.

"I feel like I lived a lifetime in the few short years that we've known one another," Nikki whispered. "Please, I'm begging all of you. Let's not allow our lives to come down to a Christmas card and a phone call on a birthday."

"That will never happen," Kathryn said forcefully. "We're family."

"Charles said we could keep our satellite phones. All we have to do is press one of the buttons and we're in contact," Alexis said.

"We'll see each other in thirty days, when it's time for the boys to go off to boot camp. We can all go out to the farm and play catch-up. By then we'll know where our lives are going to take us. Myra's farm is home. Isn't that right, Myra?" Nikki sobbed.

"Yes, dear, the farm is home. You don't have to call ahead. Your rooms will always be ready. The light will always be on. Please, just don't wait too long to come home. I feel like Kathryn. You all gave me my life back. There is no way, there are no words to thank you for that, so I won't even try."

"There's nothing I can add to what Myra said. You all gave me life, too, when I thought there was no life left in this old body. You're my children, and I love each and every one of you with every breath in my body. Myra . . . Myra is my soul sister. I hope . . . I wish . . . for all of you what I wish for myself on this new road we're about to travel, the best God has to offer all of us."

Murphy and Grady, who were standing near the door, started to growl. The Sisters knew what that sound meant. The helicopter was coming to take them down off the mountain. Two helicopters actually, courtesy of Global Securities, which would take them to Washington, D.C., and the people who were waiting for them.

Annie was the only one who wasn't going on the helicopter. She'd opted to take the cable car down the mountain, to where a car waited for her. Although the Sisters, Myra included, itched to know the why of it, none of them had asked what Annie's plans were. Nor had Annie volunteered anything.

They all heard it then, the deafening *whomp, whomp* of the helicopter rotors. Each Sister grabbed a handful of tissues before she ran to the door to snatch up her bags. Charles, his eyes as wet as the girls', had to stand aside to avoid the stampede. He thanked God that he'd said his good-byes earlier. He simply could not do it again.

"Time to go, ladies," he said quietly. "Everything is shipshape for the return of Pappy and his family tomorrow. The larder and freezer are full. The generator, all equipment, and the cable car have been serviced. If I do say so myself, it looks like we've never been here."

Annie and Myra started to wail as Charles herded them toward the door.

"Hurry," Charles urged. "We need to wave to the girls when they lift off."

That was all the impetus Annie and Myra needed. They ran like schoolgirls, their arms waving madly, tears streaming down their cheeks. They clutched at each other and somehow managed to stay on their feet when the helicopter lifted off, the winds from the rotors making the ground shake under their feet.

They looked upward to see the second helicopter hovering. They backed away as Charles appeared with their bags. Annie's bag was placed inside the cable car. The two women were locked in a tight embrace, so they could hear what each other was saying.

"This is it, Annie. Let's not say good-bye, okay? I lied to you. I could never have done the pole. Never in a million years. I am so glad we didn't have that recital."

Annie smiled through her tears. "Go!"

"You go first!" Myra said.

"No, he's burning fuel. You go first."

"Go! I'll push you off this mountain if you don't go," said Myra.

Charles patted Annie on the back, blew her a kiss as he propelled Myra forward. Once he and Myra were strapped in and settled, all luggage stowed, the helicopter lifted off. Annie watched until she couldn't see it anymore. She swiped at the tears rolling down her cheeks with the sleeve of her jacket as she walked around the compound one last time. When she felt something beside her tears on her cheeks, she looked upward. It was snowing again. Another storm was on the way, hence the urgency to leave the mountain a day ahead of schedule.

Her eyes dry, her back straight, shoulders squared, Annie marched like a recruit on the parade ground over to the cable car. She stepped in, locked the gate, and turned the switch. She counted off eleven minutes to get to the bottom, where she stepped out, removed her bag, before she pressed the switch that would send the car back to the top of the mountain.

Annie tossed her bag into the back of the Range Rover that belonged to Global Securities, settled herself behind the wheel, and turned over the engine. She switched on the GPS, pressed in her destination, then settled back for the ride that would take her to the Raleigh-Durham Airport.

Annie looked up at the airport monitor. Her flight would be boarding shortly. She looked down at the boarding pass clutched in her hand. She wanted to cry so bad, her eyes burned. She squeezed them shut to ward off the tears. She felt the air stir around her, but she didn't bother to open her eyes.

"Even when I was a little boy, my mother told me I should cry if I felt like crying," a voice said next to her.

Annie's eyes popped wide. "Fish! What are you doing here? Why are you here? How did you know I would be here?"

"I'm here to stop you from doing something damned foolish. You're as transparent as glass, Countess de Silva. I got six phone calls alerting me to what you were planning. Seven calls if you count Charles, eight calls if you count Lizzie."

"But—"

"I'm here to save you from yourself. Seems like everyone more or less, kind of, thought you would head back to that mountain retreat Myra rescued you from a long time ago. You know, that mountain where you wore a sheet and watched the weather channel."

"It wasn't a sheet. It was a . . . What it was . . . was a white robe. I don't need to be saved."

"What about all those things you said you were going to do? You were going to stick your nose into running the *Post* until they kicked you out. You said you and I were going to fiddle and diddle around at Babylon. I believed you. I had plans. Plans for the two of us. You said you wanted to have some *fun*. I haven't had any fun for a long time. I was kind of looking forward to it, and now you're kicking me to the curb or pushing me under the bus, whatever that saying is. Goddamn it, you said you were ready to set the world on fire, and I was ready to fan those flames. Look at you. There's not even a spark in you!"

"I'm not . . . I didn't—"

"Bullshit! You did. You are. You are not a woman of your word, and I do not give a shit if you can outshoot me or not. Look. I have here in my hand two tickets to the most perfect place in the world. I want you to go with me. Me and you, Miss Annie. Make up your mind right now, because they're calling the flight."

"Where?" Annie asked hesitantly.

"It's a surprise. Just trust me, okay?" Fish reached for Annie's hand. "But first, I want to know why you're here. I want the truth."

Annie's eyes brimmed with tears, but she didn't loosen her hold on Fish's hand. "They didn't need me anymore. Not one of them needed me. I need . . . I want . . . a purpose, Fish. Everyone had someone but me. If I wasn't needed, then I thought I should just go back to the mountain, put on my white robe, and . . . Well, that's as far as I got in my thinking."

"Listen! That's the last boarding call. Make up your mind real quick, Miss Annie. Just so you know, I need you."

Hope sparked in Annie's eyes. "Really? You do?"

"I purely do. So, shake it, lady. We're going to have to run before they close the doors."

Run they did.

If you enjoyed *Game Over*,
don't miss the next exciting novel in
Fern Michaels's Sisterhood series!

Turn the page for a special preview of

CROSS ROADS,

a Zebra paperback on sale in October 2010.

Chapter 1

Even though every light in the old farmhouse was on, it did nothing to dispel the gloom that seemed to shroud the house and its two occupants. Fragrant peach candles flickered on the dinner table, the crystal sparkled, and the delectable meal on fragile bone china sat basically untouched. Outside, a summer rain pounded on the roof and battered the ancient smoky windows.

"Myra, we need to talk," Charles said quietly.

"Hmmm, yes, I suppose we do. What would you like to talk about, Charles? It's raining outside. I always hated thunder, but I hate lightning even more. But then, you already know that, so there's no point in discussing it. Dinner is wonderful."

"How would you know? You haven't touched a thing on your plate. Close your eyes, Myra, and tell me what's on your plate."

"Roast beef," Myra snapped irritably.

"Wrong! It's pork tenderloin. You've always loved pork tenderloin."

"I used to love a lot of things, Charles. I'm sorry. We should just have had sandwiches and soup, or even just the soup."

"You wouldn't have eaten that, either," Charles snapped in return.

"What do you want me to say, Charles? I'm not trying to be difficult, it's just that . . . I miss my family. You know what else, Charles? I'm sorry we got those pardons. I was happy on the mountain with the girls. I cry every time I think of them. I would give anything to have yesterday back."

"That's rather cavalier of you, Myra. The girls wanted their old lives back. They didn't want that outlaw life anymore. They wanted to get married and have families. Surely you can't fault them for that."

"Of course I don't fault them for wanting their old lives back. I was speaking for myself. It's been a year and a half, Charles! Do not, I repeat, do not tell me to get a hobby. I do not want a hobby."

"I never thought of knitting as a hobby, old girl. I'd love a hand-knitted sweater."

"Then go to town and buy one! I am too old to learn to knit, and I have arthritis in my fingers. Why are you deviling me like this? Why can't you just let me be miserable?"

"Because I love you, that's why. You're starting to act the same way you did when Barbara died, and you're scaring me. I can't go through that again, Myra, I just can't."

"Oh, Charles, no, that isn't going to happen. I'll get a handle on it, just give me some time. Just a little more time."

"Myra, a year and a half is a lot of time. We need to make some decisions here. We need to join the living, to get on with our lives. We can't keep marking time like this."

"No one needs me these days, Charles. Not even you. Somehow, you manage to keep busy helping the boys with Global Securities. There are just too many hours in the day to fill. I now know how Annie felt. There's nothing worse than not being needed.

"Those old, supposedly dear friends of mine from my other life have cut us dead. Nellie spends almost all day in therapy for her two hip replacements, and even when she's home, she's too tired to do anything but sleep. Pearl is out there somewhere doing her thing with the underground railroad. I volunteered my services, and she said that if she needed me, she'd call. Well, guess what, Charles, she hasn't called once. I don't want to be a pest where Lizzie and her new baby are concerned. She and Cosmo are so happy, they don't need me fussing around them even though they said their door is always open to us.

"I love it that Lizzie is just doing consulting work these days, and Cosmo is just on call in case some emergency crops up. They're such wonderful parents to Little Jack."

"Speaking of Little Jack, tell me again why we didn't go to Lizzie's baby shower at the White House?"

"Because it would have stirred things up, and I didn't want to ruin Lizzie's day. And it's the same reason we didn't go to Little Jack's christening. Isn't it wonderful how Lizzie and Cosmo donated all the gifts to Babies Hospital and to families who need all that baby gear? They've set up so many foundations for baby care, I can't count them anymore. I can't wait for them to come back to town. Just a few weeks, and we'll get to see Little Jack again."

"You're done with dinner, right?" Myra nodded. "Get your slicker. I have something I want you to see. If you don't come with me, I'm going to pick you up and carry you. Move it, old girl!"

Grumbling, Myra followed Charles out to the mudroom and donned her slicker and Wellingtons. She held his hand as they made their way to the barn. Inside, light blazed. The horses whickered softly at the intrusion. Somewhere deep in the barn, a dog growled. "Be quiet, don't make any fast moves or loud noises. Just stay with me.

"It's just me, Charles, Little Lady. I'm coming in. Remember what I said, Myra. Look!"

Myra looked down into a mountain of straw where a warm blanket had been spread. "I don't know what her name is or even how she got here, but here she is with her newborn pups. I found them this morning. I call her Little Lady—not that she's little, because she isn't."

"Ooooh, Charles!" Myra dropped to her

knees in front of a magnificent golden retriever, who eyed her warily. She made no move to touch the mother or her pups. "Did you feed her, Charles?"

"I did, and she gobbled it all down. I'd like to bring her and the pups into the house if you don't mind. You know, just to keep an eye on her. I already called a vet, and he came out earlier this afternoon. Aside from being undernourished, Little Lady is fine. He gave me some nutrients and vitamins to give her. Like I said, it will be a lot easier to take care of them in the house."

"Of course it will, but you said we can't touch them. How will we get them into the house? Will Little Lady allow us to pick them up?"

"I don't know. I think that's up to you, Myra. She trusts me, but she doesn't know you yet. You have to make friends. Talk to her, see if she'll let you pet her. Touch is very important, so be gentle."

"It's so damp in here, Charles. That can't be good for the puppies. Find the wagon, the one we use to wheel in firewood. If you lift Lady and put her and the pups in it, we can cover them with a tarp and scoot right back to the house. We can build a fire in the living room even if it is July and make a bed for all of them. That's a good idea, isn't it, Charles?"

Charles beamed. "Splendid idea, old girl. Now why didn't I think of that?"

"Because I'm a mother, and you aren't," Myra said as she stroked the golden's head. "I don't think there's anything more beautiful in the whole world than a new baby or a new puppy or kitten. What are you waiting for, Charles, Little Lady is shivering."

Forty minutes later, the air-conditioning in the house was turned off and a fire was blazing in the humongous fireplace. Old, worn, soft blankets were spread close to the hearth but not too close, in case a spark eluded the fire screen. Mother and pups were settled within minutes. A bowl of real food was set out for Little Lady, who gobbled it down within seconds. When she was finished, she used her snout to move the bowl away from the blanket, then she offered up her paw to Myra, who dutifully shook it.

"I think you have your family, old girl," Charles said.

Myra looked up at her husband, her eyes misty with tears. "Whatever would I do without you, Charles? You always make it come out right somehow. But what happens when these little creatures don't need me?"

"An animal always needs a human, Myra. That's a given. And for your help, you get undying love and devotion. They'll never leave you until it's their time. Can you handle that?"

Something sparked in Myra's eyes. "I'm a mother, Charles, and mothers can handle anything that comes their way."

Charles turned away to hide his smile. "Well then, there you go. If you have the situation under control, I think I'll head back to the kitchen to clean up. And then I have some work

I need to finish. If you need me, just give a shout."

"Before you head down to the dungeons, I could use some coffee. It's going to be a long night, and I have a lot of stories to tell Little Lady, so she'll feel she belongs. She is ours, isn't she?" Myra asked anxiously.

"Damn straight she's ours, and so are those pups," Charles said. He didn't see any need to tell Myra the vet had brought Little Lady and her pups out to the barn yesterday. He'd called ahead when Little Lady's elderly owner passed away two days ago and asked Charles to take the dog and her pups. Sensing this was the solution to Myra's problem, he'd jumped at the chance, hoping his few little white lies to Myra would never come back to haunt him. He whistled now as he started to tidy up the kitchen.

It was so nice to have a family again.

Three thousand miles away, Annie de Silva was walking around the floor of the Babylon Casino. The customers ignored her as they feverishly dropped money into the slot machines or plunked down chips at the tables. Not so the casino staff. They imperceptibly straightened their shoulders, stood a little taller, their sharp-eyed gazes wheeling around the floor like random ricochets. Everyone learned from day one that Annie de Silva was hell on wheels, that she kicked ass and took names later. They learned it because Annie de Silva herself told them so and warned each and every one of them not to bring it to a test.

From time to time she would stop at a table or slot machine and, if the customer seemed amenable, strike up a conversation. She liked to know the people who frequented Babylon and loved hearing the nice things they said about the establishment she and Fish owned. She especially loved the seniors who came on bus trips for the free luncheons and the twenty-five dollars in chips her people handed out. The business never made any money on the little groups, but the casino counted on the goodwill the program generated.

As she ambled about the floor, Annie's mind wandered. How much longer was she going to keep doing this? It was so old hat that she could do it in her sleep, and the thrill had been gone for a long time now. She felt her eyes start to burn as she thought about Myra and the girls, and wondered if they felt at loose ends the way she did.

She was sick and tired of lying to Myra and the girls about how happy she was, that she loved working in the casino and being with Fish. Well, she did sort of love being with Fish, more or less, but she was just as happy when he took off for days, sometimes weeks, at a time to work for Global Securities. Plus, she was starting to think there was something a little screwy where that organization was concerned. Well, one of these days she'd figure it out, but not right this moment. Homecomings with Fish were rather nice but a real letdown at times, too. The bloom, if there had ever been one, was definitely off the rose these days. There just wasn't one damn thing about this new life of hers that was exciting or spontaneous. Not a single damn thing.

Sad to say, owner or not, the staff here at Babylon merely tolerated her, and that was the bottom line. It was time to take a crack at sticking her nose into the *Post*. Maggie probably wouldn't like it, but then, Maggie was expendable, just like everyone else. Annie owned the damn paper. She'd stay just long enough to stir up some trouble, screw things up, then take off for other parts. That was her life these days.

Annie stopped now where a gaggle of seniors were arguing over the slot machines. She sat down on one of the chairs and listened to the heated exchange. Half of the group wanted to cash in the chips for money so they could put it toward something or other at the group home they lived in, and the other half wanted to play with it.

Annie looked enough like some of the members that she felt she could stick her nose into their business and offer some advice. Without stopping to think, she started to chat up one of the women with a tart tongue who wanted to cash in the chips.

"Before you make a decision," Annie said to the sharp-tongued woman, "you should all play the only slot machine on the floor that actually takes a chip." She craned her neck to see that machine, standing apart from all the others. The bells and whistles emanating from it were earsplitting. She pointed to it and watched all the little old ladies and stoop-shouldered men staring at it. One of the men, who claimed to have exceptional eyesight, bellowed that it cost ten dollars a turn. His partner with two hearing aids shouted that the jackpot was $1.8 million.

These startling declarations started a whole new round of arguing. "We have to pay tax on it if we win!"

"What would we do with all that money?"

"We could prepay our own funerals so our kids don't get stuck with the bills."

"How will we get all that money back to Culpepper, Virginia, without getting mugged?"

"Then everyone will want to be our new best friends and borrow money from us."

"Who's going to manage the money?"

Annie wanted to swat all of them. "Come along, ladies and gentlemen, you can watch me play. I'll warm up the machine for you."

"Who did you say you were again?" someone asked.

"I'm a gambling addict," Annie said cheerfully, leading the way to the machine that promised untold riches. Cell phone to her ear, Annie whispered instructions, then quickly turned off her phone. She looked upward and nodded in slow motion to the unseen eyes that saw everything that went on down below.

"Hit it!" the man with two hearing aids bellowed. Annie hit it with a chip from her pocket.

Nothing happened. "Bummer," the man said.

Annie dropped another forty dollars before she turned the machine over to the members of the group home. Another hassle ensued as each of them kicked in a dollar. With two dollars to spare, it was decided that the group had to sign off on a scrap of paper that if they won, the money would be divided equally. Everyone signed their name, but it didn't solve the problem of the extra two dollars. Annie settled it by snatching the twelve dollar bills and shoving them in her pocket. She handed out two ten-dollar chips.

By this time, to Annie's dismay, a small group started to form around the famous slot machine as the seniors started to argue again about who was going to press the button that might or might not make them rich. "You all need to just shut up for one minute here!" Annie screeched to be heard over the bells and whistles. "You!" she said, pointing to a mousy little lady wearing a shawl and carrying a string bag. The lady stepped forward and flexed her fingers.

"Shouldn't we say a prayer or bless ourselves or something?" the man with two hearing aids queried.

"Absolutely!" Annie said through clenched teeth. She wished she was sitting in an office at the *Post* writing a grisly story about something or other, one that would win her a Pulitzer Prize.

The mousy lady dropped the chip into the slot and pressed the button.

"Well, so much for that!" someone groaned.

"You still have one more chip!" Annie shouted.

The mousy lady flexed her fingers, sucked in her breath, and pressed the red button.

Pandemonium broke loose as Annie backed off and headed away from the fast-approaching crowd descending on the famous slot machine.

Annie's private cell phone rang. She clicked it open and drawled, "Yes?"

"I heard what you just did, Countess de Silva!"

"I bet you did. What are you going to do about it, Fish? Not that I give a tinker's damn what you think."

"Nothing. I just wanted you to know I know. And to tell you I won't be home until next week."

"I'm fed up with this place. But I have to tell you, that was the best and worst ten minutes of my time since I've been here. I'm going to Washington tomorrow."

"You gonna screw up the paper now?"

"I am. I'm going to write op-ed pieces, cover the crap no one else wants, then I'll move on to exposés and win a Pulitzer, and by the time they kick me out, it will be time to come back here and start all over again. I-am-bored-Fish!"

Fish laughed. "You could start planning our wedding."

Annie started to sputter, but Fish clicked off in midsputter.

* * *

Maggie Spritzer sat behind her desk and thought about going home, but she really didn't want to do that. The house in Georgetown was empty, with only Ted's cats, Mickey and Minnie, in residence. She'd moved them into her house while Ted was away working for Global Securities. God, how she missed him.

She looked down at the ring on her left hand, then at the new acrylic nails she'd had put on once she kicked the very bad habit of chewing her nails. She hated the nails because they interfered with the keyboard when she was typing. She even had a French manicure that she had to keep up with, which also irritated her. The only alternative was to stop wearing the ring, remove the acrylic nails, and go back to the hateful habit of chewing her nails.

Maggie's door opened, and her secretary stuck her head in. "If you don't need me for anything, Maggie, I'd like to leave a little early."

Maggie roused herself enough to reply. "No, go ahead—things are quiet, it's summer, no news, politicians are going on recess, and we're good. Sometimes I like it when nothing is going on in this damn crazy city. I'm thinking of leaving myself. See you in the morning." She waved listlessly before the secretary closed the door.

Maggie looked down again at the sparkling ring on her finger and her beautifully polished nails. They weren't the only thing that was new in her life these days. She was no longer obsessed with food; her metabolism had somehow magically fallen back into the normal range. She wasn't sure how she felt about that, because there were days when she barely ate at all. "Crap!" she said succinctly.

Maggie heaved herself to her feet, looked around for her lightweight suit jacket, kicked off her heels, and slipped her feet into Velcro-strapped sneakers that she didn't bother to fasten. Maybe when she got home she'd putter in the weed-filled garden or go for a run. She knew in her gut she probably wouldn't do either of those things. She'd pour herself a glass of wine and park her butt in front of the television set and watch one of the twenty-four-hour news channels until she dozed off for a few hours. Result, she'd be sleepless the rest of the night. "Crap!" she said again.

Maggie turned off the lights and closed the door just as she heard the ping of the elevator. She looked up in time to see Annie de Silva step out and look around. She dropped her bag and ran squealing to greet Annie. "Oh, my God! It really is you, Annie! I can't tell you how happy I am to see you! Oh, Annie, I missed you so," she said, crushing the older woman to her chest in an agonizing bear hug. She held her so tight, Annie had to gasp to draw in any oxygen.

"I don't think I've ever had a greeting like that in my whole life. I'm happy to see you, too," Annie said, struggling to find the breath to get the words out.

Maggie released her grip and stood back, alarm bells sounding in her brain. "What's wrong? Did something happen? Why are you here? Tell me everything. Do you want to go in the office or go somewhere and get something to eat? A drink? Everyone is okay, aren't they? Oh, God, Annie, I missed you so much. I miss everyone. Nothing is the same anymore. I . . . I just hate the way it is now."

Her breathing back to normal, Annie wrapped her arm around the younger woman's shoulder, and said, "Tell me about it. Everything is fine, no problems. Let's walk over to the Squires' Pub and tie one on. By the way, I decided to try my hand at running the paper. That's one of the reasons I'm here."

"Do you know anything about running a newspaper, Annie?"

"No, but I can learn. I didn't know anything about running a casino, either, but I learned as I went along. The best thing you can say about that is they can't fire the owner. I'll stay here just long enough to screw things up, then I'll find something else to do. I promise not to get in your way."

They were outside by then, the heat like a furnace after the air-conditioning inside the building.

"I forgot how hot it is here. It's hot in Vegas, but it's a dry heat. You can keep this humidity," Annie grumbled. "I like your nails."

Maggie wiggled her fingers. "I hate the maintenance. You have to go every two weeks to get them filled in. They show off the ring." A second later, Maggie burst into tears.

"That bad, huh?"

"Yeah, it's that bad. I can't get a handle on anything anymore. Every day is like the day before, and nothing is going on. I feel as if I'm just marking time. Before . . . well, before I just thrived. Life was a constant challenge. I never knew from one minute to the next what was going to happen. Now I can tell you what's going to happen seventy-two hours in advance. Nothing." She sniffled. "Absolutely nothing."

"I know exactly how you feel. Yesterday I gave away $1.8 million to some seniors from a group home. I let them win it. That's why I'm here— figured it was time to get the hell out of Dodge. Fish was on the horn the minute the slot paid off. I really don't like him much anymore."

"You didn't! Wow! Do you have someone else on the string?"

"I did. I'm not sorry, either. No, on someone else on the string. That's what I meant about screwing up. It should give you some idea of what I can do to the paper."

"I'll keep my eye on you," Maggie said, dabbing at her eyes. "Okay, we're here. Are we drinking or eating? We can drink all night, and my driver will pick us up and carry us to the car and take us home. It's like win-win. I have never been really, really drunk. Have you, Annie?" Maggie asked fretfully.

"A time or two," Annie drawled. "Let's play it by ear, dear."

They gave their order to a snappy little waitress dressed in shorts and a bolero top.

"The food isn't even here and I can hear my arteries snapping shut," Annie said peevishly, referring to the everything-loaded hot dogs, french fries, and onion rings. And the margaritas.

"We'll eat pomegranates tomorrow, and the seeds from them will flush out our arteries," Maggie said.

"Is that true?" Annie asked.

"I read it in the *Post*. We printed it in our health section, so it has to be true." Maggie laughed.

Four margaritas later, Maggie started to cry. "I miss Ted and Espinosa, Annie. I miss the girls. Myra doesn't leave the farm; she said all her old friends thumb their noses at her. That made me so mad, I did a piece on climbing socialites and friendships that brought in so much mail I had to hire people to read it. Then I did another piece on all the boards and foundations Myra used to sit on, all the monies she pledged, and how, after she was treated like a pariah by these same climbing socialites, she withdrew all the pledges. The amount of money was staggering, and it brought another avalanche of mail. It was all I could do, Annie."

"I know, dear. If I'm not too hungover, I'm going out to the farm tomorrow to surprise

Myra and Charles," Annie said, holding up her glass for a refill.

"Life is not fun anymore," Maggie boo-hooed. "I don't mean life should be fun, but fun has its place. I am bored out of my mind."

Her eyes crossing, Annie had a hard time bringing her glass to her lips. She leaned forward and whispered, "It was the danger, dear. We all thrived on the danger, and we liked pitting our wits against all those crazy alphabet-soup groups that run this damn town. I heard the FBI has had so many screwups since Bert left that they had to ask Elias to come in and help them out. He, of course, pleaded ill health and told them they were on their own. I had a good laugh over that when I heard about it. Supposedly, they are revamping the entire Bureau."

"Do you care, Annie?"

"No-I-do-not!" Annie said emphatically.

"I think we should go home, Annie. I have to feed the cats. Good thing my driver is number three on my speed dial because I can't see the numbers to dial."

"Well, don't look at me, dear. Just do your best. This has been a very interesting evening, don't you think?"

"I hope we remember it tomorrow, Annie."

"You have a point, dear."

Chapter 2

Myra blinked, then blinked again when she saw the fur on the back of Little Lady's neck stand on end. She shivered at the low growl deep in the golden's throat. Someone was approaching the house! She ran to the security monitor in the kitchen, Little Lady on her heels. A car was approaching the electronic gates, an arm outstretched to press in the security code. Friend? Foe? So few people had the code, it almost had to mean a friend. "Shhh, let's wait and see who it is. I'm sure Charles can see the monitor in the war room." Little Lady made a sound deep in her throat again, but she remained still at Myra's side.

Myra marveled that, in less than twenty-four hours, Little Lady had appointed herself Myra's protector. She smiled. It was the mother in the golden, ready to protect and do battle. She leaned down and hugged the beautiful dog.

Myra heard the high-pitched whine of a powerful foreign car as it raced through the gates and skidded to a stop. The door swung open to reveal a pair of legs whose feet were encased in rhinestone cowgirl boots. Annie did love those boots. Myra burst out laughing as she thrust open the door and raced out to the compound to greet her lifelong friend, Little Lady right behind her. "My God, Annie, what took you so long?" she said, crushing her friend to her so tightly that Annie gasped for air.

"That bad, eh?" Annie finally managed to say.

"Worse," Myra said, refusing to let Annie out of her embrace. She finally let go when Little Lady barked, a signal she wanted to be introduced. Myra obliged. "This is Little Lady. She is the new mother of four adorable pups, who are sleeping at the moment. It's a long story, Annie. I am so glad to see you. There are no words to tell you how glad. A telephone call once a month isn't what we agreed to, Annie. I know you couldn't wait to get out into the world, so you could set it on fire, but I thought . . . I wanted . . . expected . . . Oh, hell, Annie, I just plain old missed you. Come on, let's go inside and get out of this heat."

Little Lady stepped back and barked, then stepped forward and held out a paw, which Annie dutifully shook. She ruffled the fur on the back of the big dog's neck. "She's gorgeous, Myra. I can't wait to see the puppies."

Linking her arm with Annie's, Myra led the way to the kitchen door. The new mother barreled through the door and headed straight to the pen Charles had fashioned in the living room for the newborns. "Come along, Annie. Little Lady is just like all new mothers. She wants to show off her offspring. Two boys and two girls. I'm relying on what Charles said, and you know how he knows everything. So, two boys and two girls. Be effusive, Annie."

Annie dropped to her knees and peered at the four little balls of fur all nestled together. Her eyes misted with tears as she looked at the big dog and said in a choked voice, "They're too beautiful for words, Little Lady. You take good care of them, you hear?" She held out her arm for Myra to pull her to her feet.

Both women watched as Little Lady stepped into the pen and lay down. "Her world is right side up, so we can go into the kitchen now. Do you want coffee, tea, a soft drink?"

"Hell, no, Myra. I want *a drink.*"

"Name your pleasure, my friend. By the way, that's a pretty fancy set of wheels you arrived in."

"Bourbon on the rocks, and I'm test-driving the car. I don't know yet if I want to buy it or not. It's built for speed, and I'm all about speed these days."

"You don't say," Myra drawled as she poured bourbon into two squat glasses and added ice cubes. "Is this a social drink, or are we going to get schnockered?"

"Let's just take it one drink at a time, Myra. Talk to me, tell me things," Annie said, clinking her glass against Myra's. She took a great gulp of the fiery liquid, her eyes watering.

"Annie! See that dog in there? That's my life. I am in such a funk I can't function. Charles rags on me constantly. I have never been at such loose ends. I can't sleep. I argue with Charles over nothing. My friends . . . well, the less we say about them the better. Your turn. Tell me about the trail you blazed when you left the mountain. I want to hear everything. Don't leave a thing out."

"Everything?" Annie said as she finished off her drink.

Myra poured again. "Everything."

Annie sucked in her breath and let it out with a loud swoosh of sound. "Well, when Fish picked me up at the airport in Raleigh, and we don't need to discuss the fact that I was headed back to the mountain in Spain, we went to Vegas to get ready for a surprise trip. That didn't happen for a week because Jellicoe needed him for something or other, so I hung out in the penthouse till he got back. I have a hate on for that man—Jellicoe, that is. The surprise was a trip to Tahiti. It was wonderful.

"In my quest to set the world on fire, I had this vision of myself as a smoking-hot babe, so I took it to the casino floor, picked up one of the employees, and went on a three-day sex binge. You know, to get myself ready for Fish's return."

Myra gaped at her friend and somehow managed to say, "Continue."

Annie sampled her second drink. "I think it's safe to say I got out of Vegas by the skin of my teeth. I did manage to create a bit of havoc during the year and a half I was there. No one but me seemed to think my ideas were any good," she sniffed. "That didn't stop me, made me more determined to leave my mark." Defensiveness rang in Annie's voice when she said, "I own half the joint, Myra. By the way, before I forget or get too drunk to mention it, I read in the paper on the plane that there's a bike rally going on in Florida next week for the benefit of the Juvenile Diabetes Foundation. I thought you and I could go, make a nice donation, and get out of this rut we're in. What do you say? Do you want to go with me?"

"Absolutely I want to go. What . . . what ideas did you have, Annie?"

"I wanted to tone down the outfits the cocktail waitresses wore. They fought me. Skin sells, did you know that, Myra? Their outfits coincide with their tips. To prove my point, I duded up and went out on the floor. I made sixteen dollars for a six-hour shift. The girls average four to five hundred per shift. I had to back down."

"It's okay to retreat now and then, Annie. You were new to the game. How could you possibly know how a place works and the rules they have right off the bat?"

"That's very kind of you to say, Myra. I fired a lot of people."

"I'm sure they deserved to be terminated," Myra said soothingly.

"The staff lived in fear of me, Myra. I mean that. The minute they saw me they cringed. It was like, 'Oh, shit, here she comes.' I did not like that one little bit. I initiated work-related fireside chats that the staff slept through. Everyone more or less loves Fish, but he hasn't been there too much with all the work the boys have been piling on him. He thrives in a crisis, and there's always a crisis somewhere. I was left to my own devices, so I started trouble. What would you have done, Myra?" Annie asked, peering across the table at her friend.

"I would have done the same thing," Myra said spiritedly. "Is there more?"

Annie looked down into her empty glass, then at Myra's glass. Taking the hint, Myra up-ended hers. "A little."

"Well, spit it out, Annie."

"They said I was too generous with the seniors who come to the casino by the busload. Too many freebies. I thought there weren't enough. We locked horns. I fired the lot of the dissenters."

"Good for you! Seniors need all the help they can get, and they also deserve to have fun. I would have fired them, too."

"Well, we did have a slight employment problem after that. It was . . . eventually solved."

"How?"

"I just went to the other casinos and pirated their people by offering to pay them double. It wasn't one of my smartest moves. I will admit to that."

"Lesson learned," Myra said, pouring from the bottle. "Do you have more to share?"

"Well, there was this . . . incident. I was told,

mind you, the key word here is *told*. I have absolutely no recollection of the . . . incident, but they said I showed my tattoo on the casino floor. At 12:36 on New Year's Eve. New Year's Day, to be precise."

"Oh, Annie! Do you think you did that?"

"Hell, yes, Myra. I was nuts back then. I decided to mend my ways, so I went out to the desert to see Rena Gold and visit the Institute. I wanted to be a volunteer. You remember the place down the road from Fish's place? The one we hid out in that had all the rattlesnakes. Well, I lasted a week. They said I was too aggressive. So, with my tail between my legs, I went back to the casino. Where just the day before yesterday I had the guys rig a slot so this group of seniors could win a big jackpot. Fish was on the phone minutes after the group hit it. I knew all hell was going to break loose, so I split, and here I am. Myra, I have never been so miserable in my life."

"Join the club, my friend." Myra reached across the table to take Annie's hands in her own. "I'm in the same place you are. I am bored out of my mind. When Charles isn't around, I cry. I miss the girls, I miss the mountain. I miss all of our missions. My God, Annie, what happened to us?"

"We got old. We can't accept change. No one needs us. At least you had the good sense to get a dog. You have to take care of a dog. The dog depends on you. I don't even have a dog."

"But . . . we have Charles and Fish, so in a way that doesn't compute," Myra said.

"Myra, they don't *need* us. They can function on their own. We're talking about causes and missions where we used to make a difference. No matter what you say, we got off on taking matters into our own hands and making things right. I wish to hell those damn pardons had never come through. There, I said it!" Annie cried.

"Oh, Annie, I just said the same thing yesterday to Charles. He said he understood, but he doesn't. He's a man. So now what?"

"I checked in at the *Post*. I'm going to take a stab at screwing that up. You want to help me? You can bring the dogs along. We'll each have an office, and we can text back and forth. We can take turns walking the dogs and writing editorials that will set Washington on its ear! The best part is, no one can fire us."

Myra started to laugh and couldn't stop. Finally, gasping for breath, she said, "Let's go for a walk and work off this liquor."

Annie grabbed the bottle of bourbon and headed for the door. The two old friends walked aimlessly around the farm, stopping from time to time to sip from the bottle.

Charles, a frown building between his brows, watched the women as they walked toward the barn. He felt an itch settle itself between his shoulder blades. Then he shivered.

With the sun beating down on their heads and necks, Myra and Annie headed straight for the barn, where they walked the entire length of it, stroking the horses and speaking softly to them as they walked along. The barn cats clustered around their legs, purring loudly. Myra led the way to where Charles had left two bales of hay near the door. The women settled themselves.

"So, Annie dear, what part of your dissertation was true and which part was false?"

Annie laughed, but to Myra's ears it sounded forced. "Sad to say, Myra, it's all true."

"Fish?"

"Fish is . . . I don't know, something is off-key there. I care for him a great deal. No, let's just say I more or less like him. He would like to get married, but I am not ready for marriage. I doubt I'll ever be ready. I don't know . . . I think . . . the second time around someone always gets cheated. I loved my husband heart and soul. I meant it when I said to death do us part. I know he meant it, too. I think he would be okay with Fish. I say *think*. I'm not sure if I *know* he would be okay. That . . . ah . . . one episode, I'm not sure if I regret it or it was just not for me. No one else. I was trying to prove something to myself. Whatever it was, it didn't work. I'm still not sure about that tattoo episode, either. It's all negative, Myra. That's my life, a sackful of negatives. Except for Fish; he's a negative with a little plus sign. I have to be honest, I think he's getting fed up with me, and I know I'm getting fed up with him. I wasn't like this on the mountain. On the mountain, my adrenaline pumped daily. I looked forward to getting up in the morning and never wanted to go to bed at night. I counted for something up there. We all did. It's gone now, and, goddamn it, Myra, I want it back. Do you hear me, I want it back. And another thing. If you think that dog back at the house and her pups is your answer, then you are crazier than I am. We aren't crazy, are we, Myra?" she asked fretfully.

Myra burst into tears. Annie followed suit.

"You never called, Annie. Maybe once a month."

"Because I would have started to blubber the minute I heard your voice. You didn't call, either. Why?"

"For the same reason. We have to get a life, Annie. It's been a whole year and a half. Look at us. We haven't moved forward one step. We've regressed. Even I know that is totally unacceptable. Do you see Lizzie much when she's in Vegas?"

"No. She invited me to dinner one night, and I went. The baby was about two months old. She let me hold him. All I did was cry, so I left and never went back. He is a gorgeous little boy, Myra. How many times did you see him when she was here?"

"Twice. But he was asleep the second time. Lizzie and Cosmo have their own lives now. That's the way it should be. I didn't want to intrude. I didn't go to the christening or the shower at the White House. I thought . . . well, it doesn't matter what I thought. I hope Lizzie understands."

"Do the girls call you, Myra?"

"About like you did, Annie. Do you think they're happy?"

Annie upended the bottle of bourbon, took a slug, and passed it on to Myra, who drank deeply. "I would think so. They have their lives, and they scattered to the four winds. I can't believe they forgot about us so quickly. It hurts so damn bad, Annie, I want to cry."

"You are crying, Myra. Are we saying our girls are ungrateful little shits?"

Myra pondered the question. "Yes, Annie, I think so. I tried to be fair in my heart. They have husbands and lovers who travel the globe with the girls at their sides. At this point, I am not even sure who is married and who isn't other than Nikki and Yoko. Then there is the time difference in different parts of the globe. The worst part was when none of them came for Christmas. You didn't come either, Annie. You all broke my heart that day. Charles and I worked so hard to make it all festive. We decorated and shopped and cooked till we were worn-out, and the only guest on Christmas day was Elias. Nellie was recovering, so she couldn't come. It was one of the worst days of my life."

Annie sniffed and blew her nose. Then she sniffed again. "Did you know Yoko has had two miscarriages? I think it's a rotten shame no one saw fit to tell us."

"No, I didn't know. How did you find out? That's awful. Harry and Yoko would make wonderful parents. Where are they? Do you know?"

"Maggie told me last night when I stopped at

the paper. They were in Israel. It's that Jellicoe thing. Harry goes to train the troops or whatever. Maggie said she thinks they're back at the dojo, but she isn't sure. Said no one answers the phone. She thinks they came back because Yoko was so depressed about the miscarriages, and if she got pregnant again, she wanted it to be here in the States. Because Yoko said she wanted to have her baby in Washington. That's all I know."

"That has to mean they're all in touch with Maggie but not us. What does that tell you, Annie? I don't believe this!" Myra burst into tears again. This time she reached for the bottle and took a healthy gulp. Her throat burning, tears flowing down her cheeks, she said, "Yoko needs a mother figure in her life right now if all that is true. I think we both qualify for that role, Annie. This is unforgivable."

"You're right, it is unforgivable."

The bottle changed hands again. "Where do you think Maggie stands, Annie?"

"I don't have a clue. She seemed really happy to see me last night. And she didn't get upset when I told her I was going to work at the paper. What could she say? I own the damn place. She's been calling regularly to check in. She said she did her best to help you when all your friends shut you out. But something was off-key. I had the feeling something is wrong somewhere, and she's trying to deal with it."

"She did try to help. She really went out on a limb when she published what she called her personal scoop on all those charities. I adore Maggie."

"Maggie feels as lost as you and I, and she doesn't know what to do about it. We both cried a bit. Myra, do you think it's even remotely possible that the girls were waiting for us to get in touch with them? Like they were taking their cues from us? We did moan and groan about those pardons and what we were going to do with our lives. Is it possible, Myra?"

Myra upended the bottle and gulped. "Anything is possible, I suppose. What do you think, Annie?"

"I would like to believe it. If it's true that Harry and Yoko are back at the dojo, all we have to do is pop in and see what's going on."

"I'm seeing two of you, Annie."

Annie laughed. "Ha! I can't even see one of you!"

The cats circling the bales of hay purred as they did their best to rub up against the women's legs.

"The bottle's empty," Annie said.

"So it is. When was the last time you slept in a barn, Annie?"

"When I was ten years old. I loved it. It made me feel so grown-up at the time."

"We're all grown-up now, Annie. And we're old in the bargain."

"Stop raining on our parade, Myra."

"How long are you staying, Annie?"

"Until I get tired of causing trouble."

"That long, huh?"

"Maybe longer."

Myra laughed as she teetered toward an empty stall, Annie and a string of cats behind her.

Books by Bestselling Author
Fern Michaels

___**The Jury**	0-8217-7878-1	$6.99US/$9.99CAN
___**Sweet Revenge**	0-8217-7879-X	$6.99US/$9.99CAN
___**Lethal Justice**	0-8217-7880-3	$6.99US/$9.99CAN
___**Free Fall**	0-8217-7881-1	$6.99US/$9.99CAN
___**Fool Me Once**	0-8217-8071-9	$7.99US/$10.99CAN
___**Vegas Rich**	0-8217-8112-X	$7.99US/$10.99CAN
___**Hide and Seek**	1-4201-0184-6	$6.99US/$9.99CAN
___**Hokus Pokus**	1-4201-0185-4	$6.99US/$9.99CAN
___**Fast Track**	1-4201-0186-2	$6.99US/$9.99CAN
___**Collateral Damage**	1-4201-0187-0	$6.99US/$9.99CAN
___**Final Justice**	1-4201-0188-9	$6.99US/$9.99CAN
___**Up Close and Personal**	0-8217-7956-7	$7.99US/$9.99CAN
___**Under the Radar**	1-4201-0683-X	$6.99US/$9.99CAN
___**Razor Sharp**	1-4201-0684-8	$7.99US/$10.99CAN
___**Yesterday**	1-4201-1494-8	$5.99US/$6.99CAN
___**Vanishing Act**	1-4201-0685-6	$7.99US/$10.99CAN
___**Sara's Song**	1-4201-1493-X	$5.99US/$6.99CAN
___**Deadly Deals**	1-4201-0686-4	$7.99US/$10.99CAN
___**Game Over**	1-4201-0687-2	$7.99US/$10.99CAN
___**Sins of Omission**	1-4201-1153-1	$7.99US/$10.99CAN
___**Sins of the Flesh**	1-4201-1154-X	$7.99US/$10.99CAN
___**Cross Roads**	1-4201-1192-2	$7.99US/$10.99CAN

Available Wherever Books Are Sold!
Check out our website at www.kensingtonbooks.com

DEADLY DEALS
Fern Michaels

The Sisterhood Makes Things Right

After years of trying to become pregnant without success, Rachel Dawson and her husband Thomas felt their dreams had finally come true the day they brought home their newly adopted twin babies. Though the lawyer, Baron Bell, who arranged for the surrogate mother charged a hefty six-figure fee, one glance into the eyes of their precious children told them it was all worth it. Until the birth mother reappeared, first demanding more money, then the twins themselves. Suddenly Baron Bell was nowhere to be found, and the Dawsons were once again childless, heartbroken and nearly destitute.

When the case finds its way to the offices of high-profile attorney Lizzie Fox, she can't wait to take down the so-called "Mr. Wonderful." And she knows she'll have all the help she needs, as it's just the kind of crime that really gets the Sisterhood's adrenalin flowing. Once they get their hands on the perpetrators there will be hell to pay, and it will cost a lot more than cold, hard cash . . .

A Zebra Paperback On Sale Now!

Visit us at www.kensingtonbooks.com